James Kahn's book 
and Time, *Time's*
several film noveli
and *Poltergeist*. He
emergency-room p
California.

By the same author

Diagnosis: Murder
World Enough, and Time
Time's Dark Laughter
Poltergeist
Return of the Jedi

JAMES KAHN

Timefall

GRAFTON BOOKS
A Division of the Collins Publishing Group

LONDON GLASGOW
TORONTO SYDNEY AUCKLAND

Grafton Books
A Division of the Collins Publishing Group
8 Grafton Street, London W1X 3LA

A Grafton UK Paperback Original 1988

ISBN 0-583-13509-9

Printed and bound in Great Britain by
Collins, Glasgow

Set in Times

For Ben Pesmen,
with grateful thanks

Foreword

My name is James Kahn; I am a licensed physician and surgeon. For several years now I've been engaged in the practice of medicine at various emergency rooms around Los Angeles. It's an odd sort of work – alternately exciting, depressing, and boring – and brings me into contact with a wide range of characters whom I would not otherwise expect to meet.

Such a character was Joshua Green.

The first time I saw him, in the ER of —— Hospital, he was being wheeled in by the paramedics, and he was having convulsions. This was around April 1982. A sleazier patient I hadn't seen in many months – emaciated, hair matted, filthy cuts over his face and hands. I assumed he was a derelict; I assumed he was having rum fits.

The paramedics already had an IV running, so I pushed some Valium – without success – then finally broke his seizures with a loading dose of Dilantin. After briefly examining him, I called down his old chart from Medical Records and perused it as he lay on the gurney in a groggy, postictal state. It was an interesting case history.

He'd been a paleontologist, apparently – junior faculty at —— University – and had developed this seizure disorder while on digs in South America. He'd been worked up completely on his return to this country; a frontal lobe lesion was documented. The final conclusion of the neurologist was that the epileptic focus was the result of either a scar (the patient had suffered some head trauma in the jungle), or a small, dead echinococcal cyst (an

infectious lesion caused by one of the more common South American parasites). Joshua was put on the usual medication, but his seizures remained under only partial control, largely because he didn't always take his medications.

It seems he had a psychiatric disorder as well – possibly related to the same frontal lobe lesion.

I couldn't really examine the chart in depth; other patients demanded attention. I put Joshua in an observation bed and went about my other duties – mostly sprained ankles, inflamed orifices, and failures of heart.

Over the next four hours, though, as he came around, I checked in on him periodically. Took his pulse, peered in his eyes. We talked.

He was going in and out of a fugue state, mumbling at times, at times lucid. He told me he was 'going back' – but his speech was nothing but fragments: 'time-tunnels . . . red shift . . . Scribery . . . vampires . . . Jasmine . . . getting time back into balance . . .' And so on. Intermittently, he laughed, or cried.

He began talking about seeing stars in his peripheral visual field, which I was afraid heralded the onset of another seizure – but these were no scintillating scotomas: he was simply philosophizing, it turned out, on the oddities of human perception. Not the kind of psychotic babble his earlier rantings had led me to anticipate.

He seemed to become quite alert at one point. He broke out in a heavy sweat. He pressed a small yellow, wrinkled fruit seed into my hand and begged me to keep it for him. I promised I would.

'It's from the sacred grove,' he whispered. 'But it's not the only evidence. There are documents. And the jewels, of course.'

Those would be the emeralds – stones whose shadow

may yet cross us all; though at the time I had only this barest foreknowledge of their history.

I called his neurologist, a Dr Jerome Hoffman, to discuss the case. A fascinating patient, Hoffman told me – true organic schizophrenia with an acquired seizure disorder, the bizarre ideations controlled better with anticonvulsants than with phenothiazines. By all accounts, a reportable case.

And sad as well. The young man had been a rising academician – energetic, published, adored by his students, rocketing toward tenure. Then, on the brink of what was almost certain to be a major discovery, this tragic accident. His career, his life, ruined. Other members of the party had been lost in the jungle – a terrible loss. But Joshua himself was a fascinating case. Hoffman's brother, Robert (the psychiatrist), had even added it to the galley proofs of his chapter ('Variant Syndromes') in the compendium *The Psychiatry of Seizure Disorders* (rev. ed., University Press, 1981).

In any case, it was no use to admit the poor turkey, Dr Hoffman advised me. He inevitably signed out of the hospital Against Medical Advice the same day, and wandered off to Who Knows Where until he ran out of meds again and got shipped into some other ER, grand mal seizing.

Then Dr Hoffman paused and said, 'Wait a minute. I'm being unnecessarily harsh. He's actually a rather special person. I'm just angry because he won't let me help him.'

'Special how?' I asked.

'Well, he's a mystic, for one thing.'

'So epilepsy is only *one* of his altered states.'

'I think he probably spends most of his time in one realm of the ether or another.'

'And he was such a bright teacher at the university, you said.'

'Shame, really – a fine mind squandered like that.'

To academics, lapsed academics lie somewhere between fallen angels and fallen soufflés. 'In my experience,' I said, 'intellectuals who become mystics do so in a flurry of hallucinogenic – or other controlled – substances.'

'I think there was some of that, too, yes, on his south-of-the-border investigations,' said Hoffman. 'Magic mushrooms, Don Juan, all that crap.'

'Sad when a thinker becomes a believer,' I said.

'I'll take a good disbeliever any day,' Hoffman concurred.

I thanked Hoffman for his help and went back to my patient. He was gone.

Nobody had seen him leave, though frankly, few spent time dwelling on the matter – other patients were waiting.

I found myself unsettled, though. I felt some connection with this odd patient – some identification, related, I suppose, to our similar ages, professions, demeanors. Something about him stuck with me, and all day I would keep coming back to something he said about the frailties of our perceptions or the nature of glimpsing realities – keep coming back to it, like a touchstone, or a half-open wound.

But I was – I am – a scientist – who knows a touchstone for what it is: a tender crutch.

And I was – and am – a physician, who knows an open wound is best left bandaged.

Still, I saw Joshua Green twice more – once the following week, and once over three years later. It was subsequent to that last meeting that I received his package in the mail.

It was postmarked Bogotá, Colombia, and contained numerous artifacts, including the following manuscript – a leather-bound journal, written in Joshua's hand. It's a first-person account of the events in his life spanning twenty years – 1966 to 1985 – though, of course, it may have spanned much more.

I've taken the liberty of editing the journal somewhat, for the sake of discretion in some places and for clarity in others. Otherwise I reprint it here in full for the reader to judge.

– James Kahn, M.D.
Los Angeles, 1986

FINAL JOURNEY AND TESTAMENT OF JOSHUA GREEN, Ph.D.

For Those Who Would Follow

We all were sea-swallowed, though some cast again,
And, by that destiny, to perform an act
Whereof what's past is prologue, what to come,
In yours and my discharge.

– William Shakespeare, *The Tempest*

Hypocrite reader! – my double – my brother!

– Charles Baudelaire,
To the Reader

I am dying; for I have the timesickness. I set off now on my last journey, not to save my own life – which is past hope, by all odds – but to snatch the bobbling earth, the very universe, from the indolent fires of time. You will think me mad. I pray that I am.

Here is my story.

PART ONE
The Journey

CHAPTER 1

An Interesting Find

I graduated from the University of—in 1966, then came out West to do my doctorate in paleontology at the University of California at—. I matriculated in 1969. My field of concentration was Cenozoic reptiles. The records are all on file there. My thesis paper was 'Cretaceous Homeothermic Quadripeds of the Upper Andes Valley.'

I joined the faculty in 1970. Two years later I fell in love with and married Diane Chase, a student in my undergraduate course on dinosaurs. Our life together during this period was without flaw. We studied bones, wrote joint monographs, did crossword puzzles; it was our time of innocence, of unconscious comfort.

Afer a couple of years, comfort turned to routine, and routine to disaffection. Not disaffection with each other, but with the ruts we'd fallen into – the stuffy teas, the Sunday *Times*, the monthly readings, the pompous committees, the hopeless civility of it all. What was I *doing* with my life, I'd begun to wonder. Where was I going? Was this all there was?

Di had even less tolerance for the community of intellectuals than I did. She was forever being tactlessly honest to some buffoon or painting horns on the university's most sacred cows. She was a grad student now, but she didn't really like it anymore. She'd seen every one of Myrna Loy's movies, twice; *that* was who *she* wanted to be.

I wanted to be – I don't know what. No image comes

readily to mind. Dr Livingston, maybe. Or Ernest Hemingway.

I didn't meet Lon Sanger until the winter of 1975, at a wine-and-cheese party given by the department for the purpose of preening and groveling before our big private contributors. Lon was one of those.

He was clearly different from the rest of the donors, though – grand, I would say – striking. Tall, green-eyed, coffee-skinned, a dresser – what in another age would have been called dashing. Not at all like our other benefactors at the soiree – the pudgy, polyester citrus magnates, or the old alums who'd struck it rich in the real estate boom. Lon called himself an impostor.

We gravitated to each other as if driven together by the force of all the boring chitchat endemic to such places. We clinked glasses on meeting, with a laugh and without a word – and sealed our fates on the spot, the spot being the end of the bar. We were both already quite drunk.

We bought each other another free drink, discovered we'd both been in Grant Park in 1968, at the Democratic National Convention riots – traded tear-gas and billy-club stories – then went arm in arm off into the night for some serious bar-hopping.

We'd been student radicals in the sixties, it turned out, at different colleges in the same town; briefly, we'd both even been hippies. While I'd gone into academics, Lon had become a hippie-entrepreneur: he began smuggling dope, Colombian grass at first, and then Colombian cocaine. He'd grown rich; he never got caught. Through his connections in South America, he'd gotten into smuggling emeralds, and gold artifacts as well, mostly from around Lake Guatavita. He'd grown even richer.

We grew even drunker. I told him the thrust of my latest paper, and he grasped its substance instantly –

something even some of my faculty colleagues had not appreciated sufficiently.[1] By the end of the sodden evening, Lon and I were intimates, like brothers. Blood brothers even: I accidentally cut my thumb on a broken wineglass; with a flourish, he cut his own on the same shard and pressed his bloody thumb to mine.

When I finally stumbled into bed late that night, Di was pissed off – I hadn't called, and I was righteously plastered. Worst of all, I hadn't invited her to the party. She turned a cold shoulder to me. I curled behind her, though, rubbed my hips into her backside, brought my hand around to cup her breast, kissed her neck, stroked her hair. Eventually, she softened. Even at our dreariest, we knew how to make love.

As soon as she herself met Lon, of course, she forgave me that night's sanguineous debacle – for like me, she fell to his charms.

The three of us became thick over the next eighteen months. We attended concerts together, and parties, and picnics, and museums, and taverns. Lon came to my lectures, I went to the art openings he frequented; he audited Di's classes, she researched the jewelry he periodically received, sewn into the lining of llama coats.

Occasionally, his people in Colombia came across fossils during their sorties for gemstones; instead of simply discarding them, as before, he now had the bony relics sent up – a present to me. There were, occasionally,

[1] Indeed, the very prose of my articles had recently come under attack, from no less a personage than the head of my department, who'd told me, 'There's little place for metaphor, let alone synecdoche, in scientific writing, Mr Green . . .' Such unexamined denigrations are, of course, beneath comment; still, the exchange had caused me to wonder if my work – indeed, my self – mightn't have been better loved elsewhere.

pieces of academic interest, and these seemed to give Lon as much pleasure as the more commercial booty.

He yearned, I think, to be a scholar, or at least to have that aura. To me, I'm afraid, scholarship was becoming so much pedantry; Di certainly felt that way. To us, on the contrary, Lon's life was the tantalizing one: an expensive, exquisitely appointed house in the Hollywood Hills; a glamorously illicit relationship with rare artifacts; mysterious involvement with sinister dandies, scruffy transients, rich collectors, beautiful women (I never went to his home when he wasn't surrounded by a virtual harem of exotic ladies, variously bored or attentive).

There was also, to be sure, a certain sexual tension between Lon and Di, probably all the greater because it was so incompletely fulfilled. Though I suspect they did sleep together once or twice; how could they not? Di was a natural flirt, and I a modern man. It would have been both futile and barbarian of me to object. In fact, the subject never arose – Lon was too civilized, Di too generous, I too rational.

So we were three; and not a one of us wanted to lose the other two.

Because Lon claimed (I'm sure it was a lie) to be one-sixteenth Apache, we even gave each other Indian names. Lon we dubbed Satin Tuxedo, for that most favored penchant of his; Di was Running Stocking, a trait she developed into high art at most of Lon's fetes; and I became Little Footnote. This was something of a barb, on their parts, directed toward the notion that in the articles I authored, my footnotes tended to be longer than my text.[2]

[2] Material more properly suited for footnoting only impedes the flow of thought when included in the text proper – but then Lon and Di had little appreciation for what makes good prose.

We teased one another a great deal, actually. It was all loving fun, but I think much of it stemmed from that basic ennui we were feeling – with our lives, with our selves, with each other, finally. There'd just been no change in so long, some of our nerve endings were beginning to atrophy; so we teased each other, to elicit responses. Does that make sense? Something must. Else we should not have leapt so headlong into such chaos. But I precede myself.

So in sum: I was an ostensibly complacent professor, quietly weathering the doldrums of an early midlife crisis; Di, my young wife, similarly chafing at the halls of academe, was more flamboyant by nature, and quiet weathering didn't sit well with her. Too, she secretly aspired to a life of sophistication – Lon's milieu – though to me she always looked like a little girl trying on Mom's lipstick. And Lon was just a self-educated buccaneer, not yet too jaded or self-satisfied to have forgotten why he loved to sail a ship.

So that was the setting. Have I forgotten anything? I want to get it right. Who knows what incidental fact or perception might not be critical in later years . . . but I digress. In the end, the text, unnoted, must speak for itself.

The first thing I remember about the whole business didn't really have anything to *do* with the whole business. Only in retrospect do I assign it some relevance – as a portent. Just a feeling, really – an 'aura,' the way epileptics have special auras that precede their seizures – a herald of things to come.

It was at a good-bye party at our place for Gene Caine, who was going off to medical school, from which folly I'd valiantly tried to dissuade him all evening.

'It's a snake pit,' I was saying. 'My *brother* went to med school – it turned him into an unthinking, uncaring – '

'Leave the boy alone, Joshua,' Lon scolded me. 'He knows what he's about.'

'Really, Josh,' chimed in Di, 'just because *you're* tired of academia doesn't mean you have to work out your hostilities on poor Gene.'

Gene, the sweetest of souls, tried to intervene for me. 'I'm sure Josh is only – '

'Josh is only trying to get you to be his dream-runner,' smiled Lon. 'Wants you to smuggle his contraband dream-cargo across the waters of his night.' Lon had a morbid tendency toward romantic pronouncements and literary allusions.

'I haven't got a clue what you're talking about,' I said.

'Only that you'd like to slip some of your fantasies to Gene, let him escape with them to the other side – then you could at least live them vicariously.'

'*You're* the only smuggler at *this* table,' I pointed out, 'and I haven't heard a good vicarious fantasy from you in months.'

'That's right,' piped up Margolis from across the table, 'tell us your best smuggling story.'

There was general agreement to this sentiment from the whole crowd – Lee, Stefani, Mary Barbara, Carl, Doug, Rana, Neal, Gita – they were all there. Lon ran his fingers through his long black hair and settled back with a smile. 'You mean the most valuable article smuggled, or the most difficulty smuggling?' He let his eyes defocus, mulling the possibilities.

'I mean the best story,' insisted Margolis. A movie producer, he was always looking for good stories.

Lon smiled. He was a kind, elegant man, and he had his conceits – his taste in clothes, his generosity – but

foremost was the conceit of the pirate king. 'Now once,' he began, 'I got a much-sought-after diamond bracelet back through customs, hidden inside the pacemaker of an elderly friend – of course, the pacemaker wasn't real, it was hollow – '

'Was the *friend* real?' Stefani interjected.

'No, he was hollow, too,' Lee said dryly.

'"We are the hollow men/We are the stuffed men,"' orated Lon – he was particularly fond of Eliot.

'The stuff of dreams,' said Di.

'*There* you go,' Lon declared. '*That's* the stuff. *That's* what it takes to be a smuggler. My best run? I'll tell you what it was – I smuggled out a volume of poems by a Chilean revolutionary: the distillation of his dreams. I disguised it in two books – a Spanish-English dictionary, and a trigonometry textbook. The numbers scribbled in the tables of the math book encoded the sequence of words to refer to in the dictionary – the sequence that made the poetry.'

'I can just see the translation,' Di mused: 'How do I love thee?/Cosine, log 3 – '

'You miss the point, my dear,' Lon said over the laughter of similar gay improvisations. 'To be a dream-runner, you must first have a dream.'

'That's a little heavy for me, Lonny.'

'No, they're quite light, actually, though admittedly difficult to carry.'

'How do you carry light?' asked Gita, returning from a phone call in the bedroom in the middle of Lon's remark.

'A light suitcase?' Mary Barbara punned.

'No, no, no – a box lined with mirrors,' insisted Piet – he was a magician.

'Fiberoptic cables would do it.'

'Why not just ride the light waves – let *them* carry you. Be a light surfer.'

And so it went. Not very memorable, really, except in the way it echoed off later events. And, of course, it was the last time I saw them all together – these friends who linked me to my past like old, familiar moorings, frayed yet strong.

I'm cast adrift now and can't see the shore.

But this, as I said, was just a prelude. The real beginning wasn't until a month later, at Lon's big bash.

The party was held on the evening of the Fourth of July, 1976, the bicentennial year. A glorious celebration was erupting all around the country that night, a celebration of the passage of time.

We arrived – Di and I – around nine, she in a black evening dress, I in my favourite PABST BLUE RIBBON BEER bowling jacket, burgundy velvet pants, and suede Adidas sneakers. We made quite a pair.

Lon's house sat partly on stilts, on the southern grade of one of the hills above Sunset that overlooked the entire panorama of the city. It was a brilliant summer night, the blanket of glittering lights below us, the impenetrably black sky above. Night-blooming jasmine perfumed the air, mingling with marijuana as we walked up the steep driveway to the front door. Slow, bluesy rock music poured over us there; a hundred voices danced inside; out back, somewhere, a firecracker exploded; and we entered.

Revelers filled the living room, talking, smoking. Melinda suddenly appeared in front of me, drink in hand, kissed me once on each cheek, then tongue in mouth.

'Joshua!' she said, finally coming up for air. 'Oh. And you, Di.' They wilted smiles at each other. Melinda was

Lon's most enduring, least endearing, companion. She and Di had fallen in hate at first sight.

'Oh, Melinda,' said Di, 'how nice you look . . . in this light.'

'Let's go find Lon,' I smiled, easing Di away before any more volatile fumings ignited.

We wandered into the melee. Art and artifacts adorned every surface, relics from lost civilizations decorating our own lost civilization. I saw a few movie faces in the crowd, a lot of Gucci shoes. Walls of cracked vases, patiently poised figurines, fragments of bas relief.

'Beautiful ruins,' I remarked. We were passing the coffee table upon which sat Lon's favorite Greek bust with the broken nose.

'You referring to the statuary or the guests?' was Di's response. She grabbed two champagnes from a passing waiter and handed me one.

We squeezed through a dense press of bodies to the dining room, which now served as a dance floor of sorts, a few couples moving slowly to the music.

'Let's try upstairs.' I followed her up the spiral staircase to the second floor. The crowd was thinner here, more subdued. Out a round window facing west I saw a red skyrocket explode, like a silent film. Two people came out of the bathroom giggling. One handed Di a joint, which she passed to me. I also declined, returning it to the bathroom couple, who went into hysterics and again into the bathroom. Di and I proceeded down the hall to the study. As expected, Lon was there.

He rose to greet us.

'*Mes vieux*,' he rumbled, and kissed us each on both cheeks – because he was tall, he had to stoop.

A group of four spoke quietly in the far corner. Down the hall, glasses clinked. Lon stood erect once more.

Di gasped, jumped back. We regarded her with momentary alarm.

'What is it?' I asked.

Her frozen face quickly melted into a curious smile. 'It was déjà vu,' she whispered. 'Just now. Here. This scene, this moment.'

We nodded in once-removed appreciation.

'Isn't it weird,' she continued. 'All at once, there it is, it's happened all before, it's like a picture in a familiar book, the furniture, the smells, the tilt of your head, and then suddenly you realize, Wait! This hasn't happened before, this is déjà vu! And then you think, Well, how long will this feeling go on? Is it still déjà vu now? Is it over yet? And then there's this long moment when it starts to go, and you think, Oops! There is goes! Can I hold it? Should I hold it? And you try, but somehow observing it makes it slip away even faster, and then suddenly it's gone, and you can't retrieve it even though the scene is exactly the way it was just a moment before. And then you breathe again, and smile, and somebody says, "Oh, yeah, déjà vu." And then it's over.' She took a cigarette from her purse, wedged it between her lips. 'Anybody got a light?'

Lon smiled, extracted a platinum lighter from his vest and clicked it for her. She held his hand to steady the flame, though his hands were always rock-steady.

'It's the jasmine outside,' he said, nodding toward the open window. 'That's the smell you smell.'

'It's a little like losing a dream just as you wake up,' I said.

'Maybe this is all just a dream' – Di swept her arm out across the room as if to encompass all of life – 'and déjà vu is just a half awakening, before we settle back into sleep.' She was an incurable romantic.

Lon put his arm around my shoulder. 'Come with me, both of you. I want to show you something.'

He walked us into the adjoining room and closed the door. The library. Outside, the muffled party could be heard; here were only four walls of books. He stepped across to the far wall, pulled out a volume of collected Kipling, and reached his hand into the space created by its absence on the shelf: a door-sized section of bookcase swung open on a spring. Di jumped back with a gleeful chirp, almost as if her movement had been activated by the same mechanism.

I'd never seen anything so wonderful. 'Is that actually a secret panel?' I whispered incredulously.

Di jumped up and down. 'You marvelous man,' she giggled, kissed Lon on the cheek, then ran into the room beyond. We followed directly.

It wasn't large, but it was quite majestic. And quite filled, with his finest pieces. Jade maidens holding ebony fans, golden dragons with ruby eyes, jeweled lampshades, teak furniture inlaid with ivory.

'Please, sit down,' Lon beckoned. 'I have a story.' He poured sherry as we settled on the couch.

'I love stories,' beamed Di.

'This story starts a very long time ago,' Lon began, stroking his mustache, 'but we don't pick it up until somewhere around 1948 – '

'Oh, don't just tell the end,' she protested.

'No such thing,' Lon assured her. 'In any case, this is only the beginning of the end.'

'Sounds ominous,' I whispered, opening my eyes wide.

'May I continue?' Lon arched his eyebrows.

'Please do,' smiled Di. She sipped her sherry.

'So.' Lon placed his fingertips together. 'Something around 1948 – we'll say July 1948, a day not unlike today –

an Indian from an unidentified tribe deep in the jungles of Colombia found a strange stone cube half-buried in the shallows of the river. It had frightening pictures on it, this box, so he took it to the magus of his tribe, as it was obviously quite powerful, and probably dangerous.

'The magus studied it for many years, and learned some powerful spells from it; but he was killed by his brother one day, and the box – now felt to be a vessel of great evil – was given to a traveling missionary who came to the area every other year to barter and preach.

'This missionary – Friar Bruno – carried the box with him until he reached a village big enough that it had its own priest, to whom the missionary gave the odd object. The priest was much excited and sent the box by the next caravan to Bogotá. Unfortunately, the party was attacked en route by cannibals, and everyone was eaten.

'The strange token was taken, as a prize, back to the cannibals' camp, where it was later traded to Karl Birkin for two steel knives.'

'Who's he?'

'Karl is my Colombian connection,' Lon said. 'He's a true original – half Swedish-French, half Guatec – a giant, hairy, misanthropic jungle guide and smuggler. He finds things for me.'

He stood, walked over to a cabinet, and returned with a one-foot-square object wrapped in black satin. 'Karl sent it up to me. And I now share it with you.' He set it on the table; the swathing fell away. 'Comments?' said Lon.

I touched it – cool, dark stone. Very like a box. Strange hieroglyphics were carved into its surface, magical designs of unknown meaning, that somehow portended the most extraordinary kind of power. We all touched it.

A jagged crack ran across the stone, cutting through

the three faces that formed one large corner. Lon drew his finger along the fault. 'This break is of recent origin,' he said. 'They had two days of high seas on the way up here – the object was dislodged from its niche and hurled to the floor. It broke – as you see here – into two large pieces.'

'Oh, how awful,' Di shook her head.

'Not at all,' Lon smiled. 'A case of the sweetest serendipity, if not actual kismet.'

'In what way?'

'Voilà.' Lon removed the irregular, three-sided top that had broken off the stone cube and lifted it to reveal that the cube *was* in fact a box. And there was something inside it.

He lifted the object out of the box, placed it gingerly on the table. Di drew a long, audible breath; I stared in frank wonder. Resting before us was a human skull.

But no ordinary skull. It appeared to be black ceramic, veined with gold. A huge emerald filled the right eye socket.

'It's fabulous,' I whispered. I dared to pick it up, cradled it in my palm.

'The teeth are onyx,' Lon went on. 'And yes, the emerald is real. These are not the most striking aspects of the find, however. There are two elements of even greater interest. Can you discover them? One lies in the container itself.'

Melinda wandered in just then, poured herself a drink, and looked on with mild disinterest.

Di began to examine the stone box while I pored over the skull. It was exquisitely constructed, full-sized – a perfect replica in every way. The gemstone teeth were carved to detailed shape; the leafy maze of bones that

ordinarily fills the nosehole of a real skull here was replaced with a lacy, reddish gold webbing.

'Tumbaga,' said Lon, noting my fascination with the delicate filaments in the nasal cavity. 'It's an alloy of copper and gold used commonly by many of the pre-Columbian tribes.'

I followed a gilded streak out of the nasal orifice, around the empty eye socket, across the temple, over the dome of the cranium – a glittering, jagged vein, one of many that ran like tributaries through the shiny black ceramic. There was something familiar about these lines, though. 'These are sutures,' I murmured.

'Bravo!' said Lon. 'Keep going.'

'What's a suture?' asked Melinda, though I don't think she really cared.

'It's a seam,' I replied, indicating with my finger where the golden lines connected on the cranial surface. 'They're the seams where the bones of the skull meet and connect. And these . . . they're perfect. They follow exactly where the sutures would be on a true skull. It's just a remarkable attention to detail – I've never seen anything like it.'

Lon smiled an occult sort of smile. Di now was holding the heavy stone box in her lap. 'Well, here's something even more remarkable,' she said. 'This box has *no seams* – I can't figure out how they ever got the piece *into* it. You definitely couldn't have got it out without breaking the box.'

Lon raised his glass to Di and sipped. 'That, my dear, is the first point of interest about this unique artifact.' He turned back to me. 'Joshua? Any further insights?'

Slowly, I turned the skull around, observing it from every angle: temporal, parietal, occipital. At its base I explored the foramen magnum, the large hole from which the stem of the brain protruded in life. I ran my index

finger over the lip of the hole, inside the skull. Wait, here was something – the texture was different. Not quite so shiny smooth as the glazed exterior. More irregular. More – stony. 'Do you have a light?' I asked.

Lon reached into his pocket, instantly producing a penlight. I took it and shone it inside the skull; reached my finger in again to rub a spot here, feel a bump there; then shone the light and looked again. It was hard to believe.

'It looks like a fossil,' I muttered.

Lon beamed. 'That was my thought.'

Di took the skull from me and examined it herself.

Melinda finished her drink. 'How, fossil?'

'Well . . . fossilized bone – that's just what it looks like. Bone that's been replaced with mineral over the centuries. At least it looks unarguably like the inside of a human skull, and it's composed of mineral deposit.'

'And then, you think, covered with ceramic, after the fact?'

'I . . . suppose . . .' I began, sifting for explanation. 'I don't know exactly what to think.'

'I believe it to be' – Lon spoke with a calmness that underlined the wonder of the artifact before us – 'an archeological find of the highest magnitude. It is precious as much for its materials and its esthetic as for the mysteries of its construction, its place and time of origin.' He paused, as we all continued to stare at the items. 'The glyphs on the box are in a language unknown to me,' he went on. 'The emerald looks Muisca, though I can't be certain. The ceramic is not unlike that of the death masks done by tribes near Calima. The craftsmanship is . . . unprecedented in my experience. As for the meaning of the fossil mold, the significance of the box without an

opening, the technology required . . .' He shrugged at the imponderables.

'What will you do with it?' Di asked.

Lon looked at me. 'I'd like you to take it back with you. To the lab. I suspect you can date and place it by analyzing the fossil cast at its core more precisely than I could ever trace the styles of the ceramic.'

'Ooh, how exciting,' whispered Di. She inadvertently scraped a stocking with one of her fingernails and started a run. 'Damn.'

'What a shame,' said Melinda.

'I could date the bone easily enough,' I said, 'but that wouldn't necessarily tell you much about the date of the artwork on the outside. Placing its origin geographically might be a bit more conjectural.'

'Placing its origin geographically is a bit more *critical*,' Lon corrected.

'Why? You have a theory about what tribe made it?'

'I have no theories.' Lon shook his head, wagged his finger, poured himself another drink. 'I merely intend to mount an expedition.'

CHAPTER 2

The Matter of the Skull

I took the prize home with me that night and to my office the next morning. It was summer quarter – I wasn't teaching any classes, only cataloging old material preparatory to writing another paper – so my time was really my own, with all the facilities of the university at my disposal. All the facilities I could use on the sly, I should say, since Lon had stressed the utmost secrecy in the matter of the skull.

For while my own interest was academic – and, of course, not a little romantic – Lon had his business to consider – his smuggling business, that is. If he was to find many more treasures like this one for himself, he was going to have to keep the location of the digs a closely guarded secret from the Colombian government as well as from competitors in the gold and emerald markets.

I had mixed feelings about abetting him in this essentially larcenous venture. On the one hand, I felt badly about participating in further thefts from a country whose cultures had been continuously robbed by Europeans for centuries. On the other hand . . . there were so many other hands.

Just to hold the priceless skull made me salivate; to actually be able to study it was almost a sexual delight. Moreover, it was a fossil relic, the potential importance of which I hardly allowed myself to ponder. No fossil *Homo sapiens* skull had ever been found in this perfect, unbroken condition, or with this total mineral replacement. Could it prove to be the oldest specimen on record?

And this in an area of the world not known for primate fossils? It was a paleontologist's dream, and just the prospect of Lon financing an expedition to manifest such an imagining made my heart flutter.

So stealing jeweled artifacts from pre-Columbian burial crypts was the furthest thing from my mind that morning, staring at the black-and-gold skull on my desk. What was on my mind was the materialization of dreams.

Di's job was the box. She was off photographing its six faces, showing samples of the hieroglyphics to a dead languages expert she knew, taking wax impressions, shaving bits of stone off the inner surface for mineral analysis, researching ancient South American funerary art.

My job was the skull.

I took its measure with calipers; inion to brow, mandibular curvature, zygomatic arch, temporal slope. I photographed it from every angle. I poured pink, liquid latex into it, to coat the inner surface; and when this gel had hardened, I pulled the rubbery film out of the foramen magnum in a single membranous piece, giving me a mask of what the brain might have looked like as it once sat in there, touching and denting the inside of the skull.

It wasn't a terribly detailed brain mask. But it looked terribly human. I have a crystal memory of holding the flimsy endocast in one hand, moving my fingers over the vague lumps and dips that were the echoes of its gray matter, and wondering, What did you think? Who were you?

Alas, I knew him.

Next I lay the skull down in front of the department's X-ray machine – an archaic Buck Rogers affair we'd appropriated from the dental school when it moved to the new building off-campus. I took three views – anterior, lateral, and oblique; and when the films were developed,

there was no longer any question: these were X rays of a human skull. Flawless, and composed of stone.

At the end of that first day of investigations, I slouched in my creaky swivel chair at my battered desk in my tiny office, facing the thing. It sat amid the clutter of papers and old bone fragments – this one-eyed, misplaced idol – sat there and grinned. A premonitory chill passed over me.

I locked the head in the bottom drawer and left for the evening.

We ate out that night, Di and I, at an old Deco place on Vermont called the Dresden. Someone named Toni sang 'Stormy Weather' at the piano bar while we nursed our drinks and discussed our day.

I remember both of us being oddly melancholy. Di had met with great success – her language expert was quite certain he could trace the derivation of the pictograms on the box – yet now Di couldn't shake this dismal mood. She thought she was probably getting her period.

'Maybe it's just a period of our lives,' I suggested.

'What does that mean?'

'I don't know. Just seems like the end of an era, somehow. You know – like a period of time, coming to a close.'

'Feels more like something about to begin, to me,' she shrugged. 'The way you feel the day after Labor Day, and classes starting soon.' The perennial student, she would always think of life as an extension course.

'Not a period, then: a colon,' I smiled.

Her face dropped. 'A constipated colon, maybe. All locked up, and waiting for catharsis.'

'Well. Lon's expedition is just what we need, then.' I tried sounding more chipper. 'Like a good enema.'

'Stop being so gross, Joshua.'

'Lon's Laxative Travel Service.'

'You're like a little boy sometimes.' She was half-scolding, half-coy.

'Just looking for my lost youth,' I said. Feeling wilted, I motioned to the waitress for another Jack Daniels on ice.

'God, you make it sound like you're a million years old.' She rolled her eyes.

'A regular fossil,' I nodded. The waitress came with my drink. I noticed her cleavage, we made eye contact, she smiled, I smiled, she left.

Di looked peeved. 'I suppose *she* wouldn't like to jump your bones, Mr Fossil. Or you hers.'

'Relax,' I stretched it into three syllables. 'What are you so touchy about all of a sudden?' She didn't answer, just stuck her finger in her drink and stirred it slowly. I sipped mine. 'You *must* be getting your period,' I said.

She pulled her finger from her drink, sucked on it moodily, gazed at the piano player.

Me, I just felt blue. Most likely coming down with something.

Next day I chipped away two tiny slivers of bone from a flaky section near the base of the brainpan. One I sent off – with a fragment from the box – to be carbon-dated; the other I took to the lab on the second floor that had the biggest microscope.

I kibitzed with Amy, the tech, for a few minutes, told her I had an ore sample from an old dig I wanted to check. After some obligatory small talk, she went back to numbering armadillo femurs, and I had the scope to myself.

I put the chip down over the light source and focused

in. Even on low power I could see I'd found a lucky piece. Imbedded in the sediment were three spores.

Fozzilized plant spores, deposited on the bone where it had once lain in the primordial muck. Specific spores that could be compared with all the spores that were known to have existed in that region of the world, over the eons – compared, correlated, and localized to time and place. It was a stroke of fortune.

I spent the next hour photographing the spores at different magnifications and the next hour after that developing the prints. Over a long lunch of Big Macs, I went page by page through an atlas of fossil spores and pollens, checking every documented species against the photos I'd just taken. Around four o'clock I hit paydirt – beyond my grandest expectations.

What I had in my hands, it turned out, was a variety of fern spore – *Dryopteris intermedia* – found abundantly at the junction of the Yarí and the Caquetá rivers up to 100 million years ago. The skull itself could have been nowhere near that old, of course – only a few hundred thousand years at the oldest, most likely – but it did mean that the *Dryopteris* spores had probably been deposited inside the skull within the confines of a fairly circumscribed geographic location.

There was an inset map of the region on that page in the spore catalog – nondetailed, but bounded by latitude and longitude lines. With an almost hysterical exhilaration, I noted the meridians, half ran across campus to the library, and didn't stop until I found the geography stacks. Breathing heavily more from excitement than exertion, it took me only a few minutes to locate the volume I needed.

Two atlas pages covered the territory between the Yarí and the Caquetá in which the *Dryopteris* species flourished. A small tributary of the Cahuinari seemed to wind

very near the same point, barely one degree south of the equator, giving the junction a pinwheel appearance. The nearest town was Matarca, fifty miles upriver; the rest appeared to be unexplored jungle.

I Xeroxed the pages and taped them together into a single map.

Then, feeling very clever, I sauntered back to my office, rehearsing possible entrance lines for later that evening. We were having dinner at Lon's.

'The answer is,' I said simply, wineglass raised, 'the Yarí, the Caquetá, and the Cahuinari.' Four of us sat around the dining-room table. Cooks and maids rattled in the room beyond.

'What's the question?' asked Melinda. She was at Lon's left, the consort's chair.

In the jester's seat, Di thought a moment, drank some zinfandel, and suggested: 'The question is, what were the names of the ships in which Columbus discovered mixed fractions?'

I laughed; Melinda lit a cigarette; Lon smiled politely but hurried to press me on the matter. 'The Caquetá I know,' he nodded. 'Not the others. The Caquetá cuts through Nariño territory – fascinating tribes there.'

I produced the map, with a brief explanation of how I'd arrived at my conclusion. Lon studied it, slightly confused. 'This area is hundreds of miles east of Nariño, in dense jungle – no artifacts are known to come from here. Though the skull could have been made in Nariño, I suppose, and swept downriver to this point. They're famous for their ceramics, you know.'

'Notorious.' Di loved to sport with Lon when he took himself too seriously.

Lon was never ruffled, though. 'Still, in Nariño they

used techniques not used anywhere else in Colombia. It might be a good idea to start there and then work our way downriver toward this spot you've uncovered.'

'Are we really going to do this?' Di began to get breathy as she realized just how serious Lon was. 'I mean it's really too exciting – '

'Exciting to think about, not so exciting to do,' Lon qualified. 'There'll be rains, and hostile locals, and malicious mosquitoes, and suffocating heat, and walking without end – '

'Sounds like summer camp,' said Di. 'Anyway, I've never been to the jungle, and last week I wasn't going, and now I am.' There was an almost manic quality to her speech; her recent moodiness had left her entirely. We were all being affected, I think, by the spell the skull was weaving. Starting to swirl, like iron filings in a magnetic field.

'When do we leave?' I asked quietly.

'Oh, a couple of weeks. In any case, I want you two to finish your investigations first – we're going to need all the information we can muster to try to pinpoint this thing more accurately.'

He put his index finger down on the map, on the point where all the rivers crossed. In the middle of the jungle.

I have to admit I was a little disappointed with Lon's reaction to my discovery. I'd sort of expected whoops and toasts, but Lon was pretty sanguine about the whole thing. He was right, of course – the skull could easily have washed downriver from the Nariño district. Moreover, as he pointed out over dessert, the spores could have come from *anywhere*; just because we'd only documented their growth in the single area I'd noted didn't mean the little

buggers hadn't actually thrived in lots of places over the years.

Still, it was a lead – and, as it turned out, critical to the real discovery a few nights later.

I spent the next couple of days organizing the loose ends of my life, arranging a leave of absence from the university for the rest of the summer, distributing tasks to grad students. That Friday afternoon I called Ken Campbell's office for the results of the carbon dating. What he told me didn't make sense.

He told me the fragments I'd given him – from the skull and the box – proved to be much too ancient to be carbon-dated. He'd had to run the extra chips through the potassium-argon-dating process. Sure enough, the pieces appeared to be around seventy-five million years old. I thanked him and hung up.

It was clearly impossible, of course. No humanoid skull could be nearly that old. Yet how could it *not* be that old if it was sealed inside a box that was that old, a box that seemingly hadn't been opened since the time it was made and sealed? Sealed so well it couldn't be opened.

It was all too strange to contemplate. Maybe someone had carved an ancient fossil into the *shape* of a skull? No, it was too perfect a rendering. No, none of it made sense.

I took the skull home that night. Di and I talked about it at dinner; we searched for analogies in reference texts all evening; we sat the thing on the bed between us. Giddy with mental fatigue and eyestrain, we tried to relax. We had a couple of drinks. We started to play with the mysterious toy. Silly playing. That's how we made the miraculous discovery.

First, Di did a little ventriloquist act with it. This turned lewd after a short time, with the skull making a serious pass at Di. I put one of Di's wigs on it and had my own

brief affair. Di took Polaroids. The skull demanded respect. I threatened to turn it into a lamp. The skull said I didn't dare. I said I'd seen classier lamp bases in some of the cheaper shops on Melrose and proceeded to insert the tensor light from my desk lamp up into the foramen magnum, inside the skull. With a wild giggle, Di turned out the ambient room lighting. That's when I saw it. It was madness to see such a pattern, but there it was.

'Quiet,' I whispered.

The awe in my voice cut Di's laughter flat. 'What is it?' she asked quickly, like a child ready to hear a ghost story.

I pointed to the far wall. The tensor light shone brightly through the skull's emerald eye, casting a green lattice of bright and dark lines, twisting shadows, irregular facets, all refracted by the imperfections in the crystal. But one segment of the light show somehow looked familiar to me – a fuzzy, darkling section near the center. It looked distorted and out of focus – but familiar. Almost like déjà vu.

I picked up the skull, turned it so it directly faced the wall, and walked it slowly toward the flat surface, the lamp cord trailing out behind me along the floor. Di followed silently at my side.

Three feet from the wall, the lines and shadows came into focus for me. 'Get the map,' I said. She went to get it.

I stared at the prismatic projection with a kind of terrible, momentous foreknowledge that nothing would ever again be the same. For there on the wall before me, in delicate emerald chiaroscuro, was a weave of lines that resembled unmistakably the crossing of three jungle rivers.

Di returned with the map, and I showed her where to tape it on the wall. The skull shone its green-eyed light in

a cold blaze across the paper. The markings were a perfect fit.

We stayed up all night in a state of fevered disbelief, tracing the jeweled projection onto pieces of blank paper with the skull propped at different distances from the wall. Contours began to emerge if we watched long enough: rolling hilly regions; verdant, dense foliage. The images on the wall seemed to be almost alive – respiring, changing as a real geography. I could smell the humid rain forest, hear the insects scrabbling over a dead log, feel a hanging vine brush my cheek. My fingers felt entangled in the lines I was drawing. And if I strayed, or lingered too long over a hazy shading, Di was right there to get me back on the track, to follow the next bend in the stream.

We moved the skull again. Other lines came into focus; but the illuminated area on the wall changed in size as the skull was moved up or back, so we had to transcribe these newly appreciated landmarks onto the small sheet of paper we'd started with.

The sheet was becoming our master diagram. It showed not only the major rivers and mountains that matched the library map, but numerous smaller branches not seen on the other; and unsuspected mountains and waterfalls; and what looked like a shimmering jungle lake; and one line so smooth and full of artifice it might have been a road, at the end of which was a dark, vertical cluster of shadow things I almost could imagine was a city. A city, truly.

Something about the lateness of the hour, our obsessed and wordless labor, the intense emerald glow in the otherwise black void of the bedroom – somehow it all had a dreamlike quality, both less and more than real. In fact, around four-thirty the tensor bulb blew, and I thought I

was waking up. The room stayed dark, though; only the sound of our breathing and the smell of our all-night sweat told us we were already awake.

Di didn't want to break the trance, though – even in the darkness I could feel her panic. Like déjà vu, the moment was slipping away. With a small sound like a yelp, she jumped up and raced out the door, ran all the way to the corner Thrifty to buy a new bulb, and ran back.

She was nearly crying by the time she got the light working again. The green crystal lens still projected the map on the wall – it wasn't a dream – but Di was right to weep: the trance was over.

Over, like a visitation. Yet now we had a map. And it had already taken us somewhere far away.

We sat on the floor, against the wall, both of us crying a little, exhausted, elated, ragged. Sat there until the sun started giving hints; then went outside and had breakfast at Norm's.

Is it important that I remember these things? How it felt? Who said what? I cannot know. It's important, I think, that I do *something*. These words are my fossils, the fragments of my self that will tell my story – to whom?

To you, it would seem.

After breakfast we picked up the pieces and took them directly to Lon's house. He didn't like being awake so early, though when he saw what we'd discovered, he woke up fast enough. He thought it a hoax at first but quickly realized our eyes held no humor.

We hurried him into the den, plugged in the skull, gave him a demonstration on the wall, showed him the com-

posite map we'd constructed: the rivers, the road, the city.

He was as incredulous as we had been. In fact, initially he tried to refute it altogether – but the evidence was in his hands. How could he deny what he saw, what he touched? He couldn't, in the end; he could only marvel. 'Etched in light,' he murmured.

We tried to include him in the special state we'd shared during the actual discovery, but of course it was strictly after the fact by now. It had been one of those times you just had to be there. Still, other times were coming, moments of vision or chaos that all three of us would share; I think we knew it, gazing into the shimmering green eye that morning. We hugged briefly, we three, to bond against these inklings, and began planning the adventure in earnest.

No further help was forthcoming from Di's language expert concerning the puzzle of the hieroglyphics on the box. He seemed quite baffled, in fact. Di said he told her, 'It must be a ruse, I think – I'm quite certain there is no such language.' It seemed much the same reaction I'd felt on receiving the news that the skull was seventy-five million years old: impossible. There were already enough paradoxes to choke a chaired, full professor, and we hadn't set foot out the door yet.

It took two more weeks of preparation to set foot out the door. Melinda, energized by our south-of-the-border expeditionary plans, decided to take a long shopping excursion to Ensenada. Di, Lon, and I, laden with provisions, reservations, and expectations, booked passage on Aeromexico Flight 454 to Ixtapa, to make our first contact.

CHAPTER 3

The River and Beyond

This first leg of the journey – getting down to the river – all runs together in my mind. We spent a day sunning on a beach near Ixtapa, waiting for Lon to find the only charter pilot he trusted – a parched little man named Emilio, who assured us Lon was his second cousin.

'But like a brother,' Lon swore, and the little man hugged him.

Emilio flew us to Mérida, Mexico, where we stopped only long enough to change planes. From there he flew us to Buenaventura, on the west coast of Colombia.

'Isn't this a little roundabout?' I asked.

'Want to make sure we're not followed,' Lon answered.

'Isn't that a little paranoid?'

Lon only shrugged. Maybe it was. Probably it was. We were all feeling edgy, though, and the way Lon took the edge off was with broken-field running.

Buenaventura was a bland port town, mostly fishing vessels and ferries along the coast. Lon made reservations for four people on a boat sailing up to Panamá that afternoon. Then the four of us spent all day drinking in Emilio's nephew's living room, and took the night train to Popayán.

The train was a local, so there wasn't much use trying to sleep. It stopped every fifteen or twenty minutes to let people on and off. The man in the seat across the way kept a turkey in a box on the floor, with only its head sticking out into the aisle, so every time someone walked down the aisle, the bird would get its head kicked, and

gobble. All night long. That's what I remember of the journey to Popayán.

The city itself was quite lovely, though we only spent the morning there. Classic Spanish colonial, sixteenth or seventeenth century, I think, with beautiful old stone cathedrals. Brisk, clear air. I wanted to sleep – we all did – but Lon felt we had to make Mocoa by nightfall, and Lon was the cruise director.

We bought a car – a battered, 1964 Cadillac of now indeterminate color – and left Popayán the only way out of town: across the Bridge of Humiliations. It took about seven hours of hard mountain driving to reach Mocoa.

Once near Mocoa, Lon parked the car behind an isolated shack and ushered us on foot over dirt roads, across scrubby fields, through twisted streets, and finally down to the Rio Caquetá. It was quite dark by now, and quite cold. There was, blessedly, a boat waiting for us at the docks – Lon had seen to it – and we stumbled on deck with hardly a word, as if it had always been waiting here for us.

Lon did all the dealing with the captain – they apparently knew each other – while the rest of us strung our hammocks over the deck and fell into them, shivering in the high night air from fatigue and our recent exertions. The next thing I knew, it was morning and we were nuzzling the shore at Tres Esquinas.

I felt a thrill as we walked down the pier toward the little town: this was the beginning. We all felt it. Di began snapping pictures of everything in sight – the huts on stilts over the river; the hogs wandering through the streets; the women grinding mandioca root on their doorsteps; the men cutting arrows, chewing tobacco, laughing easily. A few American-looking hippies straggled near the docks.

We walked to the water, rented a small motor launch, and took off downriver. About a half mile out, a large stream fed into the Caquetá from the north. Lon turned up into it and motored against the current another quarter mile until we reached a quiet backwater where a single, sprawling bamboo house rested on stilts half above the lapping tide, half over the muddy bank.

We tied up to a corner piling and climbed to the open porch deck along what seemed to be the front entrance.

'Hallo!' shouted Lon. No response; no movement. 'Hallo!' he called again. 'Government agents, Birkin – you're under arrest for stealing the national treasures we wanted to steal first!'

'Property is theft,' said a quiet voice behind us. 'But government property is rape.'

We turned around slowly. Standing in the shadows at the corner of the house was the largest man I'd ever seen, a blowgun poised by his mouth, pointed at my heart. Nearly seven feet tall, nearly three hundred pounds, nearly naked, nearly scowling, he wore a bushy yellow beard, with a mane of wiry hair down past his shoulders, a necklace of finger-bones, a loincloth, and a long knife at his waist. It was to my considerable relief that he suddenly broke into a broad grin.

He made a motion behind us, and for the first time I was aware of a small, leathery Indian, who lowered a bow and arrow that had been trained at Lon's back. The little man laughed wildly, then ran in the house. Karl, meanwhile, put his blowgun against the wall and walked toward us. 'Me,' he demurred, 'I am simply an honorable whore, who will accept your gifts and give you a fair embrace.'

With that he wrapped his arms around Lon in a reasonable imitation of a bear hug, and then with great good humor threw him several feet straight into the air.

For just a moment it looked as if Lon were flying; but that illusion was quickly shattered. Karl let out a solitary, raucous sound that might have been a laugh and came toward me. I took a step back. He merely thrust his hand out, though, with an ingenuous smile. Tentatively, I extended my own, and I guess we shook hands.

To Di he just bowed with the most gracious of smiles. She returned the greeting in kind.

Lon picked himself up off the deck, put his arm around Karl's waist, and spoke with many-layered affection. 'You are the worst sort of outlaw, for you live beyond the company of men.' He turned and formally introduced us to this bear of a man; then the four of us entered the house.

The front room was large, clean, spare. On the upriver side there was no wall, only the captured beauty of the arching trees, the lilies on the water. We sat on thick, woven mats in the center of the floor, around a low mahogany table. The Indian we'd seen earlier came in now, serving us fresh coffee in delicate porcelain cups.

'This is Fernando; he is a Tupi, he has no English,' said Karl. 'Or very little.' We all shook hands. Fernando's grip was iron, his smile unbreakable. 'Fernando is not his real name, naturally,' Karl went on, 'but is not my place to give you that much power over him as to know his real name.' He shrugged, lifted his cup to us, and drank. We all drank, except Fernando, who sat a little distance away with a huge plug of tobacco tucked in his lower lip, staring out the downriver windows.

I examined Karl a bit more closely as I sipped my coffee. His eyes were blue, though his skin was nearly as nut brown as Fernando's. Fine, curly golden hair covered his entire body. He was missing two toes on each foot.

'You notice my toes, eh?' he grinned. My eyes must

have widened. I began to make a polite lie, but he cut me off with his short, barking laugh. 'Is because I used to fish piranha. Is the most delicious meat, but sometimes they forget who is fishing who.' His accent was vaguely Latin, warmly formal.

'It's good you have some toes left,' nodded Lon with consideration. 'We are *here* to fish.'

'Just so?' Karl bobbed his head. 'You need a guide?'

'This was on my mind,' agreed Lon. They both sipped.

'I have only just come home from your last fishing trip,' Karl protested halfheartedly.

'This is something very special – or I wouldn't have bothered you.' He handed Karl an eight-by-ten glossy of the skull, and a copy of the map. Karl studied them both with care, and at length.

A squad of houseflies circled lazily nearby. One settled on my arm. I watched it with interest, then jumped painfully as it bit me and flew back into its holding pattern.

'They are mutuca flies,' Karl said without looking up. 'Don't let them bite you – they lay eggs in your skin.'

Behind me Fernando was chuckling so hard he had to wipe a tear from his eye. Lon only smiled and sniffed his coffee.

Finally, Karl stopped studying the papers. 'Where did you get these?' he asked.

'The skull was in the box you found for me. The map . . .' Lon made a noncommital gesture. He'd already shown the ultimate trust just to let Karl see the map.

Karl considered a moment. 'You have supplies?'

'We have medicines, instruments, goods to barter, and inflatable rafts. We need food, weapons, porters . . . and you.'

Karl scratched his beard. 'Is an unusual piece,' he

mumbled. Then louder: 'And if I don't go?'

'Then we'll just have to flounder around on our own,' Lon said with regret. To me he said, 'Karl doesn't like outsiders with him as a rule. It's just so much extra baggage.'

At that moment a snake slithered over my foot – not that I'm alarmed by snakes, really; it just startled me, being eight feet long and thick as my arm. So I jumped.

Fernando thought this was about the funniest thing he'd ever seen. He couldn't stand for laughing.

Karl smiled indulgently. 'Is only jiboa. Is for catching rats – no cause for worry.' He looked down at the documents again. Lon finished his coffee. Fernando hobbled hysterically into the next room. I sat very straight.

Finally, Karl held his hands out, palms up. 'OK, I think you are right, you need me. Let's go fishing.'

The tavern was filthy. Slow ceiling fans dangled dust streamers; a tinny radio on the bar played only static. A dozen men stood or sat around, taciturn, with flat, brown, wrinkled faces. Some were native Indians, some the mixed-breed *Triqueños*. They wore white shifts, or dirty khakis; they carried machetes, or bows with quivers of long arrows; they smoked fat, leaf-rolled cigars, or chewed coca or tobacco. Karl nodded to a few of them, and a few nodded back.

A thin, straw-haired California freak ambled in the front door and sidled directly over to our table. Torn Levi's, dusty feet, totally spaced. 'Buy some *yagé*, man? I won't rip you off, this is the real thing, it's far out, man.' He was staring at the wall; I'm not sure whom he was talking to. We ignored him for a moment, and he left.

'The hippies,' Karl shrugged. 'They come for the *yagé*, and to learn from the *brujos*. The *brujos* do not want

them, though, and the *yagé*, it eats them from the inside.' He shook his head, almost apologetically. 'Personally, I do not like them.'

Yagé was the hallucinogenic aphrodisiac used by the *brujo* mystics in these parts.

'You must understand,' Karl was saying, 'this will be a difficult trip. Lon, I trust. You and you, I do not know.' He waited for a response, got none, and continued. 'You must understand – if I say do something, you must do. In the jungle is not place for thinking maybe so, like in supermarket. *Comprende*?'

We nodded. Comprehension and acquiescence.

'Good,' he grunted. 'This way no one gets eaten from the inside *or* the outside.' He was trying to scare us, and doing a pretty good job.

'I come help you for two reasons,' he went on. 'First, Lon is my good friend, and he ask me. Two, this black skull is very much interesting. I would know its home.'

'It must be worth a fortune,' I agreed.

He shook his hand vociferously. 'No. This is not my interest. Money is nothing to me.'

'Karl is an anarchist,' Lon smiled with an expression of tender indulgence.

'Governments,' rumbled Karl, and spat on the floor.

I sort of didn't want to get too far off the track just yet. 'Then why the skull?'

'Ah, the skull,' Karl smiled. 'This jungle, you know, she is my mother. From my birth I never left her – I still curl in the wetness of her loins.'

'Karl is a motherfucker,' Lon instructed with the same endearing concern.

'Lonny, don't be so rude and tacky,' Di berated him.

'You are right,' Karl told her, 'he is these things. For

this reason also I must help him – we all must help him, I think.'

Lon bowed his head, looking more whimsical than apologetic.

Karl continued. 'My jungle-mother has a thousand mothers and a thousand thousand grandfathers, but – is said among the oldest tribes with the longest memories – only one true ancestor: he with the emerald eyes, who made the jungle green by his gaze; he with the skull of black coal which is all that was left from the fires of the last world.' This was spoken in a single breath.

'That's beautiful,' whispered Di.

'Karl is a poet,' Lon said and raised his glass to his old friend, 'and a blessing to all who know him.'

We drank.

'You think this is that skull?' I asked. It wasn't, of course. I mean, I was a scientist, not prone to believing in primitive myths. But I wanted all the history surrounding the artifact, apocryphal or not. I wanted to know all the faces of the skull.

Karl shrugged. 'Maybe. I doubt it. But maybe this skull comes close to people who can tell me better the tale of such an ancestor. I would risk much to learn such a tale . . .'

'Do you collect these tales?' I ventured. It felt like a faux pas the moment I said it.

'Karl is *not* an archivist,' Lon said.

Karl scratched his beard, looking for words. 'I *am* these tales,' he tried. Then, not happy with this explanation, he shrugged again, breaking into a deep smile, and said, 'I seek the true seeds of the mother-forest. That I may know her heart.'

Karl is a mystic, I thought to myself.

He shouted an order to the bartender, who came

around and put a few greasy paper bags on the table. Lon dipped his hand in one, took a handful, popped it in his mouth.

'Well, I'm game,' Di piped up, grabbed some out of the bag, and ate a bunch without looking. We all did. It was crunchy, tart, particulate.

'Fried ants,' said Karl. 'Is good protein.'

I could see Fernando out of the corner of my eye, grinning ear to ear. Nonchalantly, I took another handful out of the bag, dolloped a measured pinch into my mouth, and crunched away. 'Mmm,' I said.

Fernando laughed uproariously, stood, clapped me on the back, and walked out.

We slept in town that night, in a lodge near the quays. River traffic was endless, with tiny lights bobbing back and forth, up and down the waterway like magic fairies. A large riverboat, the *Amazonas*, was docked not far from my window. Hammocks crisscrossed every deck, silhouetted by hanging lanterns swaying in the damp night breeze. Like an elaborate, floating spider web.

It was an apt image, this eve of our departure.

We set out early the next morning in four rafts – three of them the inflatable rubber type that we'd brought with us, one of cork logs. In the lead raft were Karl, Lon, and an Indian whose name I never learned. They had an outboard motor, an old Evinrude 65, to help us through the rough spots.

Twenty yards of rope connected them to the second raft, which contained two porters, both Jivaros – a head-hunting tribe near Nariño. Four heavily-armed Tupis sat in the third vessel; this was for show, Karl told us, to scare off would-be attackers. It, too, was connected by

rope to the second craft, and attached to ours as well. We brought up the rear, with Di, me, Fernando, and a Yagua guide named Curicuri, who had no nose.

I remember only fragmentary perceptions of that first day. The sticky, moist heat – from that morning I wasn't dry again. It made me feel like I was drowning sometimes, as if every breath I took were filled with water.

The mosquitoes, of course. We'd pass through swarms of them; you had to get in the water and hang onto the raft to avoid being bitten. I was reluctant to do this at first, thinking of Karl's missing toes, but I was afraid Fernando would drown from laughing if I didn't.

The river itself was a constant surprise. It didn't run in one direction at all, but at times moved completely anomalously, depending on backflows from rain-engorged tributaries, dams made by newly fallen trees, and so on. Sometimes it was totally stagnant, like glass, creating a second forest in its reflection.

Giant turtles nudged the raft from time to time. A flock of screaming parrots shot overhead, changed direction like a red-and-green marching band, changed direction again, and disappeared back into the forest. The water turned from milky gray to clear ruby to black.

I have a thousand such random memories of that first day. Of the first night on the river, however, I remember every detail.

First, it was cold, and bone-seeping damp. We pulled the rafts up onto the sandy shore, pitched a large tent, and lit up a couple of small campfires. Fernando had caught two turtles earlier in the day, and one of the Tupis killed an armadillo shortly after setting up camp; so we all ate well. It tasted like chicken.

The ground was spongy. Here on land a vague smell of decay seemed to permeate everything – decay, or fecund-

ity. During dinner a foot-long centipede skittered across the edge of the firelight, then was quickly reabsorbed in the darkness.

'Oh, Jesus,' croaked Di, 'what was that?'

'A living fossil,' Lon said. He was right. This jungle had remained essentially unchanged for the past 100 million years. Protected from all the intervening ice ages by its equatorial heat, it was one of the last places on earth you could glimpse the distant past, still alive and primeval.

We huddled around the fire, braced against the chill and the shadows of prehistory, passing a small flask of hundred-proof rum I'd extracted from one of the many pockets of my brand-new L. L. Bean safari pants. I felt special warmth for our little company, for this curious human enclave in the midst of such an overpoweringly alien environment.

'The place we go to' – Karl spoke slowly, making each word clear – 'no one has gone through this place and come out again.'

'That must be true of ninety-nine percent of the jungle,' said Lon.

'Perhaps. Have been government expeditions into this place, though. Lost.'

'Cannibals, they think?' Lon knit his brow.

Karl shrugged again. 'Maybe so. But I will tell you – this place is haunted by the spirits of the dead.'

I half laughed; Di grew gleeful with fear. Lon didn't scoff, though; he only pondered. Karl was serious, quite serious, and Lon understood his tone, if not his words. As did I.

Karl continued, unperturbed by the mixed reactions. 'You may laugh. I only warn you – I have wandered at

the edges of this place. I have seen these spirits. They are very real.'

'Too much *yagé*, my old friend.'

'These are no *yagé* dreams,' Karl insisted. 'Take heed, I have seen these spirits drive men mad . . .' Did he look, for a moment, straight at me? 'And women,' he added. Di drew her knees up to her chest with a quick intake of air. 'They have never bothered me, you understand,' he concluded, 'so I do not fear them. Only I wish to prepare you.'

One of the Indians began playing a slow, funereal melody on a flute made of bone – the hollowed-out femur, I think, of a human being.

Something about that moment – the music, the rum, the shadows – gave me a sudden longing for all we'd left behind.

'Time for bed,' Lon suggested. He rose and went into the large mosquito-screened tent pitched between the two fires.

Like overtired children, we soon followed.

That was our first night. Curiously, I slept well.

Mornings on the river were full of mists, like a ghostland. We were quiet, mostly, awed by the beauty and the strangeness, floating through this dreamish place. The mists burned off an hour after sunlight, and the sweltering jungle heat returned.

Twice we had to get out and pull the rafts, the water level was so low. Karl told us the only thing we needed to worry about was stingrays lying in the mud – and only if we stepped on them. I saw one once, gliding towards me. Reflexively, I began to backstep. Karl shouted to stop – the only way I might step on the thing was if I was in motion – but I couldn't hear him for all my splashing.

Fernando raced forward to clamp a firm hand on my shoulder, but in so doing, caught his foot on the wing of the ray. Like a coil, the stinger whipped around and pierced his heel. He grunted once, slumping into the shin-deep water, weak with pain. The ray swam off.

We lifted him onto the raft. He lay there sweating, grinning, while we examined his foot. It was an angry red, already beginning to swell. Stingray venom isn't fatal, just extremely inflammatory, and the wound is terribly painful and likely to get infected. We elevated his leg and made him take a penicillin tablet. During the entire ordeal, he never lost the plug of tobacco lodged in his lower lip.

When the initial agony eased slightly, he laughed and laughed at himself – as heartily as he'd ever laughed at me. I merely felt like shit.

That was the only real incident on the river. The fourth morning – following the map – we turned south, into the jungle, leaving the rafts, camouflaged, in the shoreline undergrowth.

This, I believe – beyond the river – is when my journey truly began.

It wasn't too thick to walk at first – not at all. The top branches of the largest trees arched over a hundred feet above us; the second level, the mahoganies and the strange fruit trees, grew maybe half as tall. And the ground layer itself was fairly clear. Scattered ferns, spindly shrubs. A deep gloom was everywhere, even during the height of the day; the sunlight was diffused through the greenery, and very little penetrated all the way to the ground. The place had the feel of an immense, old cathedral.

Extravagantly purple orchids, weird fungi, straggly lianas winding around the massive trunks, or hanging,

ropelike, from the uppermost branches – it was all so prehistoric. I'd never been farther into the jungle than the riverbank on my previous dig – this was a whole new world.

The Indians peeled long strips of bark and made head slings out of them with which to strap the supplies to their backs. This left their hands free to carry rifles, blowguns, or machetes. Fernando hobbled along with half a load, leaning heavily on a walking stick he'd fashioned from a fallen branch. He refused other assistance.

The whole first morning we were followed by an iridescent bird, its call like the whine of a vibrating saw. Curicuri, the noseless one, said this was a bad omen. It was the first time I'd heard him speak.

We passed various omens, in fact, that seemed to upset various Indians, according to their tribe. A sloth, his fur green with algae, fell out of a tree directly in our path. Later a dead squirrel monkey lay curled under an outcropping, half-eaten by ants.

'It's a clean jungle,' said Lon. 'Corpses don't last a day, between the vultures and the insects.'

Clean and alive. By afternoon I was feeling woozy for some reason. I took a salt tablet and looked up to see the log before me moving: writhing, pink, alive as dying flesh. I sprang back.

It turned out to be a migration of caterpillars. I looked closer.

'Careful,' warned Karl, 'this is how Curicuri lost his nose.' He laughed his barky roar and trudged on.

I didn't laugh. I wasn't exactly frightened but increasingly had a sense of the jungle's consciousness – it was almost as if all these livid, writhing creatures formed an interconnected whole, and this totality had a sentience of its own. I tried to be at ease with it. I walked over and

hugged a tree. It was cool, smooth, stone-hard.

'Joshua, you're too much.' Di shook her head affectionately and walked on by.

Fernando limped over to me. 'Is much strong – for hold up sky,' he squinted.

I looked above, to the treetop. It wasn't hard to believe the heavens rested there, just balanced on this long arm of the jungle. I stepped back and nodded at Fernando. He was part of it, part of the consciousness of the forest. I suddenly felt in awe of this small man, and somehow deeply envious.

For lack of a more appropriate gesture, I patted him on the back – or perhaps it *was* appropriate for the awkwardness I was feeling. He took the moment gracefully, though; he was essentially without guile. He smiled, nodded back, spit some tobacco on the ground, and moved along.

I caught up with Di.

'I never thought you'd leave me for a tree,' she said as we walked side by side.

'Why not? You're always threatening to leave me for a salami.'

'A salami, I could understand – '

'Ah, but this wasn't just any ordinary tree, this was – '

'Joshua, please don't have a religious experience this trip – '

'Hey, relax, it's a little healthy communing.'

She put her arm around my waist. Sticky sweat glued her palm to my skin. I was getting used to this constant, stagnant humidity – slippery, grubby, leafy, greasy, earthy perspiration coated my body, day in, day out. It felt very animal. '*Grrrrwf,*' I said.

'Oh dear, you *are* having a religious experience,' she fretted.

'Well, maybe just a small one.'

'Do you think we're really going to find a lost city? Full of gold and bones and diamonds?' she whispered. There was glee in her eye: she was a little girl again now.

'Of course we are,' I assured her in my best older-brother voice. I filled my hand with the bottom of her khaki shorts. 'Now *this* is a religious experience.'

'Joshua, please – not in front of the bearers.'

I gave a fond squeeze and moved my arm up over her shoulder, but our packs made the position uncomfortable, so we just drifted a foot apart and continued walking in easy silence.

That night we heard the first moaning.

'What *was* that?' Di muttered. We halted; we listened. Not a sound, exactly; more the sense of a sound. An unholy, unwhole moaning deep in my brain.

It stopped us, I tell you.

'These are the spirits,' Karl said quietly. 'They are fearful, yes. But do not fear. They have not hurt me.'

We set up camp early; it seemed darker earlier.

We sat around the small fire, eating dehydrated food and being quiet. We'd had our twelve hours of light; now was the shadow time.

Karl said it would be two more days before we reached the city on the map, maybe three. I tried to make some notes in my journal but felt too fidgety to get much done. Di seemed distracted; Lon, wary. We ate tersely, and were about to retire, when the first ghosts appeared.

So insubstantial were they, I dismissed them at first as flights of imagination, or smoke dancing in the firelight. But they were more. They moved where there was no light, glowing internally with a tentative phosphorescence. So dim, they were visible initially only in my peripheral

vision; when I darted a glance straight at them, they disappeared.

I would have thought them hallucination, would have thought myself mad – but we all saw them.

'Did you see that?' whispered Di. Dear Di, her heart was on her tongue; she was ever my soul's voice.

'Pay them no heed,' advised Karl. 'It is as I've said – they will not harm us.'

One, two, and then a chorus of thin voices ululated in the darkness. 'Ohhhhhhhhhh,' they crooned, in cacophony and in unison. Faces emerged from the undergrowth and receded. Not voices, but memories of voices.

'It's the wind,' said Di, her speech thick. No one wanted to believe these were phantoms. No one wanted these things at all. But they were here. I had to account for them.

Suddenly, one of the Tupis jumped up and ran into the night. No one tried to stop him – who could comprehend any of this? We never saw him again.

Understand: I was a rationalist. I never believed in ghosts, or spirits of the dead, or wraiths, or demons. I believed in science: in gravity, and relativity, and electromagnetism, and DNA.

Yet these things of fancy were so real – what was I to believe? Only this: they were perfectly natural phenomena, whose cause simply eluded me. Chemical vapors, perhaps; firefly dust; the baying of aggrieved jungle animals. Only why, then, were these flickerings so horrible?

Not so horrible, really, as pitiable. Sorrow, truly, was the dominant feeling they evoked. Horror only because to my mind they should not have been there.

But, then, neither should we, I suppose.

They came no closer, these shapes; but they stayed all night.

Not a one of us slept well.

In the morning we left without a sound. The spirits had gone – I don't know when – and been replaced by the morning mists they so resembled.

We marched until the fog burned off and the sun crawled high enough to make breathing a chore. The jungle became thicker, with roots, creepers, rotted logs, mire. Sometime around midmorning we discovered the body. She was still alive.

CHAPTER 4

Jungle Steam

Initially, we only heard a sort of whimpering. I thought it was the spirit-illusions at first – yet this voice had substance to it. Substance, though not exactly direction. We looked all around, but something about the shape of a nearby gully made echoes seem to rise from every corner at once. With guns out we began to search.

We moved in a line, like fledgling ducks. Afraid to look behind the next tree, afraid not to. The sounds grew louder, changed timbre, then stopped.

We stopped, too, and formed a circle, peered into the foliage, heads tilted, senses primed. There was a rustling of leaves high above us. I looked up to see a gnarled vulture settle on a branch fifty feet over my head and begin to preen its ugly feathers.

There was another rustling – this time behind the tree in which the vulture was perched. A clump of ferny bushes surrounding the tree moved, then stopped moving. We stared at the spot.

Curicuri ran into the bushes with his machete and a moment later dragged an inert form out by its ankle. Bound and gagged.

It was a woman.

When we untied her bonds, she gripped me, weeping, as if I were the last piece of wood floating in the ocean: she had that twice-down look about her. We stumbled apart, finally, like similarly charged particles. She looked stunned, pursued by chaos: this was in her face, and I witnessed it. Witnessed it, witnessed her, knew her. It

was one of those instantaneous recognitions: you meet someone for the first time, and at once you feel you've known the person all your life, or you were long-lost siblings, or – something. And so it was with us.

Her hair was dark, curled by the densely humid air. Her eyes were large and brown. Her face was streaked with dirt, with tears. Her beauty was profound.

'What happened?' I asked.

She took a moment to gather her resources before speaking. 'Cannibals.'

'What were you doing here, though?' Lon pressed. I think he was concerned that someone had already discovered his secret city.

'Observing the natives,' she laughed. 'I'm an anthropologist.'

'You take your fieldwork seriously,' said Di.

'Sounds like you got caught in the uncertainty principle,' I added. 'You interacted with what you observed.'

'Only backward – what I was observing interacted with me. Actually, what I was observing tried to eat me.'

'Sounds very rude. Didn't you tell them you were only trying to study?'

'I guess they were anti-intellectual – there's a lot of that down here, I understand.' She laughed giddily – the stress of her ordeal was apparent. Di put her arm around the young woman's shoulder, and this had a calming effect. 'Rosen,' the woman said, smiling shyly. 'Torrie Rosen.'

We all introduced ourselves, welcomed her, gave her water.

'Thank you,' she said. And then: 'Can we go home now?'

'You'll be safe with us,' Lon said gently. 'But we're not going home yet.'

She nodded as if she knew this already.

And once more we set off.

We skirted a small lake – noted on the map – by walking single file along a ledge that rimmed its southern shore. As we walked, Torrie told us the story of her expedition. She'd been part of a group of naturalists and ethnologists sent in by the Colombian government to review the impact of strip-mining the area. Apparently, the natives had had their own ideas on the matter.

She was on a sabbatical from Berkeley. She was originally from Long Island (Great Neck). Her parents had been killed in a freak kitchen explosion years before. She was single, loved Mozart, played racquetball, smoked Sherman's, never got sick. By the time I found all this out, we were past the lake and back into jungle.

Fifteen minutes later we were chest-deep in swamp.

Waterlogged cypress trees rose straight up around us, anchored in mire. We had to keep moving, for if we stopped more than a few seconds, we began to sink; yet movement was incredibly slow. Leeches began sticking to my arms and legs. Not so painful, really, but disgusting.

'Are we sure about this?' I asked the group. Our silence had been intense, we'd been concentrating so much on locomotion.

'Is very difficult,' agreed Karl.

'Maybe we could go *around* the swamp?' Di said.

'No,' Lon shook his head. 'This map is too erratic – I'm afraid if we stray off course, we'll never recover the real track again.'

'There's another possibility,' suggested Torrie. Mixed feelings were clear in her voice, but I think she had decided it was better to get this trek over with, the sooner to go home.

'Such as?' said Lon.

'The canopy.'

'What about the canopy?'

'The first-level canopy of this swamp – if you haven't noticed – about twenty-five yards up, is composed of a particularly thick net of vines. They lace the cypress together almost like a web.'

'So?'

'So I've had some experience up there – with our entomologist – and I think, if we're cautious, we can cross the swamp like little spiders.' She spoke slowly, her words chosen with uncertainty.

We kept walking.

'How would we get up there?' Lon asked finally. 'These trees have no low branches.'

'It shouldn't be a problem,' Torrie insisted. 'But we have to go back to dry ground.'

Off to the left, a caiman thrashed out of the water, clamping an eel in its teeth, then plunged back into the depths of the swamp. The surface boiled a moment longer.

Without comment Lon made a wide turn to the right and kept turning until he was walking back in the direction from which we'd come. We all followed.

Twenty minutes later we once again stood on muddy ground. Another five minutes of walking brought us to a leaf-strewn area of even more solid earth, and finally to a cluster of strange, giant trees that Torrie seemed to recognize. At the base they varied from ten to twenty feet in diameter, braced by sloping, planar, buttresslike roots that tapered up to a narrower columnar trunk rising up to the canopy.

Torrie pointed to it, smiling.

Lon frowned. 'There's no way we can climb that thing.'

'Climb, no,' Torrie pursed her lips. 'We take the

elevator.' She walked up between two root-buttresses and knocked on the wood with her knuckles. It sounded hollow. 'This is a strangler fig,' she continued in a somewhat academic tone. 'Its seeds get caught in the upper branches of a tall tree and send down roots. The roots encircle the tree until they reach the ground, completely fusing around the original tree; and then when their base on the ground is solid, they squeeze the tree at their center until it's dead. The dead tree is eaten by termites and fungus, and disintegrates – the strangler now has a hollow core.' She took a machete from Curicuri and began tapping around the circumference of the tree until she came to a spot that sounded more resonant that the rest. She attacked the place with the weighted blade. With just a few hacks she was through it, into a hollow, dark space. After another minute she'd created a thin, shredded opening to the center of the tree.

Lon shined his light in. A thousand tiny creatures scuttled up out of sight.

'So,' Torrie went on, 'we make a bigger door here, we make a big fire inside, to drive away all the spiders and bats, and then we climb – put your back against one wall, and your feet against the other, and you push yourself up, like an inchworm. The top is open – we just climb onto the canopy, and crawl across.'

Lon scratched his head. 'Damnedest thing I ever heard.'

Karl mulled it over. 'Is interesting way to see the jungle. Is something to try.'

'Seems like a long way to fall,' Di suggested.

'It'll seem a lot longer from up there.'

So we did it. The Jivaros quickly chopped a big hole in the side of the tree. Inside, we piled dry leaves and branches, and lit them. Soon a huge bonfire was blazing

within, sending flames and sparks high up the living shaft. Atop the fire we threw moss, lichen, and mushrooms, which generated a great deal of smoke. There was a lot of squealing; high up, I could see dozens of bats swarming out the top of the tree, scattering into the forest.

Di sprinkled some insect repellent on the smoking blaze – she said she hated to think of what might still be lurking there.

When it had burned itself to embers, we scattered the coals, put our packs in our laps, wedged ourselves into a cramped supine position, and began the slow ascent. It was tough at first, primarily because the inside of the tube was too wide to be able to get much leverage – my legs had to be nearly straight, just to hold myself horizontally in place.

The core of the strangler quickly narrowed to a diameter of about four feet, though, so as we got the hang of it, we jerkily pushed out way up in a dark, halting procession. The smoke stung my eyes, and the people above me continually dislodged showers of rotten wood, bat shit, or plant debris down on my head. No insects, though, and no spiders.

At the top we squeezed through a lattice of crisscrossing roots, which split up into thick, arching branches. We scrambled atop them, one at a time, until we were again assembled in the daylight.

Real daylight. It was brighter up here than it ever got down on the jungle floor. You could actually see the sun through the second canopy of leaves above us.

I looked down. Eighty feet below us the ground shrank into green halftones.

'It's better if you don't look down,' Torrie suggested.

And off we went. Sure enough, the vines of this level were thick, crossing in every direction, forming at times a

net that we could walk across with ease, at times a matrix that we weaved our way through, our feet balanced on rope-thick lines as we held on to guide-wire air roots strung between higher branches.

In a short while we were again over swampland. Lon indicated the direction he wanted, and there we went. A stragglier bunch of primates never branchiated through the treetops. I wished for a prehensile tail as I watched the marshes glittering darkly below. Fernando, on the other hand, looked like he was born to it; his old smile returned as he swung here and there.

The jungle seemed more in perspective from this height. Caimans glided far beneath us, anacondas draped distant trees, peccaries nibbled roots in the shallows – all far removed, almost in a different world. After a while it lent a false sense of safety to our meandering through this web-land. I was cured of that quickly, though; I nearly walked into a bothrops.

Only ten inches long, the thin green snake was dangling from an overhanging branch like a broken twig. Above its eyes it had little horns that might have been thorns on the twig. Karl pulled me back just moments before I would have hit it with my face.

'Listen, please,' he warned. 'Do not be so interested in what is down there. Be more interested in what is up here, where you are walking.'

'What is it?' I asked.

'Bothrops,' said Lon, coming near, but not too near. 'It's a two-step snake.'

'You mean it strikes in two stages?' I asked.

'I mean after it bites you, you can walk two steps before you die.'

One of the Jivaros gave the snake a brisk thwack with the flat of his machete blade, and the critter dropped,

wriggling, to the swamp eight stories down. We continued on. I walked behind Karl.

Periodically, there were gaping holes in the netting, necessitating roundabout detours, slowing our progress. After some time, I noticed the air seemed a little chilly – darker, too. I looked up to see the sky beginning to fill with masses of slate gray clouds. With the sun now blotted out, the swamp below got very dark. The water churned as a thousand new night creatures came alive; the beings of our underworld. Unformed shapes darted, or masquer-aded as stumps, or dissolved and reformed.

Fireflies came out. Blue green sparks hovering near the water's surface, they blinked on, blinked off, tiny souls in cryptic motion.

Marsh gas, too. Vague flickerings of greenish yellow light – puffs of burning methane exuding from the swamp, visible now in this eerie darkness, looking not so different from the spirit-forms we'd seen the previous evening.

'Keep moving,' Lon goaded us.

We moved. The sky got darker; the clouds seemed to come almost to the trees. A bit of wind picked up.

I let myself down slowly on a hanging vine for a yard or so until my feet touched a large branch, then walked along the branch fifteen steps, following Torrie, who seemed to know the ropes, as it were. Eventually, it got too thin to support our weight, so we sort of half-climbed, half-scuttled across a skein of nettles intertwined with a wild tangle of airoids.

It went on for hundreds of yards this way.

Periodically, someone would slip, and plummet a few feet, always to be snagged in some awkward position at the next level of vines. As the wind started to rise, this happened more often.

'Well, this is all totally out of control, if you ask me,'

said Di. She was just behind me, hung up in a jumble of hyacinth.

The wind really started blowing now. I felt a few raindrops whip my cheeks; the suspended forest began to rock.

'I don't like this,' Lon called out, ten feet below me and to the right.

'Maybe is possible to go lower,' Karl shouted back from up ahead.

'Not too much lower,' Torrie answered. 'The canopy gets thinner quickly.'

Lightning cracked nearby, shaking the trees all around us. In a matter of minutes, it was a storm, and soon after that, a torrent.

Sopping, I held on to everything in the neighborhood. We all did, twisted around vines, branches, leaves, roots. Yet inexorably, we sank.

With the weight of the cascading water, with the random dislocations of the wind, with the gravity of our own unexpected presence in this canopy, we were sinking toward the jungle floor.

Sometimes vines broke; sometimes we slid down slippery footholds; sometimes the webbing just sagged. I looked down, and the water was fifty feet below me. I looked down again, and it was forty.

My grip failed. I plunged ten feet to an air root draped between two banyans. I grabbed even as it was snapping, and bounced down a trellis of something for a while until the root I was holding got caught and I slid along its length, burning my palms, and then it was a freefall twenty feet, flailing all the way, holding my breath, until my back slapped the water and I was submerged.

I coughed on impact, tried not to inhale, spun over, hit mud, pushed up. Air again. I treaded water but hit bottom

with my knees. I stood, gasping for breath. The water was only thigh deep.

Around me all the others were either falling or jumping. We collected ourselves in the lee of a grandfather cypress and found, miraculously, that nobody was seriously hurt.

The wind was so loud we couldn't even hear each other shout. Tall trees bent under the force; one lost its rooting completely and toppled with a sucking crunch.

We pushed on.

The rain diminished after a time, and the swamp water shallowed. We trudged ahead, silent, soaking – refugees. At least all the other creatures of the forest had sense enough to stay hidden, so we felt little threat from predators.

It wasn't too long before our bruises began to tell, though: my back, Di's ankle, Lon's shoulder, everyone's hands – sprained, strained, abraded, contused. Our walk became listless, uncomposed. We couldn't have made more than a mile the whole remainder of the day.

Eventually, the rains did stop, however, and at last we did reach high ground. And as it was near evening, we halted our march, set up camp, and ate the last of our dehydrated food.

We lit no fire that night, trying to keep as low a profile as possible. Instead, we huddled together, using body heat and companionship to ward off the cold.

'Well,' Lon smiled, 'I'd say we were ill fated, if I believed in fate or illness.'

'I think I have a fever,' Di whispered, wrapping her arms around herself.

I held my hand to her forehead. She was warm.

'Nonsense, my dear,' Lon beamed, 'you're just flushed

with excitement. We're very near now. We've come through a lot, and we're very near. I feel festive, in fact. I wish I'd brought my tux.'

'Can you tell me,' Torrie inquired politely, 'what it is we're looking for?'

'A city, we believe,' Lon eased in. 'The place of origin of an artifact that's come into our possession.'

She was about to say something else, then only nodded, as if she didn't really want to know the rest. There seemed, in fact, little to say, and sleep came quickly.

The Jivaros slept arm in arm, for warmth. Curicuri slept sitting up. Di and Torrie dozed propped against each other; Lon slept alone, his back to a tree. Karl bedded down under a huge fern. And I settled, by starts, into a troubled unconsciousness.

I was awakened some hours later by the sound of rustling. We all were.

'What was it?' I rasped, jolted out of thick sleep. 'What's happening?'

The sounds came closer, like a recurrent nightmare.

We formed a tight circle. Torrie's teeth were chattering.

Di was silent, licking her lips. She grabbed my hand, squeezed it, needing something familiar to touch, needing to touch something that loved her.

Suddenly, a form stepped out of the darkness. The shadow of a form. Like a man, but bent over with pain or hiding. When he was ten feet from our huddle, within the flicker of the torchlight, he stopped; he faced us. Slowly, he straightened.

He looked nearly solid to me, yet somehow lacking substance. His eyes were dark as coal; his mouth opened and closed soundlessly as he seemed to stare at our little

group. He wore pants, and a torn shirt, and jungle boots not unlike my own.

In fact, to my dense, cold horror, he looked a great deal like me.

Sounds issued from his mouth – muffled, broken, like a station from another country heard over an old radio.

'What *is* that?' whispered Di.

'Jungle steam,' Lon murmured. 'No more. Josh's reflection. It's a trick of the moonlight.'

'Quiet,' I said, 'quiet. He's trying to say something.' I felt quite weak and dizzy at the appearance of this specter – somehow almost as if I'd manufactured him from the stuff of my unconscious, and this dream-coagulation process had taken its toll on my stamina.

'Noooo . . .' moaned the wraith. 'How can . . . be? Whaaat . . . doing here?' His eyes seemed to grow darker, he shrank away from us. 'Goooo awaaaay . . .' he wailed. Suddenly, he brought his hands up to his face and began crying, the most pitiful, disconsolate weeping I'd ever heard. It took my breath away. It made *me* want to cry, want to comfort him, and be comforted. I started to reach out, to touch him.

All at once he bolted back into the night and was gone.

We stood motionless for a minute, the eleven of us, straining to see into the blackness. It yielded nothing.

Karl shook his head. 'I must insist we douse the fire . . .'

Before anyone could respond, a spear flew out of the dark, impaling our Tupi squarely in the chest. He fell dead.

In an instant the cannibals were on us, issuing from the forest like leaves of night blown by an ill wind. Screaming warriors – some in bark masks, some with faces painted in fluorescent swirls with a paste made from firefly tails –

descended from the trees. Terrible battle ensued.

We were firing in all directions. Our Jivaros went wild, slicing off heads, yowling ferociously. Fernando was thrashing with a machete, backstepping toward the torch on the ground. I shot an Indian behind him.

Karl was incredible. I was totally unprepared for his strength. He leapt into the brunt of the assault and with bare hands started throwing our attackers into the air, into each other, knocking weapons from their grips as if they were children. He caught one cannibal from behind, broke his neck in the crook of his elbow, then continued to hold the man's dangling, dead body in front of him as a shield – held it up by the neck, in his elbow – while he bashed others who came near with his free arm. He threw one such assailant against a tree – I heard the Indian's back snap, and he slumped.

One of the mask men tore me to the ground. I fired off several rounds from my revolver, and he fell to the side. I stood again. Lon was being wrestled down by three of them; I shot two, but then my gun was empty. Something hit me in the forehead and I sank to my knees.

Everything was swimming in circles around me now. It looked like the savages were fleeing, uphill then downhill. Karl's blowgun darts hit a couple. I turned my head to steady it; warm blood flowed down my left cheek. I saw Torrie being dragged into a tangle of bushes. Everything turned dark red. I tried to get up, but vertigo held me flat. Soon I could neither see nor feel, but only heard the gunshots all around me, exploding deeper and deeper inside my skull, until all was void.

CHAPTER 5

A Remarkable Likeness

When I awoke, it was early morning. To my great surprise, I found myself lying in the same clearing we'd occupied all night. I sat up with a start, but a splitting pain in my head kept me grounded. I groaned.

'Go slow, *mi amigo*,' came a growly voice.

I opened my right eye – the left was stuck shut with crusted blood – to see Karl standing before me. He handed me a canteen of water, from which I drank. I immediately threw up.

I looked around: heads, bodies, blood – it was too grisly. I burst into tears. It was all more than I'd been prepared for; never before had I actually fought in battle, actually killed people to defend myself. Death littered the ground.

I noticed, for the first time, our group had diminished, all of our bearers but Curicuri and one Jivaro slaughtered. It made me starkly alert in an instant.

'Where's Di?' I rasped.

'Taken prisoner,' said Lon. I winced. 'Torrie, too.'

'We could do nothing until light,' Karl added. 'Now we can follow. They have perhaps an hour lead.'

Fernando moistened a rag with water and roughly swabbed my face. My other eye came open.

'So let's follow,' I said.

Fernando smiled and handed mc a rifle.

I was wounded in the leg, too, it turned out. I bandaged the laceration – it wasn't very bad – and took some penicillin. Fernando's foot appeared to be festering, but

he only laughed it away, and clapped me on the back, pointing to my own cut calf as if it were a badge of honor.

Everyone was pretty much the worse for wear. Karl had an ugly gash down his side. Lon's back was all cut up, and Curicuri and the Jivaro were badly bruised.

But we were still moving.

We carried only weapons and light packs now. I had a pistol at my waist, and a shotgun – these were the only arms I trusted myself with. The others were loaded to the teeth, though: automatic weapons, flares, and our explosives, originally intended for use in blasting open jewel-rich tombs. It was this firepower that had saved our lives the night before; I prayed it would save the hostages now.

It was an easy trail to follow, marked by broken foliage and blood. The kidnappers had no reason to think we would pursue them, I suppose – probably no one else ever had – so they'd simply made a straight line back to their camp, carrying their wounded captives. Yet it soon became apparent that their track followed the same path we'd been tracing on our own map.

These Indians were heading for the city we sought. The city I'd seen in the glint of the emerald eye.

The track ran into a straight, limestone road – it must have been built who knows when – that corresponded to the road on our map. It was half-covered with leaves, but nothing else impeded our progress, so we made good time for several miles.

After an hour of this, the highway abutted a fast river and stopped. We tramped through a shallow bend to the far bank, but no footprints emerged there.

'Upriver or down?' I asked.

'It's pretty fast water,' Lon rubbed his cheek. 'Be hard

to carry hostages up it. Easier if they had canoes waiting here and sailed down.'

It made sense, what he said. We were about to start trekking with the flow, when something glinted at me ten yards upstream. Something golden.

I ran back. There at the edge of the water lay Di's wedding ring. It couldn't have fallen – she'd have to have pulled it off.

So they'd gone upstream. And Di, at least, was still alive.

I showed the others, and we set off along the shore, against the current. Three of us walked on one side and three on the other, to make certain the tracks didn't come out again. The river stayed fairly shallow, though in twenty minutes it had become white water, and ten minutes beyond that we came to its source: a two-hundred-foot waterfall, crashing down the face of vertical cliffs that extended in either direction as far as we could see.

'You sure they didn't leave the water back there?' Lon shouted over the roar of the falls. We all backtracked a hundred yards, then returned. No sign.

Cold spray filled the air. Above the churning surface, where the sunlight stabbed, rainbows shimmered in the mist, then disappeared, or shifted position – except one. One rainbow remained motionless, a thin streak of red and blue, still as a line, firm as an arrow sticking out of the rock that protruded . . .

The rock.

It was a great boulder, actually, jutting out of the cliff face, through the falls, about twenty feet above the surface of the river, making a cleft in the cascading water, a dark vertical gash in the center of the falls. Protected from the tons of pounding water by this rock was a dark,

dry, sheltered space which, to my eye, looked very much like a portal.

Without reflection I leaped off the shore onto a table of stone sitting in the rapids. Here I stood and motioned the others to follow, as the river crashed all around me.

'Where the hell do you think you're going?' screamed Lon, but I only grinned smugly and turned back toward the falls.

There was a series of flat rocks sticking up out of the river – stepping-stones, you might call them – and I jumped from one to the next without problem. When I got near the waterfall itself, the wind of its tumult nearly dislodged me. But I kept my footing, and as the stones veered close to the protected area beneath the boulder in the waterfall's midst, the air became curiously calm.

Another promontory of stone extended, like a wharf, under the overhanging canopy of rock above me. I sprang onto this natural pier and walked a few steps in. Sure enough, this was no solid cliff, but a cave.

I turned around to face my friends. Falls thundered on either side of me, a giant boulder poised over my head, a yawning cave mouth opened at my back, rainbows played before me on the water – and for just a moment I felt like the potent wizard of a magical kingdom.

The moment passed. The sun dropped another degree; the rainbows vanished. My comrades stared at me in disbelief from the shore. Lon shouted something, but I couldn't hear him. Finally, Karl threw up his arms, threw his head back with a laugh, and jumped down onto the first stepping-stone. Presently, the others followed.

When we all stood together upon the stone lip of this entrance, we entered the cave, flashlights first. It turned out not to be a cave per se but a sort of cavernous foyer leading to a whole myriad of tunnels, conduits, under-

ground rivers, shafts, basins, and catacombs of every description perforating the stuff of these cliffs. It was pretty overwhelming.

'Uh-oh,' muttered Lon.

Fernando found the blood, though – drops of it, leading directly to the second tunnel on the left. We followed the trail, having to hop across a narrow stream that cut through the rock floor. Into the tunnel.

A paleontologist is never without a piece of crayon with which to number his fossil samples. I took mine from my side pocket and, as we entered this first turning, drew an arrow on the wall to show the direction we'd come. Now we could find our way back if the bloodstains got washed clean.

'Well done, *mi amigo*,' Karl remarked.

I felt ridiculously proud – but this was the first time I'd contributed anything since we'd begun the journey, and it was a great relief to be something besides useless baggage.

The blood-drop trail took us through aimless tunnels, past multiple cross-turnings, into rooms of stalagmites, along subterranean rivers – in absolute darkness save for the beams of our lights. Bones cluttered the floor in places, some of them fossilized and some of them quite large. We didn't stop, though – not for my academic curiosity or Fernando's foot, or for the occasional blind moaning that emanated from a number of the tunnels. We'd been through more than unhuman wails already. We pressed on.

At every cross-tunnel I made a mark with my crayon. Every third turn we doused our lanterns to see if any other light sources had become apparent. At the ninth decussation we saw the light.

Barely a glow at first, diffusing from the far end of a huge, vaulted chamber. The bloodstains headed right to

it. We ran softly, along the wall, until we came to the spot – it was another cave mouth, opening onto daylight. A thin sheet of water poured over the outside of the cave, like a translucent curtain obscuring what lay beyond. All we could see on the other side of this unimposing waterfall was a soft, sunny green.

'Wait here,' I said. I don't know why. I'd never been particularly brave; my adventures all came from books and movie screens. But I was living an adventure now, so I suppose I was behaving the way I imagined I should. Besides, I could barely stand to think of what might be happening to Di in there, and the agony of these imaginings alone was enough to propel me forward.

So I held my breath, plunged through the fall, and opened my eyes on the other side. What lay before me was a valley.

Not an enormous valley, but large enough. And luxuriously verdant: spotted with plantano trees, mango trees, groves of tamarind and pomegranate. It was ringed on all sides by high cliffs over many of which grand waterfalls poured – thirty or forty falls around the entire perimeter, some of them emptying into streams that flowed into the valley, some of them apparently coursing back into the tunnels that honeycombed these cliffs.

And in the center of the valley was the city.

Ancient stonework ruins sprawled over the grassy slopes, starting perhaps three hundred yards from where I stood, extending a mile across the craterlike valley. The nearest of them were completely untended – crumbling half walls, piles of rubble. A little farther in, stone houses were visible, small, square huts with flat roofs and open doors. From some of these, smoke could be seen curling up out of tubular chimneys.

Finally, at the core of all this, was the castle. A great,

falling-down, hulking ruin of a Gothic stone castle. One whole side appeared to be leveled, while another rose from mounds of its own debris to form spires, towers, walls, and turrets, starkly silhouetted against the green cliffs that circled the basin.

I was absolutely stunned.

A moment later the others joined me. We sat in the tall grass beside the stream that flowed down from the waterfall through which we'd just passed – sat and stared in wonder at this impossible sight. We could make out people moving in the distance, too, scurrying around the castle like ants investigating a child's broken toy.

Karl shook his head slowly. 'I have never seen such a thing.'

'It doesn't seem possible,' I said. 'A medieval French castle just plunked down in the middle of – '

'Not French,' Lon muttered. 'And not medieval. It's a fifteenth-century Spanish castle.'

I was a bit nonplussed by this out-of-the-blue assertion, but Lon quickly continued.

'Chuvalo, a great conquistador – he's said to have discovered a magical valley, surrounded by falling waters. He forced the tribes here to carry a city, stone by stone, into the canyon, and to build the castle he left behind in Castille.'

'I have never heard of such a thing,' rumbled Karl.

'It's referred to in a few monographs – I didn't think it was near here, really. These waterfalls, though, and that fortress. Chuvalo sent word requesting a priest for his new kingdom, but the return ship never found the place.' He paused. 'But I think we found it.'

We crawled three hundred yards along the stream to the most outlying structure: a deserted stone wall, three or four feet high, twenty feet long. It afforded us complete

invisibility from the village. The little river actually made a ninety-degree turn at this point and headed back into the cliffs a quarter mile to our left. I peeked over the wall. The castle seemed much closer already.

'There's some kind of small forest over toward the right,' I whispered. 'Just behind the castle. If we could hide in there, we could scope it all out better.'

Karl and Lon squinted at the scene, calculating, guessing. Karl spoke first. 'Two houses we must cross near to get there – one, at least, I see people.'

I began moving along the wall. Fernando tried to follow but immediately broke out into a white sweat.

We looked at his foot. 'He can't go on,' said Lon. 'This looks terrible.'

It did. Purplish red and puffy to the ankle, with angry streaks moving up the calf. Fernando winked at me, or maybe he was just blinking away the sweat. In any case, he never complained.

We decided to leave him at the wall with some food, a rifle, and two sticks of dynamite. He could see pretty much everything from here, so he'd be good surprise cover for our escape if we had to make a fast exit – which seemed likely.

We gave him a double dose of penicillin, propped his leg up on a big rock, said our farewells. Fernando just spat tobacco and peered at the city through a hole in the wall.

We backtracked to the base of the cliffs, then scuttled through the grass counterclockwise along the perimeter of the canyon, flat against the cliff wall, trying to be inconspicuous. Apparently, we succeeded. We reached the point along the cliff which put the dense grove of trees between us and the castle.

On nearing this spot, we found a reasonably deep river

flowing out of the cliff – it appeared to pass by the small forest before exiting somewhere on the other side of the valley. We slid in and floated downstream, only our heads and weapons bobbing above the water, then emerged once more hardly thirty yards from the edge of the grove and scurried across the open space without mishap.

I felt scared and excited. This was farfetched for me, yet what could I do? My wife had been kidnapped by cannibals; I was in the general vicinity of nowhere; I'd been attacked, I'd killed people. It was all utterly insane, totally out of control – but what was I to do? How to act? I had to more or less invent it as I went along, drawing on instincts (largely atrophied), old movies (of mixed genre), and the actions of Karl and Lon, who seemed to have done this sort of thing before.

I had a vague sense of fatigue, propped up by lots of adrenaline. And I was aware of an increasingly relentless headache where I'd been hit during the fighting.

These were the elements that comprised my mood as we entered the grove that sunny noon. The grove itself was cool, dark, heavily scented with the flower of the fruit that filled the trees. The fruits themselves hung low on the branches – red, bulbous, opalescent things, they looked almost ornamental and sort of unsettlingly erotic. Slowly, we walked.

It was like a fairyland: strange flora, clackering birds, sweet breezes. Time felt stilled. Step-by-step, we moved, listening to each moment. A leaf fell. I watched its intricate tumble to the ground, watched it nestle, finally, into its new place in the universe. We walked on.

After perhaps a hundred yards, we stopped suddenly at the appearance of a figure among the trees. I stood, gun poised, certain our discovery was imminent. The figure

before us was equally motionless, though, and it quickly became clear why: it was a statue.

We approached from behind and walked gingerly around to face it, not knowing what to expect. It was incredible.

It was the statue of a man, life-size, cast in what appeared to be solid gold. And when I say life-size, I mean *my* size, not the size of the natives we'd run into in these areas, who averaged closer to four or five feet tall.

His eyes were emeralds. On the ground before him rested an open chest, literally overflowing with jewels of all kinds. Lon filled his pockets. So did I.

But the most amazing thing about the statue was his dress – he was clad in the armor of a Spanish conquistador. On his head was the characteristic helmet, sporting an ostrichlike plume. In one gloved hand he brandished a saber; in the other, a quill pen. He had a certain disturbing familiarity.

'*Madre mio*,' whispered Karl.

I felt the same way. We all stared in lame awe.

Ten yards before him was a large stone slab that could only have been an altar. It was covered with dry, and not very dry, blood.

Out of the corner of my eye I saw something move. I whirled, dropped to one knee, pointed my shotgun – it was another statue. Thirty feet away, half-hidden by a tree, it stood there as eternally still as the golden man beside me. It wasn't movement that had caught my attention, only humanness.

I walked over to it. It was carved from some kind of stone, covered with moss and lichen: a woman, naked, European, poised in mid-step. She looked just as if she'd been frozen while strolling through the woods. I touched her cheek and she seemed to gasp. I jumped back,

bumping into the Jivaro: it was *he* who'd gasped, standing close behind me, watching me touch the statue.

As we resumed our march toward the castle, it became apparent that this part of the wood was in fact filled with statuary: human forms, animal forms, intermediate forms. I felt watched. I think we all walked a shade slower under their stony gaze. Curicuri held an amulet before him.

The grove began to thin after another hundred yards. We could see a large courtyard – perhaps fifty yards deep, surrounded by small stone buildings – on the far side of which was the ruin of the castle.

The courtyard bustled with natives of a variety I'd not seen before. Like the statues in the grove, they were taller and lighter-skinned than most Amazonian tribespeople. Their garb was an odd mixture of tribal and European; they were bare-chested, sometimes painted or tattooed, yet many wore long pants. Some even had knee boots.

For several minutes we sat there staring, mute.

Finally, Karl said, 'Could be you are right about this conquistador nonsense.'

Lon indicated a long, low structure with bars on the windows and two guards, spears crossed, standing at attention on either side of the single door. 'If that's not a stockade, I'll eat these jewels.'

'You will eat them anyway if you expect to smuggle them through customs, *mi amigo*.'

'Most likely,' smiled Lon. 'But that blockhouse is my bet for where they hold prisoners.'

I was getting edgy. We appeared to be heading for a plan of action. All my perceptions seemed heightened: I felt the breeze ripple every hair on my neck; pungent vapors filled the trees.

'Is too crowded to rush,' Karl said, squinting, scratching his beard. 'I think better we wait for tonight – will be more quiet, more dark.'

Lon nodded. 'We could use the daylight hours to scout the place a little more – look for shelter, secure some alternate exits.'

'Tonight, then,' Karl agreed with himself. 'If we can slip in to the prison, we slip in. If not, maybe we just try to kill the chief. With these colonial governments, when you kill the chief, the society crumbles. Is like *any* government . . .'

He was saying something else, but I didn't hear what. My attention had been diverted to a profusion of sparkling lights near the center of the square: pulsatile spots, vibrating like electrons, whizzed in and out of my peripheral vision, accompanied by a tantalizing scent. I took two steps toward them – toward the castle – to the top of a rise at the edge of the clearing.

'Hey, watch it, Josh!' I heard Lon's voice warning me in a fog, felt his arm restraining my shoulder as if from far away. A feeling overcame me, though, like a compulsion – to *be* in this city, to shed myself of these strangers I was now with, these faceless so-called friends, and plunge my inner self into the soul of this place. All in a moment I felt these things.

I broke free of Lon's grip and ran dizzily out of the woods, into the square.

'Get back!' Lon whispered after me as loud as he dared.

'Leave him,' I heard Karl growl. 'Follow me, there was a cave. . .'

And then I heard no more. I stumbled, rolled down the shallow slope, got up running, fell again, arms akimbo and grunting like a gibbon. Before I knew it, I was standing in the middle of the square, facing the remnant castle, swaying, trying to grasp the compulsion that had led me to this spot.

My sudden appearance immediately became the main

attraction. Everyone stopped, gawked at me, and began jabbering all at once in a strange, totally foreign tongue.

I felt very odd. My head seemed about twice its normal size, which probably accounted for the echoes that wouldn't stop. The two guards who ran up to grab me developed a waxen, turquoise sheen to their skin; their mouths began to melt.

A man stood before me. He was naked save for a weave of feathers girdling his loins. His height exceeded mine. His flesh was the color of dark, tarnished copper. He was extensively tattooed with ornate designs, some of which included gemstones sewn into his skin. On his face he wore a mask: wooden, intricately carved, adorned with jewels. It was the face of a wildman, with animals growing out of it: its thick tongue was a screaming lizard, snaking from its open mouth; an eyeless, snarling iguana stood upright on human feet that emerged out of the mask's brow: serpents curled around the eye slits, demon women stretched across its cheek.

This man was the *brujo*.

He poked me with a staff of some kind, but I didn't feel it – didn't feel anything. My body was all numb, my mind distorted. A musky, perfumed smell filled my nostrils. It was all too bizarre. I was trying to think of something to say, but could not think.

I noticed my left hand was twitching. Nerves, I thought. But then the whole left arm began to jerk, and then my left leg as well. I saw the *brujo* jump back, gesticulating, babbling. I felt the left side of my face go into spasm. I began to topple. My vision faded. The last thing I remember before consciousness left me was a labyrinth of tunnels, opening before me into forever.

I awoke curled in the dark corner of a vast, dimly lit room. A few high windows admitted early evening light,

augmented by two small hearth fires. Shadows spread out across the floor. When I blinked my eyes open, I could see they were bodies.

I didn't move except to focus. Sprawled everywhere, the bodies seemed to be sleeping – at least, many did. Some were so motionless they could have been comatose, while others appeared to be having seizures – quietly, repetitively convulsing. I stared at one unmoving body for two minutes; its chest never rose, it never drew breath. I finally realized it was dead.

I jumped to a sitting position with a gasp and immediately heard another gasp behind me, which made me gasp again and lurch around. Sitting there to my side was a woman – middle-aged, wall-eyed, pale – looking every bit as surprised to see me as I was to see her.

'You're alive,' she whispered, her accent distinctly British.

'As far as I know,' I whispered back. 'Am I supposed to be dead?'

She laughed – more of a wheeze, really. 'And you speak English to boot.'

'Well, I speak American, actually. But I understand English.'

She laughed again, and held my face in her hands. I could see her eyes moisten in the firelight.

'Well, understand this, American,' she rasped. 'You've gone and stepped in it this time.'

We both had a wheeze over that one. I felt pretty tearful myself, in fact, but kept it at bay. She gave me a cup of water, which I downed to steady my throat. 'I'm Darwina S. Vine,' she said as I drank. 'You can call me Dar, though, and I'll pretend you mean "Darling."'

I told her my name.

She extended her hand, and I shook it. 'Special UN

envoy. I was sent down here with the Colombian government expedition – nearly a year ago, dear Lord – to investigate charges that the government was committing genocide among the indigenous tribes of the interior. Funny, now – the locals killed us all but me. Still, turnaround's fair play, I suppose. But that's the gist of it – the rest are dead, and I've got the fever. There, I've talked enough for a while. Now what's *your* story?'

She was frank, with a hint of lunacy, it seemed to me. Maybe it was just the way her one strabismic eye stared off into the corner, but she made me think of mad dogs and Englishmen.

'Well, I'm not exactly sure *how* I got here,' I began, suddenly realizing that I couldn't remember anything I was doing before I woke up. I had amnesia.

'Oh, I can tell you that,' she said. 'You've been having fits. You know – convulsions.'

'No, no, that's impossible,' I dismissed. 'I don't have – '

Darwina S. Vine smiled and put her hand over mine. 'I watched you twitch right here beside me for an hour. And then another hour still enough I thought anyway you were dead. You startled me so when you sat up, like to put *me* in my grave.' She patted my shoulder. 'Easy, you're postictal now. It's the time after the fit – you'll be feeling logy, and your memory's addled, but it'll come back, in patches anyway. Still, be glad – it's what saved your life. It's what saved mine, I know – I've got it, too, you see. Epilepsy, that is.'

She was going way too fast for me now. I held up my hands with a half laugh. 'Whoa, I don't have epilepsy.'

She shrugged. 'Well you've got *something* that gave you seizures, and you couldn't have picked a better time. We're *revered* by this tribe.' She furrowed her brow,

brought her fingers gingerly up to my forehead. I winced in pain. 'Nasty bump,' she nodded. 'Broken, I shouldn't wonder. Bad sign, I'm afraid – if that's the knock causing the seizures, there's bound to be bleeding inside.' She looked tense for a moment, then broke out in a hopeful smile. 'They do good trephination here, though – very sophisticated surgical instruments, really. For relieving the pressure, you know . . . that is, if you do develop any intracranial bleeding . . . damn, now I've scared you, I'm sorry, here, let me . . .'

Scared wasn't the word. I was petrified. I think I turned quite pale. She lay me down.

'You're doing just fine,' she whispered, soothing. 'You've got this far, and now there are two of us to fox the bastards. So you just lie here and rest up, and I'll tell you the story of this bloody tribe and their bloody gods and goblins.'

I tried to slow my breathing down, tried to order my thoughts. The natives were definitely hostile, but I knew I'd make it if I could only keep a clear head. I tried to clear my head.

Darwina continued. 'Goranchacha, child of the Sun, born of an emerald – he's the god these Guachetá pray to. According to scripture, the Sun himself impregnated a village girl, and she gave birth to an emerald, which turned into Goranchacha, a beautiful, yellow-haired boy. Why's it always yellow hair, I wonder? Anyway, he went wandering, and everyone was waiting for him to show himself, but he was the coy one – and then what happens but five hundred years ago he shows up here with his disciples.

'Well, these villagers were ready. According to informed sources, in fact, they'd already *built* a golden statue of the sun-child, generations earlier, they were so

sure he'd return. Keys to the city is what they gave him, but if the truth be known, I'll lay odds this Goranchacha who showed up was a vagrant Spaniard. Probably Pizarro, or some lieutenant of his. He appeared one day with his little army and just decided to stay. He heard the locals threw a lot of good parties, and before long, the castle became a "temple to the sun-god," and old Goranchacha was going native. I'm reading between the lines a bit, of course, but that's the prerogative of the historian.

'The point is, old Goranchacha-Pizarro-whoever had the fits. DTs, most likely, but there it is. And that fact got passed on from *brujo* to *brujo* over the generations: the god incarnate was epileptic! Of course, epileptic isn't what old Gor called it. He had a clever cover for the natives. "Visits from God" is what he had them believe.' Her tone was one of controlled mania – an intense involvement with the narrative, as if she'd been waiting to tell this story to someone all her life. A bit more slowly, she went on.

'Now the plan was, old Goranchacha was to marry the queen – Queen Namsháya, Goddess of the Moon, Jaguar-Woman – and the two of them would spawn a new race of beings. Trouble with that plan was, the queen was only three years old.' She smiled thinly. 'So they had to wait. But before the queen reached a proper age for marriage, old Goranchacha had to leave the valley – to meet his own high priest "from across the water." Some bishop, I expect, on the latest armada.

'So Goranchacha told everyone here to stay here, he'd be back, and he left. Left a small garrison of men, too. Only he never did come back. Never heard from again. But – the Guachetá are a patient people. They're still waiting, you see. They fully expect the sun-child will return, and take the *new* good Queen Namsháya Moon-

Goddess Jaguar-Woman for his bride, and father a whole new world. But in the meantime, in the meantime, Joshua – and this is key – the Guachetá believe Goranchacha has been sending down little emissary godlets to keep watch over his tribe. And the way these spirit-beings make themselves manifest is by inhabiting the bodies of select individuals, their presence being expressed by the appearance of seizures.

'So that's your basic background – this tribe worships people who have convulsions, whom, it is believed, are possessed by the gods. And it is our great fortune, my dear boy, to be stricken with this holy occupation.'

My fascination with her story was beginning to override my multiple anxieties. Confusion still fogged me, but I temporarily kept it cornered.

'Fact is,' she rolled right on, 'I've had epilepsy since I was eight. Well controlled, too, until I lost my pills when we were captured. That was the end, I thought, but I've had two seizures a week ever since, and that's the only reason the *brujo* lets me live. They'll keep you intact for the same reason, long as you throw a fit now and then. I'm not certain *what* they have in store for you, of course – not exactly anyway. Heard some talk about Goranchacha's idol out there, but I doubt they'll sacrifice you – you're too well possessed.'

I had to laugh, though it hurt my head to do so; it seemed like a pretty good pun under the circumstances. I sat up and faced her again, feeling somewhat rejuvenated. The sun had set now. The only light was from the two small bonfires crackling in the middle of the big room. Shadows jumped and shrank along the floor like uncertain thoughts.

'How do you know all this?' I asked.

'Learned the language,' she said. 'Knew some of the

local dialects already – I've got an ear. And these other poor specimens here, they've taught me.' She motioned at the shapes huddled around the fire, then brought her face close to mine, her bad eye staring over my shoulder. 'Say, you wouldn't happen to have a cigarette, would you?'

I shook my head as I looked at our darkling companions across the room, and a queer thought struck me. 'But surely they don't . . . you're not saying these people all have epilepsy.'

'This bunch does.'

'But how – '

'Now that's another story,' she smiled. 'Think you're ready for another story just yet?'

I nodded.

'Glutton for stories, are you? Well, this one will fill your belly right up to your throat.' She scowled as if she took a certain delight in her grim existence here. 'These people are all prisoners, like you and me – from different tribes, mostly, captured in battle. Special prisoners. Special for reasons discernible only to the *brujo* – I haven't a clue how he reaches his decisions; they probably come to him in dreams, or the Watcher tells him, or the current Queen Namsháya. I'll tell you about the Watcher some other time. In any case, the prisoners in here were selected for special treatment. Very special treatment.

'See, the *brujo* did brain surgery on them. Quite a ceremony. First, he drills a little hole in their head, then the queen of this happy village, Queen Namsháya – God save the queen – dear Queen Namsháya scoops out a little bit of their brain and *eats* it – eats it, by God, to imbibe the power of this special captive. And then the *brujo* heats up a small emerald until it's red hot, and he plops it back into the hole where that bit of brain was – the "jewel

of the gods," it's called – and then he sews the chosen one back up.

'And guess what? Shortly after the ceremony, the patients all develop seizures. Now it's no surprise to you and me that some poor clown is going to start convulsing when someone sticks a burning rock in his brain – but to *these* little Indians, it's a holy miracle. They believe this victim of unnecessary surgery is actually a sacred vessel, now inhabited by one of the deities.

'Of course, half of those specially chosen get meningitis, or encephalitis, or brain abscesses, or cerebral bleeding, along with the seizures. Actually, most die within a week of surgery – but *they* are said to have abandoned their earthly bodies, so they could go back to live with the gods. And then, of course, those who *don't* die merely continue to have implanted emeralds – sort of like seventeen-jewel alarm clocks that rattle off at odd times.

'They're given special attention, special meals, special license – until they get sick. Fever, vomiting, coughing – these are all taken as signs that the god is trying to leave the body, to go live in the stars again. When that happens, the sickie is put in here. Sick bay. It's kept isolated, so the straining spirits can help each other out of the chains of their unwanted bodies. That's why I'm here now – I've got the fever; my god wants out. I'm not sure why you're here; it might have something to do with that blood trickling out of your ear there . . .'

I reached up quickly to touch my right ear. It was sticky, warm, crusted. With a sickening sense of vertigo, I brought my hand down again: dark blood oiled my fingers; there *was* bleeding inside my head. The shadowy forms sitting around the fire grew ominous to me; but also pathetic, like souls in hell. It began to dawn on me that I

was probably here on a one-way ticket. Then I had another sickly flash.

'They did this operation on *me*, didn't they?' I whispered.

'Not a bit of it,' Darwina said, steadying me. 'You just got a bad whack. Now buck up. I've had the fever before and made it. Things could be worse. If we *didn't* have seizures, they'd have cannibalized us right off. Or vampirized us – they love a bloody drink here. Fact is, that's what they were doing to me when I threw my first fit of godly possession. If you're real lucky, they might even want to use you for copulation – of course, inbreeding is a big problem here, you can imagine – and believe me, there's worse ways a prisoner of war might spend his time – '

I straightened up, pulled myself together. 'It's just – this is just a lot to assimilate all at once,' I said quietly.

'Right,' she smiled. 'And so it is. Well, it's not all that bad a life for us, really. If we don't make waves, we're treated well. I try to look at it as just another phase in my life. I wouldn't have a prayer out there alone in the jungle if I made a run for it – probably wouldn't even make it through those caves to get out to the jungle. So I take this for an altogether strange experience and make the best of it. One ought to keep a sense of balance about these things. If I see my chance to get out of here, I'll take it and nothing will stop me. Like if the marines show up. Until then – well, I've got you now, at least. Who knows what next year might bring? So don't look so god-awful glum, and tell me what you're doing here.'

There was, at that moment, a commotion near the door. Natives carrying torches entered, dumped a flaccid body onto the floor, and left.

Darwina stood up. 'Come on, then. That'll be some

poor initiate with the dry heaves who needs tending. We take care of our own in here.'

I stood and accompanied her across the room to where the new body was slumped. We crouched down to examine the chosen one. Good pulse, breathing okay, unconscious. Head was shaved bald. A bruised, three-centimeter incision was newly sutured above the right ear, oozing a little blood, a little serum.

'New victim,' muttered Vine. 'Just bejeweled. Waiting for the god to come.'

We turned the body over. It was Torrie.

And suddenly my memory came flooding back.

I gasped, took her in my arms, held her. She was totally limp.

Rage paralyzed me. Had we saved her for this? It was incomprehensible. I looked blankly at Darwina.

She called two people over from the central fire. The three of them stood talking in subdued tones for a minute, then the two natives gently took Torrie from me. I resisted at first; I wouldn't give her up. But Dar touched my shoulder and nodded, and I relaxed my hold on my lost orphan.

'They'll take good care of her, Joshua – they've had lots of practice. And Umboro was a medicine man in his own tribe. He's a good soul, you needn't worry.'

'But . . . she . . .'

'No use brooding over what might or might not happen. She's got a chance, just like all of us.'

Before I could answer, the medicine man who'd taken Torrie came back. He peered strangely at my face, spoke in a low voice to Dar, and looked at me again. Dar looked at me, too. She squinted a bit, smiled an odd smile.

'What is it?' I said.

'Umboro here just said something funny, but I half believe he has a point.'

'What are you talking about?'

'You know that golden idol of Goranchacha you passed in the sacred grove?' she said with an amused lilt. 'Well, I'm damned if you don't bear it a striking resemblance.'

CHAPTER 6

The Watcher and the Stars

'That's ridiculous,' I told her.

She chuckled softly. 'Well, maybe. I suppose that's the reason you're getting such funny stares, though.'

I hadn't noticed it before, but now everyone seemed to be darting surreptitious glances at me. It was unnerving.

Full night settled, crisp and expectant. My head began to clear; I was only just realizing how foggy I'd been for the past hour or so, like waking from a dream. Something still caught in the back of my mind, some dream shred I wanted to recall but couldn't quite. Something important. Suddenly, I remembered.

'Listen,' I whispered, 'is there any way we can put out a signal, to let my friends know where we are?'

'Friends?'

'They're out there in the grove. I forgot all about them, I'm so spaced out. They're going to make a rescue attempt late tonight. You think there's some way we might coordinate our efforts?'

She gaped at me. 'You have friends out there? You weren't *all* captured?'

'No, I forgot. I mean I got all mixed up when I woke – '

'Are they armed?' Her withering disbelief had moved rapidly through incredulity to daring.

'Yes, of course they're armed, they – '

'My God, we've got to help them.'

'That's what I was just suggesting,' I offered tentatively.

Fear and excitement mingled in her features: this was

potentially the end of captivity, but equally the specter of hazard. It was danger and hope. It was the marines. She called out several names to the natives around the fire.

A cluster of men and women walked over to us, slowly, uncertainly. Dar spoke for a minute in the words of this strange language: '*Mondawe guetze quachina boro dom* . . .' Her little audience listened attentively, though for the most part their faces remained impassive. A few of them replied, a few nodded their heads.

When these exchanges were done, she turned back to me. 'Well, they're ready to help. They want to get out of here as much as you do. Much as I do, if I let myself consider the option.' She seemed to wilt for a brief second.

'Okay, what now?' I asked.

She regained her composure with a breath and a smile. 'Right. Now the main thing, as I see it, is to let them know where we are.'

'I don't see any phones.'

'No, but the thing is, you see, we're given an awful lot of leeway here, due to our "special condition." So I think if you just started singing very loudly – something unmistakably "you" – your friends would get a good fix on your position. Then if any of the *brujos* become annoyed with your performance, I'll just insist it's the god in you trying to get out, and they'll damn well leave you alone.'

It sounded kind of farfetched. 'What will I sing? I can't sing.'

She rubbed her chin. 'Something quirky, I should think, so it sounds sufficiently alien to their ears.'

'But I don't know anything quirky,' I whined, beginning to panic. 'All I know is old Beatles.'

'Perfect,' she beamed. 'We'll start as soon as the moon

breaks over the cliffs – that should give the cavalry plenty of light.'

She discussed possible escape routes with our native confreres, while I hummed dismally in the corner, trying to recall fragments of the few tunes I could half carry. I settled on *Lucy in the Sky with Diamonds*.

With Dar's help I even managed to teach two of the natives to sing backup of a sort – they crooned, on cue, the "Aahh's" at the end of each chorus, in whatever key suited them. This increased the volume of our broadcast so as to make it easier for Karl, Lon, and the others to hear us.

When the silvery glow of the three-quarter moon came through the window, I began to sing what I could remember, at the top of my voice. I could only dredge up the first verse, so I kept singing it over and over, with my two native accompanists wailing the 'Aahh's' at each coda.

It was certainly the only performance of its kind in the history of rock and roll: a terrified American paleontologist bellowing John Lennon out of tune, backed up by the sporadic atonal moanings of two native Amazonian epileptics, conducted by a slightly fevered British UN investigator, before an audience of sullen prisoners, dead bodies, and variously convulsing, vomiting, or febrile captives, all by firelight.

At one point some guards stuck their heads inside to see what the commotion was, but Dar waved them away, explaining it was merely my god trying to get some air. They were apparently used to all kinds of rantings so they left without a fuss.

After about fifteen minutes of this, my voice began to crack, and I paused.

'Intermission?' asked Dar.

'My voice,' I croaked, pointing to my throat. She gave

me a cup of water, her wild eye glittering in the firelight.

I took a few sips, then walked over to where Torrie lay, still unconscious, near the fire. Curious dark faces watched me as I knelt beside her, held her head up in my hand, touched the edge of the cup to her lips, and poured a little water into her mouth. Much of it spilled down her cheeks, but she swallowed some, too. It gave me a comforting feeling – somehow connecting me to all the friends and healers over the centuries who had ministered to the lost or wounded. The faces around the fire continued to watch as I stroked her temple, held her head to my breast.

Her skin was cool, and for a brief horrible moment I thought she was dead. I put my ear to her chest, though: the heart was strong. For a minute I just listened to it. *Dhub-dhup, dhub-dhup, dhub-dhup*. Like an ancient engine. *Dhub-dhup*. I pulled my head back, looked at her – shaved, pathetic. Sleeping Unbeauty, waiting for a kiss. I kissed her softly, on the lips.

Dhub-dhup. I heard it again. Dar was standing beside me now.

'Drums,' she said.

Like the jungle heartbeat, I heard them, getting louder. 'What does it mean?' I asked.

'It means the ceremony is tonight. In honor of the new kids in town, I expect.'

'New kids?'

'You and yours. Well. This changes things, then, doesn't it.'

'How so?'

'They'll be moving us from here. To the grove. To the image of Goranchacha.' She gave me her hand, as if it were the last time we would touch. 'For the ceremony,' she whispered.

* * *

A short time later two guards came in to escort me away.

'Wait, where are they taking me?' I protested. My eyes felt wild. I retreated behind Darwina.

'*Mongalu dwanai?*' she barked. One of them answered. A brief conversation ensued; then Dar turned back to me. 'They're to take you to the Watcher.'

'What's that?'

'It's a who. She's their chief diviner. She reads people, and she reads stars. Wants to read you, it seems.'

'Can't you come with me?'

'They say no. It's a private audience. I'm not certain, but I think what happens in the ceremony later may be influenced by what transpires in this reading.'

'But I don't know what to do!' I began to panic. 'How should I be?'

'Nothing for it but to be yourself. Anyway, you'd best get going – the Watcher is waiting.'

Before I could ask anything else, one guard took each of my arms and walked me out into the courtyard.

Some kind of priest fell in behind us. His head was shaved, his face tattooed; he wore a shredded monk's cassock woven through with feathers; he carried a torch.

The courtyard itself was filled with people and lightning bugs, all blinking curiously at me. Children whispered to each other; old women in doorways made gruff pronouncements; all eyes followed my promenade. As nonchalantly as possible, I checked my fly.

Slowly, we crossed the public square, moving toward the ruined face of the castle. Stone huts marked the perimeter. Warm fires glowed from within each; the rattles of cookware, families shuffling. Beyond this cluster of dwellings I thought I discerned a field of crops, row upon row of some maizelike vegetable, and, to my surprise, what looked like an irrigation system: straight,

furrowed canals connecting several streams tracking along the rows of corn.

We passed between a number of the houses. Thin waterways had actually been dug, feeding off the larger rivers – waterways that entered each home and exited its other side. So all the houses had running water.

We curved around to approach the castle from the back side. On the way, a breeze came up, cool, dry, rattling me awake. Okay, I was on my own now, time to get with it, snap alert, think sharp. Okay. Okay.

A broken stairway rose to the wide, doorless opening, as if the wall had once been breached with a battering ram. I took the stairs carefully – they were full of holes and discontinuities – so my eyes remained mostly fixed on the ground. At the main landing I looked up and involuntarily halted, causing the priest at my rear to bump into me.

It was a wall of skulls. Human skulls: literally thousands of them, piled side to side and top to bottom, with some kind of rough, dark mortar congealing them in place. Old skulls, new, large ones, infants, whole and riven – all facing out into the night, forming a loose, ragged arch above the aging staircase, making this opening in the wall resemble nothing so much as a gaping mouth. The priest shoved me through.

Inside, a torchlit hall loomed up. I was taken across it to another set of steps against the far enclosure, and again we ascended.

At the next level we entered a long corridor, followed it around through a series of cloisters, walked across a wide wooden plank that spanned an area where the floor no longer existed, and came finally to another large hall with a dozen exits. We took one that led to a smaller room filled with furniture. The priest said something and

put me in a chair, and the three of them left.

I sat there for a while, just looking and listening. Old oil lamps were spaced along massive wood tables, illuminating everything. The chair I occupied was carved teak, dark with years. Artwork decorated one wall: woven feather tapestries, animal masks, stone bas-relief, broken clay vases. Another wall contained a large, open, exterior window. I went over to it.

Five stories directly below me was the courtyard; beyond it, the woods. Torches were alight everywhere, dancing about the clearing and the grove to the ceaseless cadence of the drums. I walked back to examine the room.

A large open-topped, cylindrical receptacle of some kind stood in one corner. I looked inside, but it seemed to plunge down into the depths of the castle; I couldn't see the bottom, even using one of the oil lamps.

The table was filled with arcane apparatus of unknown purpose. It looked alchemical. Glass beakers, opaque with dust; cracked flasks, rusted coils; illegible, ancient books reduced to flake and mildew. I picked one up and it crumbled in my hand. I put my ear to the two doors. Silence. I tried one of them; it opened. Might I leave? Was escape possible? No way to know – but I didn't think it could hurt to learn a little about the layout of the place. So I slipped into the next room.

Torchlight shone over the walls, which were covered with murals – and with weird writing, like the characters on the box Lon had shown us in his library so long ago. One entire section seemed concerned with a cryptic mathematics or astronomy: orbs and constellations swept over the curved ceiling – arcs, lines, geometric shapes, arrows, numbers, figures, symbols – it was fascinating.

But not helpful. I went to a long shelf, covered with

paraphernalia, that ran around two walls. There seemed to be centuries of booty, probably taken from previous interlopers like me: an astrolabe, a sextant, rusted-solid Spanish dueling pistols, cameras, cigarette lighters, a thermometer, a wristwatch, a broken radio: the unfathomable, captured magic of foreign marauders.

I turned into an adjacent alcove. There, in a cage at the far wall, huddled Di. I ran over, wrapped my hands around the bars of the prison cell, and tried to pull open the door. It was locked.

'Di,' I whispered urgently. She jerked awake, saw me, rushed up to the gate. Our hands clasped across the barrier; between the bars, we kissed.

'Joshua, get me out of here,' she whispered, hugging herself. She was sweating; her eyes were dark.

I nodded and began to search for a way to get her out. The whole wall was floor-to-ceiling cells, like animal cages, but Di was the only prisoner.

I looked for something I might use to break open the door. No hammers or crowbars, no functional firearms, no chisels, no keys – but there was something: a long, pointy quill pen, from a vulture feather, maybe, but hardened with some black enameling. Maybe I could pick the lock with that.

I grabbed it, scuttled back, knelt on the floor, and inserted the top of the quill into the keyhole of the thick iron lock.

'What are you doing?' she whispered. 'Do you know what you're doing?' Her voice was scratchy, pulling wildly in different directions.

'Sort of. I used to pick the lock on my father's rolltop desk with a bobby pin when I was a kid.'

She kneeled beside me, just the other side of the bars. 'Whatever for?'

'Just snooping. I figured if it was locked, there was probably something nifty inside.'

'Was there?' She sounded desperate, or confused, or angry, or something.

'Nothing I ever found. That lock was easier, though.' I twisted the quill up against a likely catch; it seemed to give a bit. 'Are you okay?'

'I don't know.' Her voice cracked. 'They washed me and fed me this sweet-smelling fruit and herb salad, and I wouldn't eat it at first, but they made me. Josh, what's going to happen?'

'We're getting out of here, that's what. Lon and the others are hiding in the woods – they'll rescue us tonight.' I felt a spring latch slide out of the way and levered the quill point upward. There was a loud choonk as the bolt snapped open.

I pulled the door wide, and we embraced.

'Come on; I know the way back, I think,' I said into her hair. She didn't let me go for a moment, though; she held me there like her last memory of home.

Finally, we turned to run back through the door I'd entered. But we stopped dead. Someone was standing there, just watching.

A woman, impossibly old, disconcertingly tall, preterminally thin. She reminded me of a walking stick, or some ancient bird with a dire hunger. She wore a long, gauzy robe torn in many places. Her eyes were black as infinity; her nose was a broken beak, her mouth a broken laugh.

'*Guetzieh lonos*,' she uttered with a voice like wind in dry leaves.

From behind her, through the door stepped two muscular guards and Darwina.

'The Watcher greets you,' smiled Dar. 'Seems I'm to be here after all – as a translator. They saw us talking, so

they know I know your language. She sees everything, the Watcher does – been watching you since they sat you down in that room by yourself.'

'Tell the Watcher I was admiring her collection.' I spoke as calmly as I could. Di's glance darted from door to window like a cornered rabbit's.

Dar translated. The Watcher laughed, I think – like claws rattling in a hollow gourd – then answered.

'The Watcher admires your admiration. She invites you to watch the stars with her. Up on the roof.' Dar tilted her head toward the ceiling.

Hesitantly, I nodded. The Watcher, Dar, and one guard accompanied me to the second door in the room. The other guard escorted Di back to her cell.

'Wait,' Di rasped. Her face was expressionless with fear.

'Wait,' I echoed.

The Watcher spoke. Dar said, 'Your friend is temporarily becoming part of the collection you so admire.'

'Tell the Watcher nothing must happen to her,' I said.

'I'm not sure . . .' Dar began. She was tense, uncertain. I gathered she didn't want to jeopardize her position here, in case all else failed.

The Watcher spoke. Dar nodded. 'She says not to worry – your friend is being prepared for greatness. Come on, Joshua. It won't do to insult her hospitality, even if you are one of the blessed possessed.'

We walked out, leaving Di incarcerated in a state of bleak horror. The next room seemed to be a bath, with sunken tubs. Beyond that was a chilly hallway leading into the strangest enclosure yet – one entire wall appeared to be a melted-down, half-corroded console of some sort, partly metal, partly stone, full of frayed wires, bent switches, fused glass, crushed rubble. It was incredible.

'What . . . what . . .' I began, but we kept walking.

The next room was a throne room quite clearly. The massive stone chair at its center was encrusted with jewels, elevated on a dais, surrounded by long ebony tables. The Watcher approached a blank wall behind the throne, pushed up on two irregular bricks, and a door-sized section of wall opened before us. We passed through this secret stone panel to a circular stairway whose helical rise we followed up for several score feet, emerging at last on a flat, open tower that overlooked the entire city and underlooked the entire galaxy.

I'd never seen so many stars. Even the brilliance of the low-hanging moon couldn't diminish their luster. White, yellow, bluish, reddish, they glinted like a million burning gems tumbling back forever into the dimmest reaches of the cosmos. It made me reel just to look. I got truly vertiginous, felt the stone floor tipping up beneath me, and actually started to fall – but the guard caught my arm, held me upright.

The Watcher chuckled; I thought of torn paper, snagged and blowing in a dead branch.

They walked me over to the edge of the tower. There stood an elegant, antique telescope. Brass, intricately worked, with a four-inch-diameter lens.

'The Watcher wants you to look,' said Dar.

'At what?'

Dar spun the scope on its tripod so it came to rest pointing down. 'At what you will.'

I tentatively aimed the telescope back up at the sky and peered through it. The stars multiplied. New, more distant flecks winked and guttered; white sparkings took on hues invisible to the naked eye – faint violets, pale greens. The Watcher spoke to Dar in a sere and ancient scrabbling, as if it were the sound of spoken hieroglyphics. The

stars above me danced. I felt like falling again, like I was getting caught up in the dance, spinning and flying to this special secret music.

I sat down hard, panting slightly. The Watcher smiled.

'The Watcher says your choices are meet.' Dar spoke slowly, selecting her words with care. 'That in the first room you touched only the book, that in the second room you picked up only the quill; that here, through the Eye of the Watcher, you chose to gaze upon the bloodstar – these things have import.'

'What's the bloodstar?' I fixed on the last thing she'd said, although none of it made much sense. The things I'd done, I'd done for no particular reason, or for my own reasons – none of which had any import as far as I was concerned. I felt vaguely annoyed.

'The bloodstar is Mars,' said Dar. 'That's apparently where the telescope is pointed.'

The Watcher rambled on again in her parched phonations.

'She says it's a night of . . . auspicious wonders,' Dar repeated. 'Not only is the bloodstar strong, but the dreamstar as well – that's Jupiter, I think. But most wondrous of all, she says, is that the birthstar has been eaten by the moon-goddess.'

'Could you translate that translation?'

She shook her head. 'I'm not clear on that. The birthstar is Venus – I think because it appears in the evening and then fades out, and then gets "reborn" just before morning. And the moon-goddess is the moon itself – they believe it's the spirit of Queen Namsháya, who reigns in earthly form down here – the queen of the tribe, I mentioned her earlier. But the moon eating Venus? I don't know – '

'Look, just give me a clue – is this good or bad for us?'

Not good, I thought – I was beginning to feel odd again. Disjointed, unwhole.

'She does you honor, I think. Not sure why, though, and I could be wrong.'

'Tell her the god in me is attended by the god in Di – I need Di to be with me, or I'll have to return to the sky.' Have to return *somewhere* – I was feeling twitchy. There was a funny smell.

'Don't get too cocky boy, you'll spoil our best chance.' She looked severe, her cocked eye cautionary.

'This may be Di's *only* chance.'

She considered a moment, then spoke tersely to the Watcher. The Watcher took a crystal from under her robes – a jagged hunk of emerald the size of a softball. Enraptured, she gazed into its depths. Enraptured, I watched her. The bulky crystal seemed to catch bits of starlight, whisk them around within its facets, displaying patterns of fire, patterns that the Watcher read, patterns reflected in her eyes. Sparkling lights fluttered across my field of vision. My hand began to shake; a strange aura overcame me. I suddenly knew I was only moments away from a seizure.

Slowly, she lowered the jewel to the stone floor, walked up to me, took my head in her hands, brought her face to mine, our mouths nearly touching, and stared into my eyes.

I stared into hers. It was the blackness of night in there; it swept me away. Flecks of crimson swirled around me, dazzling, disorienting. I was engulfed. I was in the void; I *was* the void.

The seizure was upon me.

I was the bloodstar: carmine power, seething with intent. Aurora Corporealis, dawn of flesh.

I was the dreamstar: camera obscura, camera lucida,

planet of passions, its bands of color shimmering through the ether like the wandering world's own crystal dreams.

I was the birthstar: borning, dying, borning, dying . . .

I was the void.

The void . . .

I opened my eyes. Above me the Milky Way spanned the heavens like fine muslin as the moon hovered near its zenith. A sharp chill brushed my face. I knew my convulsions had passed. I sat up warily, testing the ground with my hands.

It was the same stone tower – two hours later, by the rising of the moon – only now I was alone. A cold wind had come up, clarifying the night, giving me a sense of acuity. I looked across the sky; it no longer made me dizzy. I felt no longer beneath the stars but among them. It was a feeling of integration – and power.

I peered over the edge of the tower, at the city below. Like the stars through the telescope, the torches had multiplied a hundredfold. They swayed in a kind of organic unison to the tidal rhythm of the drums that swelled out of the darkness. It thrilled me: the lights, the pulsing rumble, the musky air, my connection to it all, my potency within it.

I stood. The wind caught my hair, splayed it like fire. I felt immortal. I felt the crowd below sense my presence, touch my spirit. My vision extended beyond the city, beyond the occult jungle, beyond the spinning stars. I held – I was – this moment.

I closed my eyes, savored it, breathed it into my lungs.

For just that instant, the universe was within me.

I exhaled. The earth came rushing back to my feet. I wobbled, but maintained. Solid ground once again.

Still on the tower, still alone; what next? Time to get out of this place, no doubt about it.

I checked around the corner. Nobody there. With as much stealth as I had left in me, I scurried down the long spiral staircase. It was deserted. I retraced the route by which we'd come, room by room, until I reached the place where Di was being kept. Only she was gone.

The cell was empty. I ran through every room on this level. No Di, no nobody. I picked an old knife off one of the tables, slipped it into my waistband. My pulse was quickening. I wiped my palms of sweat and ran down the next flight of stairs.

These rooms were all empty too. The castle suddenly felt as if it were a huge mausoleum, cold and lifeless. I crept down to the ground floor. The drums outside were quite loud, throbbing like an open wound. I eased around the lip of the outer door.

Immediately before me stood the Watcher. Beside her was Dar, and beyond them were hundreds of natives bearing torches, faces, uplifted, swaying to the sonorous drumroll.

'You – you were waiting for me.' The words caught in my throat.

Dar nodded stiffly. 'It's time for the ceremony.'

CHAPTER 7

The Ceremony

We marched through the streets of the city. Torches burned at every doorway or were wedged in between the bricks of crumbling stone walls. A thousand townspeople joined in the procession, more coming at every corner. We went twelve times around the castle. I felt like a comet, crossing the sparks of its own tail, circling a dark sun, until finally we spun out of orbit and headed into the woods.

The drums were louder and faster now: the heartbeat of a lover anticipating a caress. Darwina stayed beside me, surrounded by naked warriors holding spears and beaten-copper shields. Torches were planted every five yards throughout the grove, casting strange shadows in the trees, reflecting off the dozens of watching statues. We passed them slowly, to the depths of the small forest.

Ten yards from the altar that stood before the golden idol of Goranchacha, we stopped. The crowd stopped. The drums stopped.

'What is it?' I whispered to Dar. My eyes strained into the darkness for signs of rescue. 'What's going on?'

'It's to be a sacrifice, I'm afraid, Joshua.'

It gave me a hollow, giddy feeling to hear her. 'Hey, my singing wasn't *that* bad,' I joked, but the air felt thin and my forehead was moist with fear.

Suddenly, the *brujo* stood before me. He still wore his mask that sprouted lizards – there was even a live iguana crawling among its interstices. Around his tattooed body

he wore a mantle of teeth, and in his hand he held an ornately carved thigh-bone.

Behind him stood his minions: dozens of ominous natives, dressed like renegades from a nightmare Halloween: black ceramic death masks; shattered human skull masks; bark-hewn devil masks; mythic beast masks constructed of bone, feathers, jewels and rawhide. They were costumed as vampire bats, king vultures, minotaurs, dragons. Some wore the tattered, yellowed dresses of archaic Spanish *señoritas*, sporting mantillas in their hair; some wore the cassocks of old Spanish monks. One carried a large scroll; one wore the head of a horse down to his shoulders; one looked like a giant tortoise, one a crouching reptile, one a monkey with antlers on his head, one a . . . they stretched back indefinitely, into the depths of the night.

'Who are they?' I rasped, my throat dry.

'His parishoners,' answered Dar.

The *brujo* screamed something. His followers began beating the ground in slow unison with bones, with spears, with their feet. It sounded like the earth's own clock.

The *brujo* started talking to me in a loud, reedy voice; Dar spoke along with him, giving simultaneous translation.

'He says as head *brujo* of the Guachetá, it's his responsibility to look after the spiritual well-being of his tribe,' Dar told me. 'He says, "Welcome." He says – wait, now let me get this straight – he says the signs are clear, the Watcher has told him – tonight the birthstar was eaten by the moon-goddess in the western sky, just prior to your arrival. Then *you* arrived. It is without question now – you are Himself: the Sun-God Emerald-Child Goranchacha, consort of Moon-Goddess Jaguar Queen Nam-

sháya, returned at last to his people, as prophesied for ages beyond time.'

There was a stunned silence. I looked to Dar uncomprehendingly.

The *brujo* continued, Dar interpreting. 'If there be any doubt of this truth, let him who doubts gaze upon the faces of these two.'

With this I was picked up bodily by the *brujo*'s henchmen – truly, I didn't resist – and deposited beside the golden statue of their wandering god. There was another prolonged silence, as all who could see peered intensely at my face, next to that of the long-lost Goranchacha.

I heard Dar mutter, 'Unbelievable,' and all at once the crowd broke into a wild frenzy. The costumed demons began dancing, keening, writhing on the ground, waving torches. Drums were beating, women ululating. Hordes of people were having seizures, and mock seizures, on the ground. I was terrified.

Dar managed to squeeze beside me. 'I'm afraid it was a perfect match, my darling Goranchacha. Damned if I understand it. We're probably both damned in any case.'

I looked at the statue, its saber raised in one hand, its quill in the other. Its emerald eyes sparkled in the light of the swaying torches.

It did look like me.

Looked like me. How was it possible? It had all the aspects of a horror dream from which I couldn't escape, whose course I had to follow to the end, until I awoke screaming.

But it wasn't a dream.

I looked the idol up and down. My size, or a bit bigger. For the first time, I noticed hieroglyphics intaglioed into the statue's chest – the same kind of scribblings as those

on the stone box Lon had originally shown us, the box that had sucked us into this royal mess.

Lon. I looked for him now in the jabbering crowd. Nowhere. Only these mad shadow dancers, whirling souls, ghoulish creatures foaming in ecstasy.

The *brujo* raised his bone staff, and in ten seconds the gathering was hushed. Once more he spoke to me.

'And now,' translated Dar, 'as further prophesied, before all eyes, and before the lesser gods who dwell in the forest, you will mate with Queen Namsháya, that your children will be true gods on earth and begin a new race.'

Before I could ask her to repeat this, my clothes were torn from me, my body slathered in a thin, clear, reddish oil; I was carried ten yards and placed upon the stone slab altar.

I tried to get up, but a large warrior in a crocodile mask pushed me back down. That was the last of my strength. My heart was pounding, my legs felt like jelly – I'd have fallen over flat if I'd taken a step. The drums were thundering, in perfect synchrony with my heart. I began to tremble.

The *brujo* stepped up. Three large men held me in place, another pried my mouth open, while the *brujo* force-fed me a fine powder. I squirmed and gagged, but some of it went down and some of it I even inhaled. They stepped back. I lay there on the altar, on my back, panting, shivering, grunting a little, as a thousand glazed eyes, jangling with dark fire, stared at me from out of the trees.

I looked down at the foot of the altar.

The queen stood there.

Glistening, naked, magnificent – I could believe she *was* the moon-goddess. Such a creature of power, magic, and strange sensuality I had never beheld. On her head

was the ornate bronze helmet of a Spanish conquistador of the sixteenth century, replete with plumes. Over her eyes and nose was a half mask, made of a jaguar's half face, including the upper fangs. Her bare, oiled skin seemed to radiate, rather than reflect, the firelight. Jaguar claws adorned her fingers; black, Spanish leather knee boots covered her legs. She stepped up onto the altar and stood above me.

Still supine, I pushed myself backward a few inches, scared nearly senseless. I looked to the left and right: darkness moved, eyes became jewels. The statues of the gods appeared to be coming to life, twining with the trees, merging with the earth, twisting in each other's arms.

It was the *yagé* they'd just given me; I was starting to hallucinate.

I felt all my membranes begin to ooze: my eyes, nose, mouth, all watering. Lights exploded in my brain. I turned my head and looked up.

There sat the queen, straddling my hips with her own, riding me, joining our bodies in a fluid of motion, her breasts filling my upraised hands, her jaguar fangs poised above my neck. We were both drooling.

I felt – no, *we* felt, for we were a single beast now – swollen with lust, swollen to bursting, as though nothing existed but our own wet heat, moving on itself, pushing inside out, pressing parts until they melded in a sweating frenzy – and we burst. Exploded in spasms of light.

Next thing I knew, she was standing, one foot either side of my outstretched legs, once more towering over me. Then she stepped down. Then she was gone.

I sat up. The ceremony was in full swing. Wild, fantastic creatures coupled in every pose of light and shadow. Statues turned into animals, dancers shrieked. People had seizures, visions, strokes, disintegrations. Trees burst into

flames, which turned into dragons, which flew off into the night.

I saw Karl – now masked, body painted in magenta designs – roaming, glassy as a wraith, through the melee.

I saw Di being passed from goat-man to serpent-woman, each one drinking from a bloody puncture at her neck.

I saw Lon, stained ruby from head to foot, sitting cross-legged in the fork of a gnarled old tree.

I knew all was lost.

On wobbly legs I stood beside the altar. Before I could really focus, though, I was grabbed, lifted, taken to the idol of Goranchacha. To the rear of the idol. They began fussing along its side, making little tapping sounds, and then, with a numbing horror, I understood what they were doing. They were opening the statue.

Opening it on hidden hinges, from behind. It was totally hollow inside. Not a statue at all, in fact; nothing but a thin metal shell. A suit of armor fashioned into the shape of their god. No, not exactly a suit of armor either. Rather, a coffin.

For at a brief invocation from the *brujo*, they wedged me into the thing, and closed it at the back. And locked it. It was a nearly perfect fit. It felt like I was buried alive.

My first sense was of intense claustrophobia. My arms and legs were immobile, extended fully into the limbs of the image; I stuck out my tongue and could taste the inside of its lips. Cold, bitter metal. I started to gag but forced the bile back down. My breathing quickened. I was going to die.

Yet I could see.

How was it possible? I squinted; hazy, green shapes twisted before me like smoke in a dream. Was I already unconscious? I blinked.

It was the eyes, of course – the statue's emerald eyes. I could see through them. They distorted and fragmented what I saw, but it was all so unreal anyway, these new alterations hardly mattered. What mattered was that I was dying.

The air seemed to thicken. Chaotic emerald figures swam past my vision. A young woman – was it Di? – was flung to the altar, surrounded by convulsing forms.

Something distracted me from this morbid vision. Not twenty yards away, walking toward me, emerging from a cluster of saplings, was Death. Gaunt, robed with bottomless eyes and empty nose socket, he stalked me. Moved around to the right, circled slowly, lips parting for that final kiss. Ten yards. Into the glare of the firelight he came, when in a flash I saw it wasn't Death at all. It was old noseless Curicuri, slyly grinning.

He nodded across the clearing. I looked out, and left, to see – was it possible? – Lon, Karl, and Dar, converging slowly upon the altar. I shouted but only managed to deafen myself.

Lon scooped Di off the altar, slung her over his shoulder. Karl collected a limp body that looked like Torrie, then approached Dar, said something to her, and pointed at – me. The three of them, carrying the two bodies, began to walk toward me.

Thank God, they knew where I was. Tears filled my eyes, shimmering everything even further. My friends came closer. In the churning confusion nobody paid them any attention. Nobody except the *brujo*, who was himself approaching with a cadre of his own. I strained in my metallic suit to warn my friends, stretched every muscle beyond pain, beyond air hunger, to reach them, to help them. And in so stretching, I pushed together the fingertips of my right hand, the hand in which the idol was

clutching its quill pen. Pushed my thumb against my index finger, to no avail, my strength failing, my vision fading, this was madness – but wait.

There was movement.

Movement in the fingertip. My fingers came alive, palpating the inside of the copperish glove. It was a wheel, a small wheel in there, like a gear. I turned it over and over, feeling it loosen more and more, turning it in a fever of hope, when all at once the mouth on the idol's face dropped open. I could breathe.

Before I could shout, my arms fell down to my sides like lead weights, my knees began to buckle. Lon and Dar ran up to support me. Without thinking, I took a step toward them – I could walk! Suddenly, the body mold had become jointed, the joints unlocked by some long-dormant mechanism I'd released by turning the catch in the finger. It was now truly a suit of armor.

'I'm okay, I'm okay,' I panted.

'Can you walk in this thing?' shouted Lon.

'I think so.' I was still feeling the effects of the *yagé*, but by concentrating intently, I was able to keep the visual imaginings to a minimum.

The armor suit was inconceivably heavy, but Lon advised me he couldn't find the locks at the back to let me out, so I had little choice. I stumbled forward and Lon caught me; then, slowly, I began to walk.

This had a miraculous effect on the native populace; to them it was Goranchacha come alive. They ran away, they bowed down before me, they trembled abjectly in my presence. Even the *brujo* and his crew stopped in their tracks.

I strode among them, insofar as it was possible to stride. Jewels were thrown at my feet.

'Gather up the troops,' I said to Lon, near my right arm, 'and let's get out of here.'

Lon, Karl, Dar, Curicuri, our last Jivaro, and our new native cohorts formed ranks behind me, carrying the slumped bodies of Torrie and Di. I plodded, robotlike, through the woods.

On the far side, where the grove thinned to open ground, the moon was bright and stark. I headed directly back toward Fernando.

On arriving there, at his duck blind behind the low stone wall, we were greeted by a horrible scene: Fernando locked arm in arm with the Watcher, each clasping a knife buried deeply in the other's side. Karl pried them apart. The old diviner was dead; Fernando still breathed.

We walked up the stream carrying Fernando, Torrie, and Di, and with a nervous glance behind us, plunged into the falls.

Once inside the cave entryway, Lon turned on his flashlight. Torrie was coming around, moaning and retching. Dar rolled her on her side. Fernando was coughing blood – he really looked bad. Karl patched up his old friend's chest would as well as was possible. Di lay still on the floor.

Darwina's native companions turned their attentions to finding the latches at the back of my suit as Lon fired up a little Coleman lantern he'd packed away. We could see an occasional torchlight through the curtain of running water that now separated us from the valley. Thcy moved back and forth, these lights, but like uncertain memories, never came closer.

One of the Indians finally found the hidden locks on the armor and unbuckled me. I pried myself out and sat down hard. The armor kept standing, though it slumped a bit. I squeezed my eyes – all of a sudden, back in the

real world. No more distortions of color and shape here, just solid floor and a warm light, friendly faces, quiet breathing.

Lon sat down beside me and put his arm around my shoulders. 'How are you?' he asked in his gravelly baritone. 'Are you okay?'

I nodded. My head was throbbing, but I felt in control of my faculties at last. The hallucinogen the *brujo* had force-fed me was apparently a short-acting one. I formally introduced Darwina to Lon and Karl, and they all shook hands, like team captains before the game.

'What about Di?' I asked. 'And Torrie.'

Lon hugged me fiercely. 'Di is dead, Josh.'

It didn't register at first; I didn't even understand the words. 'Oh,' I said. I felt slightly confused. 'Is she okay, though?'

He nodded. 'She's okay. We'll just leave her in the narrow tunnel there. Nobody will ever find her.'

I nodded back. It was starting to sink in; a big void was filling my chest. I crawled over to her body and sat beside it, holding her hand. She looked so pale in this light; so alone. I wanted to cry, but nothing came. I tried so hard to cry. Later, I would weep for days.

I lay down beside her as the others gathered up the equipment and the wounded. I kissed her on the cheek. I held her face to mine. Don't go, I thought. Don't leave me, Running Stocking. Her skin was already cool, though. Her . . . Must I tell you these things? Even this? It wrenches me to resurrect these moments; rather would I let them sleep, troubled sleep though it be. Her sudden absence – how can I describe its effect on me? I can't, that's all. Suffice it to say, it was the final casting adrift. I no longer had heart for any of this.

'Those torches outside are inching nearer, I'm afraid,'

said Darwina. 'They won't like it when they find the Watcher dead – be looking for your feet of clay, I expect.'

I didn't move, though; only continued to lay there beside my lost love.

Lon pried the emeralds out of Goranchacha's eyes with his knife. Karl gave me an extra pair of pants from his pack. Torrie and Fernando, still only semiconscious, were slung across the strongest backs available. Lon pulled me up; I resisted at first, but my resistance was low. I felt like a sleepwalker. So off we set, flashlights leading, into the tunnels whose path we'd marked with crayon on the way in.

It was cold, but I was still too much in shock to feel cold. Lon gave me the two jewels to hold. I held them in my hand, rolling them around like dice, wondering if I'd ever wake up. Maybe I *was* the god Goranchacha, and all this silly world was my dream, and when I *did* wake up, the world would disappear, and everyone in it. Maybe I'd been just starting to wake up, and that's why Di vanished. Maybe if I went to sleep again, Di would come back.

'Are we there yet?' I asked like an overtired child. A rather deadly silence followed.

'The arrows,' said Lon blankly. 'The arrows are everywhere.'

'It is not possible,' protested Karl.

It was true, though. Crayon arrows had been marked in every tunnel, in every direction. It was impossible now to know which one to follow, which way to go.

Fernando muttered something to Karl. 'Fernando says it was the Watcher,' Karl growled. 'He says was too late to stop her. He says she stole the crayon and did this thing before he could prevent it. He begs our forgiveness.'

'What are we going to do now?' Dar said. 'We're lost. We have to go back.' Her voice held an edge of panic.

'Go back to what?' demanded Lon. 'That's a useless idea. There's nothing to do but go on.' His jaw was in knots.

'Go on where? We're in a labyrinth here.'

'It's this way, I think,' said Lon, and set off. And truly, there was nothing to do but follow.

Turn after screwing turn, we wound deeper into the coils of the maze. It got darker, or maybe our flashlight batteries were just getting weaker. And colder, too; I began to shiver.

The caves we passed through seemed somehow sentient, as if we were creeping into the mind of the mountain. We crossed rooms full of reddish phosphorescent algae, glowing the way a nerve cell must glow, transmitting a thought. Here was the earth's gray matter.

'Wait a minute,' Lon said at one point. 'I didn't see any glowing caves on the way in.'

We stopped; he was right.

We were lost.

I sat down on the stone floor, light-headed with fatigue. I needed sleep badly – we all did, of course. But sleep was not to be ours.

There was a scream at the rear of the group: scouts from the city had found us – the shout was to call our location to their warriors. Karl and Curicuri killed them after a brief scuffle, but too late: in a not too distant tunnel, dozens of footsteps could be heard giving us chase.

Lon dragged me up to my feet, and we ran.

Ran without direction, as fast as we could, deeper into the maze. We'd put the hunters behind us for a time; we'd slow down, rest; then the footfalls would reappear, and we'd set off in some new direction.

Hours passed in this way. Finally, it seemed, we'd lost them.

At last, we came upon a cavern that was open to the sky – hundreds of feet above us, the dome of the cave was pierced by a great shaft that exposed the starry night.

And cutting across the floor of the cavern was a river – probably eighty yards wide, gently flowing, warm, and fragrant. It must have been fed by hot springs somewhere along the line and filled with aromatic esters of some kind, because it smelled like lilacs, or some summer oil.

It smelled like the summer I'd met Di. At least I think it did. I think that's why I jumped in.

I wasn't thinking at all, really – it was just an impulse, a way to recapture something we'd had together. A way to be with her again. I certainly wasn't much of a swimmer; and though I wasn't actively contemplating suicide, neither did I feel that I had much to live for.

I looked up at a galaxy of brilliant stars whirling through inky space – to my eyes, fixed as a memory, vivid as a dream. Was Di's spirit up there now? Could I hope to be with her again someday? I felt tears trying to flow, but once again, none came.

That's when I heard the footsteps return.

We all did – louder by the second, accompanied by a horrific chanting. Suddenly, they burst into the cave – two-score war-painted natives, out for our blood.

With three long strokes I swam back to shore and pulled the half-conscious Torrie by the arm into the water – better for her to drown here with me than suffer Di's fate. Holding her head above the surface, I dog-paddled out to mid-river. Lon dove in to assist me a moment later. Karl did the same for Fernando. Many of the others on the bank weren't quick enough, though: poison darts felled them in a matter of seconds, or they were taken captive.

The rest of us, including Curicuri and Dar, swam for

the opposite bank, arrows flying all around. For reasons that soon became obvious, the natives didn't follow us into the river. We were more than halfway across when I first felt it grab my ankle.

It was sticky, warm, and strong, and it wouldn't let go.

'What's the matter?' said Lon. He saw the sudden panic in my face.

My chin was touching the waterline now; I was thrashing. 'There's something . . .' I began. But before I could finish, Lon and Fernando were sucked down out of sight; and a moment later I was pulled under, still holding Torrie.

Fierce churning. I tried desperately not to breathe, wished angrily I'd taken a bigger breath. I tried to wrestle with it but found nothing to grab. Crosscurrents pulled me, tugging my arms in different directions, rolling me upside down, disorienting me. There was violent activity around my legs, making me lose my grip on Torrie. I was swung around, doubled over, yanked with great speed along an unknown course. My air was running out.

Spinning, sinking, I strained to stay conscious, flung my limbs wide, clawed at the constriction around my waist. To no avail.

I decided to stop resisting. The effort was only draining my oxygen. If I went limp, maybe the thing would let me go, maybe I'd float to the surface.

I went limp. Everything twisted around a bit longer; and then suddenly it was all in slow motion, as though I were suspended in molasses, turning at half speed through some viscous brew. I exhaled my last but one; the dark veil drew near.

And then there was a final wrench, and I found myself gasping on the shore.

Unsteadily, I sat upright. Lon and Karl lay beside me.

A few seconds later Fernando spurted out of the water like buoyant flotsam and crawled onto the sand, followed directly by Curicuri, Dar, and Torrie.

All crumpled on the beach.

I scraped the ground with my fingers and came up with a fistful of sand. Not the stone shelf from which we'd slid into the river. White, limy sand. Confused, I looked up. We were surrounded by people.

Thin, tall, white-skinned people. They wore robes of animal hide. They stared at us curiously for some seconds, and then walked away.

CHAPTER 8

The Awakening

I stretched for comprehension. What had just happened? We were swimming, got pulled under, shot down some rapids . . . I noticed Lon peering upward incredulously and followed his gaze. There, a hundred feet directly above us, the river ran straight across the sky, with no visible means of support. And through it I could see, high above, dimmed and shimmering, the stars.

It had to be an optical illusion.

Beneath the river, just beside us, was a large, still lake. In the meadow beyond, mostly ignoring us, were scores of people, occupied with their own business: playing games in a field of lilacs, sitting around campfires, talking, making strange music on reedy instruments. Here and there among them strolled two kinds of animals: a squat, multicolored, wingless bird and a three-foot-tall, horselike creature with a single conical horn, looking like nothing so much as a unicorn.

'Lon?' I said.

'Don't ask me' – he shook his head – 'I've never been to this country.'

'It is my judgement that we were caught by the undertow of those falls and washed down here,' said Karl.

I looked to where he was pointing. At the far end of the river in the sky, a wide, thick waterfall cascaded down into the lake beside us. Not only that – I saw now – an equally massive geyser shot straight up out of the other end of the lake until it joined the river above.

'I don't know what grabbed *you,*' I said, 'but what pulled *me* down was big and muscular.'

We surveyed our surroundings more carefully from where we sat. The lake was bounded by a short, sandy beach strewn with unicorn horns. The place itself seemed to be a huge cavern, with the river covering most of its ceiling. Catalpa trees grew in clumps beyond the lilac field; ferns sprouted up in all the outlying areas. The enclosure extended hundreds of yards, illuminated by dozens of small bonfires.

We began tending Fernando and Torrie – they were still barely half-conscious – when one of the people approached us. He wore a white suede jerkin and a bland, nonthreatening smile. 'I'm Symeau,' he said in a soothing baritone. '*Yu r welcm.*'

'You speak English!' I exclaimed.

'*We spk Lakish,*' he corrected. '*Yu r welcm tu mi fyre.*'

'Thank you,' I said.

'I'll be damned,' muttered Lon.

Carrying our wounded, we followed him. Walking past the lake, I noticed dozens of children throwing lilac blossoms into the water. So that was where the river above us got its aroma. We walked past a saltlick where two unicorns were lapping peacefully – at the salt and at each other. It made me feel quite tender.

We came to Symeau's fire and sat down. Another villager was there, names Desireau – I hesitated to say man or woman, they all looked so androgynous to me; and two small unicorns, whom Symeau introduced as Belame and Blancame, though they didn't stop munching ferns long enough to utter a syllable. Over the fire was a roasting bird of the type we saw waddling everywhere – screal, they were called.

It tasted delicious. We ate, nursed our wounds, dared

to relax. Torrie seemed to perk up a bit. Fernando winked at me and spat a plug of tobacco. I kept glancing around. These people somehow didn't look quite human – the shape of their heads, the color of their skin . . .

Nobody spoke during the meal. When it was over, Symeau smiled a greasy smile. '*Screal s gud. Hiir s a bowl of screal fat.*' He lifted up a large bucket of thick, yellowish lard, scooped out a handful, and rubbed it on his belly. *It heels. It s gud fr mny ting.*' He belched and laughed. '*Now, yu whish tu takk?*'

'Yes, Symeau, the screal was wonderful, thank you,' said Lon. 'But now I must tell you – we're lost and need to get home. Can you help us out?'

'*Nunn r lost hiir,*' he beamed. '*Th lak s hohm tu all.*'

'We are lost,' Lon insisted. 'We have enjoyed your hospitality, but when our friends get stronger, we have to go. Can you tell us the way out?' He spoke as if to a young, precocious child.

I admired Lon's manner. It was at once direct, and yet still in keeping with Symeau's attitude; he even took on a little of Symeau's inflections. I was usually pretty direct, but frequently without tact or delicacy. In any case, I was still in shock from our recent catastrophes.

Symeau thought a moment, considering the alternatives. '*Com. Vieileau will kno wht tu du. Th lak wil speke thru her.*' Three of us got up and accompanied Symeau and Desireau across a ferny dell, leaving the others to rest beside the fire. After a short walk we entered a cabin built of catalpa logs.

Coals burned in a pit at the center of the hearth. In the glimmer of their burgundy glow, I saw an old woman sitting cross-legged on the dirt. The light of the red coals reflected from her face, throwing every line in shadow.

'Hiir s Vieileau,' said Desireau proudly. *'Thru her th lak told us tu wahtch fr yr shadoh.'*

Lon spoke. 'Vieileau, we are lost. Please help us to go home.'

'Hiir s th lak,' said Vieileau in a cracking voice, *'n hiir r its peepl. We liv n th luster uhf th lak, its wundrs tu perform.'*

Cups of incense burned either side of her, sending thick plumes of smoke around her head, like smoldering dreams. Slowly, she stood and exited the hut. We followed.

She walked to the lake. On the shore stood the entire community – humans, unicorns, and screals.

'Yu mus wahtch,' Vieileau said. *'Hiir s th feest.'*

An old man was carried on the shoulders of several others to the edge of the lake. Tied around his neck were five squirming screals. The people all chanted in an atonal drone that made my hair stand on end. At a sign from Vieileau, the man was thrown into the lake, screal and all. He sank like a stone.

It was quickly evident where the birds got their name. In unison they emitted one long, squealing, screaming wail and then were silent again.

The lake suddenly began to churn. Where it had been flat, now dark, roiling waves rose in ten-foot peaks. It made its own sound, almost an animal moaning. Huge swells climbed straight out of the water, then slowly curved around and dipped back on themselves, merging with themselves, sinking back into the liquid mass, looking – to me – like huge, groping pseudopods. After some time, a whirlpool appeared at the center of the lake and sucked all the remaining debris down into its cold black core, then rose, intact, out of the substance of the water,

like a mad funnel cloud – roared, swelled, and finally plunged back down into the lake.

Once again, all was quiet.

The surface of the water, now devoid of floating lilac petals, was motionless as ice and deep turquoise in hue. Vieileau smiled at us. *'Th feest s ovr. Now I mus go awhake th Ol One. Th Ol One wil whish tu see yu.'* Whereupon she walked away, as did everyone else.

Leaving me, Lon, and Karl staring dumbly at each other.

'What do you make of it?' said Lon.

'Is beyond my understanding' – Karl shook his head – 'but I think we are all safe here.'

'All except Di,' I said.

And finally, I cried.

For many days we did nothing but recuperate. Fernando mended quite fast – fortunately, nothing vital had been severed by the Watcher's knife. Torrie was slower to heal, but gradually she, too, woke up, took food, and grew stronger. She had a petit mal seizure from time to time, but she was alive. Apparently, screal meat *was* good for many things.

The rest of us explored this cavern. It was immense and enclosed. No way out. The people were polite but unhelpful. As far as they were concerned, this was the world. Twice a week they would have a ceremony in which one of their dead or dying was tossed into the lake, never to rise; but aside from that, they mostly did little: ate, played games, slept.

We examined in detail the two columns of water that rose out of the lake to the river above. They were actually clear, giant tubes, with water rushing up inside one and down inside the other.

'Some kind of crystal, I think,' said Lon, rapping his knuckles against the translucent tube. The humming geyser gushed up inside it; outside, it was moist with a continuous lavage of cool water flowing down from above.

I felt it, tapped it, smelled it, tasted it, and frowned. 'I don't think it's mineral. It's thin, and pliant, I think. Some kind of plastic, maybe?'

'Can maybe cut a hole in it,' Karl suggested, drawing his knife. He brought his arm back and stabbed the dagger into the crystal casement. Incredibly, the entire tubular column pulled away as soon as the blade pierced it – jerked away in withdrawal, like a contracting filament. The movement pulled the knife from Karl's hand and knocked it to the ground. For a brief moment a hole was left in the membrane where the knife point had punctured it. A stream shot out as if from a nozzle; then suddenly the hole closed off, and the waterspout stopped. The tube seemed to relax and resumed its original position.

I examined the spot where the knife had entered, now smooth, hard, and uninterrupted as before, without even a trace of a scar.

Karl shook his head slowly and picked up his knife. 'Is crazy,' he whispered, 'but felt like a great animal twisting from my knife. Like a bear.'

I took his blade and studied the tip. A tiny bit of sticky, slightly gelatinous goo stuck to it. I walked over to a nearby campfire and held the point momentarily in the flames, then brought the charred smoking substance under my nose.

'Smells organic,' I said. 'It's unbelievable, but I think this thing is alive.'

Lon looked at me uncomprehendingly. 'What thing?'

'The lake,' I said.

We went over to it and kneeled at the edge. I dipped

my cupped hand in it, brought it to my lips, tasted it. 'Tastes like river water.'

'Just what do you mean by "alive"?' said Lon.

I sat on the bank and dangled my feet into the still waters. It was almost the last thing I ever did.

In an instant I was being pulled, with a horrible smacking noise, into the lake. The strength of the suction was enormous; it took Karl's quick reflexes and every ounce of his strength to extract me before I'd sunk far below the level of my thighs.

They laid me on the ground. The skin on my legs was uniformly red with first-degree burns. It was excruciatingly painful.

'Something . . . got me,' I said. 'Clamped my legs.'

Lon crawled back to the bank. Gingerly, he stuck a long piece of driftwood into the water. Ripples spread out across the surface. Slowly, he advanced the branch. At a depth of one foot, he seemed to encounter some resistance, then forced past it.

All at once, the wood in his hand was pulled rapidly to the left, then back to the right, and finally extruded from the water amidst a flurry of sizzle and foam.

I examined the driftwood. Its barky surface showed signs of chemical burn, like my leg, but it looked not so much chemical as proteolytic. Enzymatic. I shook my head. 'It can't be, but it acts like a gigantic one-celled animal filling up that entire lake.'

'A one-celled animal,' said Lon. 'Your brain is leaking.'

I didn't know where this would lead me, but I decided to just follow the thought and see where I ended up. 'Sort of like an amoeba,' I said. 'It has a membranous, malleable cell wall that sort of oozes all over, in different shapes and directions, through the pond water it lives in. It eats by pinocytosis. It sort of engulfs its food with out-

pouchings of its wall, then pulls the meal through the wall into the cytoplasmic jelly it's made of; then as the wall instantly reforms, the food is set upon by enzymes in the cytoplasm and digested whole. That's what it was starting to do to my legs, and that's what it does to the guys they throw in there twice a week.'

'And those columns?' Lon pursued. He was only half-amused by my explanation. Bizarre as it was, it made some kind of internal sense.

I tried to stay within the logic of my postulate. 'Maybe the columns are tubular extensions of the cell wall – like long, erect pseudopods. The thing has made its walls thicker there, to hold its own mass up against gravity. And that stuff inside the membranous tube isn't river water rushing down or a subterranean geyser shooting up – it's streaming cytoplasm, and it squirted out when you broke the thick cell membrane with your knife.' It was making dream-sense, at least. 'Probably the two columnar pseudopods form a bridge between themselves way up at the top, and that bridge is the riverbed up there. The river is completely supported by the joined pseudopods; and we're down here watching the river flow over that protoplasmic support, held up by those protoplasmic buttresses, and it's so clear that we can see right through it, through the cell wall and the cytoplasm and the river, all the way up to the stars.' I shook my head in amazement, speaking these conclusions as they came to me.

'And the river water runs down the outside of the pseudopod columns to coat the membrane so it doesn't dry, and the runoff fills this pond and covers the beastie[1] with a foot of water. And probably the thing stuck another

[1] I took the appellation 'beastie' from Van Leeuwenhoek, the inventor of the microscope, who first saw and characterized the microorganisms of pond water.

little pseudopod way up into the river while we were bobbing there and pulled us down, and then spit us out on the shore here. I don't know why it didn't just eat us *then,* of course. But we sure see it eat those dudes they toss in every week, and we saw it mend its wall as soon as Karl tore it with his knife, and then it goddamn near almost *did* eat me.' I shook my head again.

Darwina began to laugh uncontrollably, and then to cry.

'So it's a huge blob of protoplasm masquerading as a lake,' said Lon. 'I wonder why I find this theory unappealing.'

'Just tell me how we get out,' Dar said abjectly.

Truly, the prospect of dealing with a giant amoeba as the door monitor of this place didn't exactly fill me with optimism either. It seemed unlikely that we'd be able to reason with, bribe, or step on it. 'I'm not sure,' I said, 'but if we can't outsmart a single cell, we might as well pack it in.'

That's when Vieileau walked up. *'Th Ol One wil see yu now,'* she said. Without waiting for an answer, she walked off. We joined her.

We entered the hut, where it was now apparent a secret trapdoor led into the earth. We walked down a flight of earthen steps to a chamber below.

Candles lined the walls, casting a moody sort of light. The must of ages lingered in the air. The room wasn't large, but somehow it felt massive.

In one corner was the crumbling, mummified skeleton of what looked like a half-man/half-beast of some kind – four legs, two arms, human head, body the size of a deer or lion. Maybe it was two animals, torn apart and twisted together. Maybe it was . . . Then the other corner caught my attention.

Standing there watching us was a woman – light-skinned, red-haired, lovely. She couldn't have been more than thirty. Her eyes were sad but wondrous, filled at once with great loss and great hope.

The seven of us stood there staring back at her for a long moment. Then she walked directly up to me and spoke.

'You must be Joshua,' she said.

It was a pretty remarkable opening line, but she went on before any of us could respond.

'My name is Jasmine. It's good to see you all . . . again. Josh, Lon, Karl . . . I've been asleep . . . so long . . .'

She half-collapsed. I ran forward to catch her and let her down to the ground. For a long second we held each other's eyes. She felt so familiar.

'Thank you,' she smiled. 'Your impulses were always good. Please, all of you, come close. I'm weak from disuse, and words will come slowly at first.'

Everyone came near.

'Who are you?' whispered Lon. His gaze was transfixed.

'Dear Lon,' she touched his hand, 'we were lovers once.'

He squinted hard. 'You I'd remember,' he joked. But he seemed almost to be remembering.

'What I have to say is far beyond your experience,' she said, 'and possibly beyond your understanding. But listen for a while, and put aside what you know to be true. Because much depends on what you think to be fable. The universe depends on it.' She breathed deeply. 'First of all, I'm sixty-seven million years old.'

'The dinosaurs,' I said.

'What?' Lon sounded annoyed with me for interrupting.

'That's when the dinosaurs died,' I said. It was, after all, my field of interest.

'That's right, Joshua,' Jasmine continued. 'In fact, that's when nearly everything died, except me and a few thousand survivors. That was the Cataclysm, when the earth reversed its rotation, and gravity changed, and . . . that was the end of the last cycle of time – like now. We're nearing the end of another cycle now.'

'Preposterous,' said Dar. She was outraged that after all she'd been through, some moron would have the gall to even suggest such a hoax.

Lon seemed to agree. 'I don't believe a word of this. This is crazy, utterly . . .'

'More crazy than an ancient statue with my face on it?' I said dryly.

'More crazy than a lake that's a bug?' said Torrie.

'Yes, more crazy than that, more crazy than – '

'Please,' said Jasmine. 'Remember my prayer – put aside for a while what you know to be true.'

We were all silent again. She went on. 'I'm what we called in my time a Neuroman – the only thing organically human about me is my brain. The rest is all microcircuits and polymers, and it allows me to go into suspended animation for long periods of time – that's what I was doing until Vieileau brought me through my awakening process.'

'Like an android?' I asked.

'I don't know that word. My time was quite like your time but not identical. I had compatriots with your faces and names, and we had our own quest, as I'm sure you have yours. Time is cyclical, but it doesn't make perfect circles – there are patterns, and forms, which repeat over and over, but always with variations; the specifics change

with each go-around.' She looked at Lon again. 'For example, you were a vampire last time.'

Lon's nostrils flared.

'Yeah, you used to do that a lot,' she smiled. 'Actually, we had a lot of species you probably don't have now – for one thing, genetic engineering had become a very popular science, so new species were coined every year, just by splicing together the genes of preexisting creatures – that's how centaurs were made – with humans and horses – and minotaurs, and vampires, and dragons, and . . . Anyway, it was all wiped out in the Cataclysm, and then the new revolution of time began.'

She seemed so clear about it, so fundamentally sane in some intuitive way; it was quite disarming.

'Was it beautiful in your time?' asked Torrie. She had on her dreamy, preseizure expression, but even so, I think we were all a little shocked at the question. It implied a belief in Jasmine's narrative, a belief at face value, a leap in faith that the rest of us just hadn't made.

Lon looked aghast, Dar's crooked eye seemed to be vibrating wildly, Karl and Fernando remained unequivocally skeptical, and Curicuri sat alone in the corner, trying to break the curse we were obviously under.

'Was it beautiful?' mused Jasmine. 'It was lovely, until the last couple of hundred years. But then there were wars, plagues, mutations – it got ugly. Except for my friends – you – you were always beautiful.' Her smile warmed us. 'Especially my dear Beauty – that centaur whose bones lie in the corner there. His sense of balance and loyalty kept me whole in a time when nature herself was being torn apart.'

We looked at the mummified skeleton – the four legs, two arms, human skull – encrusted with cobwebs. Torrie

walked over to it, to stare at the fantastic creature, and began to weep.

Jasmine stood, put her arm around Torrie's shoulder, spoke softly. 'Yes, you loved him, too – back in my time. Once you were his woman, and your name was Rose, Rose Centauri, and your love was young when the world was already old, too old.' She paused to look at us all. 'I only hope we're strong enough to make it young again now.'

'What do you mean?' I asked. She seemed so compelling, I wanted to understand every word. I found her strange, beautiful, romantic, unsettling, and entirely unlikely.

'Tell me,' she said, 'how did you come to find me here?'

I told her about the skull Lon had showed us, and how we'd dated it at 75 million years old ('Only eight million years off,' she said. 'Not bad.') I told her about the map in the emerald eye, the jungle expedition, the ghosts in the rain forest, the city where we rescued Dar, the prophecy of Goranchacha, coupling with the queen, Di's death, the escape through the tunnels, and finally getting pulled down into this strange, landlocked city.

'Landlocked and time-locked,' Jasmine said. 'But one thing at a time. First of all, the skull that came into your possession is the skull of the man I knew in my time as Joshua. Toward the end of the Cataclysm there were many fires, and his coal-hardened skull I kept with me, into this new world.'

Something clicked for Karl with this – something about the ancestor with the emerald gaze, risen out of the fires of the last world, I think. In any event, I noticed a sudden change in his attitude toward Jasmine from this point on.

'Anyway,' she continued, 'long after Joshua died, I coated the skull's interior with clay, enameled the outside,

and placed that special, carved emerald in its eye. Then I sealed it in a seamless clay box, wrote some hieroglyphics on it, and oven-fired it. This book is Joshua's, by the way.' She indicated a large book on the floor beside her. 'It's his personal journal. It documents the story of all his adventures in those olden times. You should read it, Joshua, it may be instructive. The fossil *skull* of your previous self has already brought you a long way. Imagine how far his *words* might take you.'

I picked the journal up, leafed through it, and shivered: it resembled my handwriting. Too weighty to read yet, I closed it.

'That's all right,' she smiled. 'You have time.'

'And those hieroglyphics on the box,' posed Lon, 'mean what?'

'They're from an archaic civilization of my time-cycle. They mean, simply, that if you can follow the map in the eye of this skull, then time has come full circle, and closure is near.'

'But the map led to that city in the jungle – what do those natives have to do with it?'

'The tribe you discovered in the valley of waterfalls – well, now, that's a tribe of a different color. Right after the Cataclysm there were orphans of all kinds running around. I found a community of primitives wandering in the wilderness, dying of fear and disease and such. I pulled them together and hid them away in that basin. I gave them a religion, showed them how to plant and harvest, and gave them a written language – those ancient hieroglyphics. And I left them that gold idol, in Joshua's image, and left them the legend and prophecy of "Goranchacha," that their sun-child would return to them someday. That's my tribe, and my myths, and they've lived there ever since – waiting for you – because I knew

that eventually time would bring you around. Of course, the valley has shifted its position over the globe a bit since then, what with tectonic drift and all, but it's still the same time-locked valley it always was. The fact that some crazy, lost conquistador accidentally showed up five hundred years before you and was *mistaken* for you – well that's happened several times, over the millennia. Like you, he discovered the lake, and once he came down here, Vieileau's grandmother woke me up, as all the eldest women of her family are instructed to do if someone even vaguely fitting your description shows up. Of course, I could see immediately he *wasn't* you, so I had him thrown into the lake, and I went back to sleep for five hundred years – until now.'

In the quiet that followed, Torrie leaned forward and spoke softly. 'When you call that city "time-locked," what do you mean?'

'That city, and this one, too. Surrounded by a network of time-tunnels I've constructed, a network that keeps this entire area locked out of the natural flow of time, we've aged only hundreds of years down here, really, instead of millions. Of course, that wasn't my *purpose* in constructing the time-tunnels, that was just a side effect. No, the purpose of the tunnels, the nodes, is quite different.'

'"The nodes?"'

She looked us over, calculating. 'I think I've talked enough for a while. Let's go up to the lake, and maybe you can tell me a little bit of what *your* world is like.'

We sat by the edge of the lake and I told her. I told her what the continents were, and the oceans, and where. I told her about the earth's place in the solar system, in the galaxy. I listed major countries, with brief descriptions of

their political and economic stances. I talked about the developments of the twentieth century: telephones, electricity, cars, airplanes, skyscrapers, nuclear power, satellites, moon rockets, space probes, computers, lasers, particle physics, astrophysics, subways, ski lifts, movies, television, freeways, roller coasters, napalm, nerve gas, pistols, rifles, machine guns, tanks, bombs, atom bombs, hydrogen bombs, neutron bombs, X rays, chemotherapy, antibiotics, intensive care units, respirators, flashlights, flash cameras, videotape, adhesive tape, ticker tape, teletype, telegrams, holograms, electrocardiograms, candygrams, candy underpants, rock and roll, electric guitars, electric pianos, electric Kool-Aid, THC, DMT, MDA, PCP, DDT, BHT, Red Dye no. 2, sodium nitrite, nitroglycerin, Häagen Dazs ice cream, nylon stockings, ballpoint pens, digital watches, submarines, pacemakers, kidney transplants, birth control pills, electric chairs, hair transplants, oil wells, motor oil, love oil, love-ins, be-ins, sit-ins, walkabouts, holdouts, holdovers, takeovers, roll-overs, walk-ons, rubouts, standoffs, stand-ins, stand-ups, layoffs, layovers, layaways, runaways, runoffs, run-ins, shut-ins, hideaways, takeoffs, write-offs, write-ins, income taxes, profit-sharing, employee saunas, Nautilus machines, sunlamps, microwave ovens, supermarkets, Superbowl, Superman, microchips, microfilm, electron microscopes, radio telescopes, geodesic domes, solar energy, geothermal energy, refrigerators, central heating . . .

It was an exhausting tale. Darwina didn't hear any of it. She refused to take part in this madness, merely shuffled around the lake and sulked, but Lon and Torrie got into the spirit of my narrative, joining in periodically with their own additions or versions, variably excited or cautionary. At one juncture Lon launched into a long

two-part historical digression: (1) the history of Western civilization with overviews of Greece, Rome, the Christian Era, the Dark Ages, the Middle Ages, the Renaissance, the Enlightenment, the Industrial Revolution; and (2) the history of Eastern civilization, from Egypt to India to China. Torrie elaborated a bit on the development of the major world religions. We all discussed the variations on the human condition, the nature of the human character – good, evil, aspirant, hopeless, willful, empathetic, self-conscious, behavioristic.

It took hours and hours; it took a moment; I don't know how long it took. There was a momentum to it, though – the more we talked, the faster it came.

And Jasmine listened, enthralled.

And the rest of the village went on about its business, caring not a whit what we were talking about or who this new person was in our midst.

'What is the *story* with these people?' Lon demanded of no one in particular. He was more annoyed with their apathy than the rest of us. He was more of a romantic, I think, and romance wilts quickly under the chill of indifference.

'They've just stopped evolving, that's all,' said Jasmine. 'Partly it's the time-clot, and partly the ecosystem. They have no predators here, no aspirations. No threats or hopes of any kind. They're perfectly content, and perfectly stagnant.'

'So what are *you* doing here?'

'I chose to go into suspension here, because I could see it would never change. At least, not before you showed up.'

'And you knew we would.'

'I'll say it again – time is a cycle. We *had* to meet again in this life. At least, I was counting on it.'

'So, I presume, you have some way of getting us out of here?'

'You presume correctly.'

'You are perhaps not aware that during your sixty-million-year repose the lake has become infested with a giant amoeba?'

'Slime-mold, actually, but amoeba is a very good guess.'

'Slime-mold?' I felt sick.

'Yeah, I genetically engineered it myself – just manipulated a few regulatory genes, spliced in some plasmids. Not so hard if you have the maps.'

'And you did this for a reason?'

'Sure – it's sort of an organic gate, to let you in, but then keep you down here. I didn't want you running off before Vieileau could wake me.'

'Must be a pretty intelligent slime-mold.'

'Well, I did engineer some interesting features into it. For one thing, it loves the taste of anxiety. What I mean is, emotions have biochemical correlates in your body, and the chemicals you circulate when you're anxious happen to be the chemicals that enhance this slime-mold's functions – and the mold knows, like any organism knows, what nutrients can help it. You could say an organism has a taste for such nutrients. This mold loves the taste of anxiety. And I knew that when you showed up in the neighborhood, you'd be on your quest, so you'd be just nervous as anything. So the mold would be sure to snag you.'

'Let me get this straight,' said Lon. 'You genetically engineered a sixty-odd-million-year-old slime-mold to thrive on the subtle spice of human anxiety. I'm supposed to believe that my neuroses are suitable as herbs in the main course of an omnivorous prehistoric parasite.'

'Not omnivorous,' she corrected. 'It doesn't eat inert materials, like plastic – like my skin – '

'So you'd just float around in there like a bit of fruit in a Jell-O-mold – '

'Slime-mold. And also, it doesn't eat human flesh until that flesh has been detoxified of its noxious ethers by some highly saturated fish or bird oil – '

'Like screal fat?' I ventured.

'Right. So you were safe inside the slime on the way in, but once you'd eaten screal fat, the slime's enzymes could digest you easily. These villagers feed their decrepit or dying citizens to the beast, to keep their population controlled and to keep the slime well fed – but they're not an anxious people, so drop-ins like you can be real tasty morsels to an old slime.'

'How disgusting.'

'I have no anxiety,' Karl said without expression.

Jasmine shrugged. 'Well, no matter what your psychological state is, I can't imagine it's very pleasant to be digested alive by a mammoth slime.'

'So how do we get out now?'

'Hemolube,' she smiled.

'Which is what?'

'The oily polymer that runs through my veins. Keeps me lubricated, carries oxygen. Has a Teflon base, which means inert as far as slime-mold is concerned. Vieileau refilled me to wake me up – I have gallons of the stuff downstairs, though. Just oil up your bodies with it and we'll all swim through the mold, up to the river. Make sure you cover everything – drop some in your eyes, too – it'll leave a protective film long enough.'

So we brought her cans of Hemolube to the banks of the lake and smeared the clear, viscous fluid all over our bodies.

Night was falling fast on the little city. Fires were sparking up; songs were being sung and evening meals prepared from one end to the other. It was an ancient and human scene, and I took a long look at it.

We walked quietly to where the upstreaming tube entered the lake.

'Hang on tight,' Jasmine said. 'And if we get separated, swim for the moonlight.'

I smiled; we all held hands tightly. Then in unison we jumped in.

I could feel myself almost immediately drawn slowly up the pseudopod by the capillary action of the cytoplasmic stream. In spite of the oily polymer covering my body, I was aware of a warm tingling from the moment I entered, especially over my feet, which had lost some of the lubricant as I'd walked along the shore. Opposing currents pulled me in different directions, but I held on to the hands that anchored me on either side – in the primitive single cell as in life.

We passed a darkened area at one point. I wondered momentarily if it was a nucleus, with giant chromosomes sensing our alien presence. As we neared, I saw it was only human bones, though – a skull, a couple of ribs, half a pelvis. Floating above them, I looked down. Far below, I could see the fires of the village flickering peacefully. Through death to life. To life again. I felt somehow as if I were being slowly reborn on this journey. Through the raw protoplasm of time.

Suddenly, I was slammed out of my slow-motion contemplation by the impact of warm, rushing water, tumbled and bounced along the riverbed, torn from Jasmine's grip, and swept away in an uncontrolled spin. In another moment I unexpectedly hit the stone riverbank, coughed up half my air, and pulled myself out onto a slab of shale.

One by one, the others dragged themselves up. I looked around: we weren't fifty feet from where we'd left our packs. I looked down: through the river, through the cytoplasm, I saw the tiny sparks that were the bonfires of that timeless place. I looked up: a circle of stars rested high above us, just winking on in the twilight.

I felt newly born.

CHAPTER 9

Time and Timefall

We dressed, checked our supplies, checked our selves. All intact.

'Well, anyone have a clue about how to get out of here?' said Lon.

'Do we still have a compass?' I suggested.

'Actually,' said Jasmine, 'I know the way. But I was hoping to convince you to stay.'

'Stay?'

'Stay here? You kidding?'

'What's on your mind?' said Lon.

She fixed her gaze on him. 'You once loved an adventure,' she said.

'I just had an adventure,' said Lon. 'It's time to go home now.'

She paused. 'I could take you to your home in an earlier time.'

'I've been living in this bloody jungle camp for two years,' said Darwina. 'My home in an earlier time was London, thank you very much, and that's where *I'd* like to go now.'

But Torrie had a strange glaze to her eyes. 'An earlier time,' she whispered.

'Speak your meaning,' said Karl. His voice was stern, as if he didn't wish to be toyed with in these matters.

Jasmine seemed to be trying to choose her words carefully. 'This is going to be hard for you to understand, but I want you to stay here with me and put your lives at risk. Great risk. But great matters are at stake.'

'We've risked enough already for *ten* expeditions.' Lon shook his head. 'We've risked enough.'

'We've *lost* enough,' I added. Di's memory was still fresh; it wouldn't settle. Or more accurately, it *would* settle, for two or three days, and then suddenly bubble up again to sting my eyes like acid vapor.

'We've *all* lost much over time,' Jasmine went on. 'You no more than I. What's at stake now is time itself. The end of time. Of everything, maybe.'

'Maybe if you just skipped the melodrama and told us the story . . .' said Lon.

But he got no further before we heard footsteps and looked up to see more warriors than I could count running toward us at the far end of the cavern. We fled into the nearest tunnel – but not before Curicuri was hit by the first volley of arrows and fell dead. I saw him slump at the tunnel entrance, his spear outstretched to try to slow our pursuers in his dying effort. Fernando paused just long enough to touch the dying comrade – a long, tender touch – and then rejoined our flight.

Jasmine led the way – she seemed to know every turn and backtrack through this maze. 'I'll take you out to the jungle again,' she panted. 'We'll be relatively safe there. These tribesmen have the timesickness badly outside the tunnels, so if we can just outlast them there for a few hours, they'll have to go back.'

Nobody bothered asking her what she was talking about. We were all too scared and breathless.

After about ten minutes we were able to slow a little – we'd put some distance between us and the bad guys. 'I know a shortcut,' she said. 'We'll be out of here in no time.'

She took us down this corkscrewing slope, then through a passage so narrow you had to exhale to make it. Then

across a six-inch ledge overlooking a bottomless drop; then around two sharp corners to . . .

'This is the tricky part,' she said.

The tunnel here was a good ten feet wide, but the central five were occupied by a pit; and out of the pit shot a column of fire, like a retro-rocket, straight up to a flue in the ceiling. Even from twenty feet away, it felt like a blast furnace.

'We've got to get past it,' she said. 'Too bad, I thought it was at low burn this time of year.'

'Great.'

'No problem, though,' she smiled – with some strain, I thought. 'My skin is fire-resistant. I'll just walk each of you by, one at a time, you stay on the far side of me.'

'We'll be cooked alive.'

'Simmered, maybe. Come on, you can only die once. Or twice.'

Nobody moved.

'No faith,' she grumbled. 'Definitely a problem with the people of this cycle.' Whereupon she walked to within a foot of the fire, then came back to us. 'See? Just toasty.'

Her skin was flushed and sweating but nothing worse.

'Take me,' said Torrie. She looked a little *petit mal*ish to me, but Jasmine said, 'Let's go,' and they went. Inched past the flaming blow hole, Torrie pressed to Jasmine's back, Jasmine's face toward the fire; they slid around the column to the other side.

A few seconds later Jasmine ran back to us. 'Next?' she grinned. She looked a little the worse for wear, though – her face seemed sunburned, her eyelashes singed.

'I'll go,' said Lon. Like he was taking a dare.

Like an imp, she kissed him on the lips, then backed up. 'Come on, handsome.'

He was rather taken aback – we all were, a little – but

he went with her, and they made the passage.

Dar was next. By the time it was my turn, Jasmine's cheeks were starting to char pretty badly, and her hands were blistering. Her clothes had burned away during the last pass, too.

'I better face the other direction this time.' She smiled but was obviously in pain.

So she walked me around the column with her backside to the fires, me pressed to her bare breast, face-to-face.

It was a beautiful face. Deep green eyes that seemed unendingly sad, yet full of humor, the wisdom of centuries. Our lips touched as the flames roared just behind her. Something else touched, too. Something like a memory.

And then it was over.

We reached the other side. She went back for the others. When we were all together again, we rested a moment while she got a new set of clothes from Lon's pack. It looked like she'd sustained several bad burns, but she denied any discomfort and simply covered them with Hemolube. 'This is all-purpose stuff,' she said.

I was really starting to like her. She was stoic, tender, cavalier, brash, vulnerable to her own feelings, and I found her quite dear. All she'd seen, and all she'd done – was it possible? On the one hand, of course not. On the other hand, there was an ingenuousness about her that nearly radiated. Without question, she was guileless – how, then, could I not believe her?

In any case, we trudged on through the labyrinth for a good ten minutes before we saw the raiding party at the opposite end of our tunnel. Fortunately, they didn't see us.

Jasmine quickly, silently back-stepped us to a side

tunnel, then thirty feet around a blind corner. She looked tense for the first time.

'Look, I didn't want to do this yet, to show you this before I'd told you about it, but I'm afraid we have no choice now. Those natives can only come this way, and we can't go back very far now.'

'Show us what?' I said. I felt edgy.

She took us around the next corner to a dead end. Dead except that the entire wall seemed to glow. A dull red glow.

'This wall,' she said. 'This wall is a doorway. Now I want everyone to hold hands, keep your back flat to the wall, and follow me. Okay?'

We shrugged, or nodded, held hands and put our backs to the stone wall that abutted the radiant cul-de-sac. Jasmine was at the head of the chain.

'Ready?' she said.

I was scared, excited, and confused. But I smiled.

And Jasmine walked into the glowing wall. Walked through it, actually. And me, right behind her, holding her hand tightly, and holding Torrie's in my other hand, I walked through the wall, too.

Momentarily, it felt like I'd lost my body. Like I was nothing but a – consciousness. Unattached to anything physical or directional. It wasn't an unpleasant sensation, exactly, but it wasn't any party either.

And then we were through, to the other side – all of us at once, it seemed like. I looked around. We were in a hallway.

A sterile, white, hi-tech, dimly lit corridor.

'What is *this* doing here?' whispered Lon. The place made you want to whisper.

'It's always been here,' said Jasmine. 'Come on, let me

show you something.' She walked down the hall. Tentatively, we followed.

The walls were metal of some kind, hung periodically with framed pictures of strange design. Triangular doorways, nine feet tall, marked about every thirty feet of corridor. We entered the fourth one, walked up three flights of stairs – big steps – and went out another door.

What we found was rather hard to assimilate.

It seemed to be a huge room, filled with people bustling there. Except they weren't exactly people, and they weren't exactly there. What I mean is, they looked pretty human, but they were eight feet tall and dressed quite oddly. And there was something insubstantial about them. You could almost see through them.

It seemed to be a war room of some kind – maps on the wall, tables full of diagrams and model ships, a large central space with numerous cubbyholes around the perimeter. We were standing in one of these cubbyholes, a darkened one. Watching it all, without being seen.

'Where *are* we?' said Lon.

I knew before Jasmine answered, though. I knew as certainly as if I'd always known, as if I'd always known and she was just jogging my memory.

'We're in a different time,' she said.

We gawked, silently for a minute, at these strange aliens. They spoke an odd language. It sounded just like English – all the inflections were the same – but none of the words made any sense.

Four people walked near our doorway. We pulled back, but as they passed, I saw their faces clearly. It made me gasp and stumble. Jasmine caught me, lowered me to the floor.

'Those people . . .' I said.

Jasmine nodded. Lon had seen it too, though; his mouth hung open.

The four giants who'd passed – three of them were Lon, Di, and myself.

At least, they had our faces. And the one who looked like me was speaking to the fourth man – the man I didn't recognize – speaking to him, and I understood the words: 'But you're my *brother*,' he was saying, 'you've *got* to understand.'

I looked at Jasmine for some explanation. She smiled sympathetically. 'That,' she said, 'was you in a previous cycle of time.' She spoke slowly. I tried to listen, but it was hard – seeing myself like that; seeing Di, alive, animated, with me again – my chin began to quiver.

'Pull yourself together, man,' Lon's voice whipped at me. I could see he was scared, though, barely holding it together himself.

'I can explain this in detail later on,' Jasmine began, 'but what it is, is this. The axis of time rotates. It sweeps in great, wide arcs through the warp of space, and when it makes a complete revolution, it comes back close to the same point in time where it started. Not the same point in space, but the same point in time. Time repeats itself. Time goes in cycles. Time and time again.'

Dar clenched her teeth. 'No, no, no, no . . .'

'It just makes no sense,' I shook my head.

Karl crossed his arms over his chest. Torrie squinted. Fernando, on edge from all our intense reactions, crouched as if ready to spring.

I kept staring out the doorway. 'But who . . .'

Jasmine kept her voice calm, like an older sister on a spooky night. 'Those people you just saw were your counterparts in one of time's previous revolutions – a cycle that crossed very near your own time. Crossed near

enough that I was able to construct a bridge between that time and this one.'

'It's not possible,' said Lon.

'It's well recorded,' Jasmine insisted, 'though I admit frequently denied, or at least misinterpreted. You've all had experiences in your lives that are a function of this phenomenon, though.'

'Such as?'

'Such as precognition. Some people claim great skill at being able to see into the future. But in fact, precognition isn't foreknowledge of something that hasn't happened yet – it's a perception of a similar event that *already happened* in a previous cycle of time and is about to happen again, because time's axis is about to come full circle.'

'I've never believed in fortune-telling,' said Dar.

'Well, *déjà vu*, then – the feeling that you're seeing something that seems to have happened before, yet you know it *couldn't* have. Well, in fact, it *has* happened before – during another cycle of time. And you're just vaguely, fleetingly aware of it.'

'And those people . . .' I said again.

'Have you ever met anyone you felt as though you'd always known? Like you were old friends from the start?' I thought of the feeling I'd had when I first met Torrie. Jasmine continued. 'Like you'd been with them before, in another time and place? Or what about the sensation of reincarnation – the feeling that you've *been* someone else before. Well – you *have* been. You've been essentially the *same* person, in a different, but overlapping time. A different *cycle* of *time*. Those people out there – you *were* those people, eons of eons ago.'

'Well, the one who looked like me was talking to a man

he called his brother – but he didn't look anything like *my* brother.'

'Nothing is ever *exactly* the same,' said Jasmine. 'The cycles always vary. Once that man was your brother – this time, maybe he's someone else. We all have ways of sensing our pasts, though, and translating them to our futures. And the more clearly we can see and hear those pasts, the more surely we can take part in shaping the future of this cycle.'

Torrie was nodding. 'Like intuition,' she said.

'Exactly,' smiled Jasmine. 'Intuition's just the recollection of a pattern that was laid down in an earlier cycle and is now being repeated, with variations. Always with variations. That's what myths are, too – just racial memories of events from earlier cycles.'

'But how . . . how . . .'

'Look, let's get out of here,' she said. 'Those hostile natives are gone by now, and the longer we stay here, the more timesick we get. And we can't afford to get timesick until the work is finished.'

'What work?' I didn't care what work, though. All I cared about was Di, seeing her again, talking, laughing – with me. I went over to the doorway, just to glimpse her, even to touch her. But Jasmine held me back.

'Come on,' she said quietly. 'There'll be time enough for that.'

So we left. Back downstairs, along the corridor, through the glowing wall, into the catacombs once more. The natives were gone.

Jasmine took us quickly through the tunnels and finally to the original entry cave. There we walked through the waterfall, and then across the stepping-stones in the river to the jungle shore. And there we rested, in a grove of trees secluded from view.

When had we first passed this way? Only a few days ago? A week, perhaps. It felt like years, though. So much had happened, I couldn't begin to deal with it. Even Di's death seemed suddenly a distant memory, buried years before. I knew I was repressing, but at the moment that felt like a good protective reflex.

I was a little surprised, then, to hear Lon say, 'God, I'm tired, it feels like ten years have passed.'

'More like five, I suspect,' said Jasmine.

'What's that supposed to mean?' I said. Every time this woman spoke, she turned my stomach upside down.

'Just means time's different out here in your world than it is back there in mine. I told you, those cliffs are time-locked by the network of tunnels that connect us to earlier cycles – time moves much more slowly in there. In there a few days, out here a few years.'

Night was falling. We drew close for warmth, all looking at Jasmine with equal parts of awe, disbelief, and anticipation. Karl and Fernando remained taciturn yet intently focused on the ageless woman. Torrie seemed hypnotized, Lon scared but excited. I simultaneously believed her completely and believed I was hallucinating her. Dar seemed to be the most disoriented of anyone. 'Wait a minute,' she said. 'What year is this?'

'Fall of 'seventy-six,' I said.

She drew in a breath. 'When those bloody natives captured me, just last year,' she whispered, 'it was 1947.'

We were silent in the gathering twilight.

'I guess I'd better lay it all out for you,' said Jasmine.

'I guess you'd better,' said Lon.

'Well, first of all, if after hearing this any of you *do* want to go home, the way is very simple. This river leads – it has always led – to the sea. You just float downstream at night, and keep that red star' – we looked where she

was pointing, at a brilliant red dot low in the southern sky – 'in front of you at all times. Whenever the river forks, take the fork that follows that star, and in time enough, you'll reach the sea.'

Dar suddenly jumped up, laughing, and ran toward the cliffs.

'What's the matter with her?' said Torrie.

Not knowing, we gave chase, uncertain if she'd seen something or just gone 'round the bend. I suspected the latter.

By the time we caught her, she was already digging frantically in the brush at the base of the cliffs. 'It's got to be here,' she said, 'this is just where we left it before they captured us.'

It wasn't a minute before we saw it, too, and then we all helped her dig. It was a large aluminum canoe, buried shallow, filled with supplies. We pulled it out of the ditch and over to the river.

'This is near where they raided our expedition,' she said, sniffling with joy, escape within her grasp. 'It's just been sitting here waiting for me this whole year – '

'Thirty years,' said Jasmine. That hushed us. 'But as I was saying, here's the story.' We sat around her, leaning against the canoe. 'I was born, as I said, many millions of years ago. My time was a grand and terrible time. Humans were nearly an extinct species, trying to stay alive, while the world was ruled by the races they'd genetically engineered – creatures who were the materialization of their dreams and nightmares. You, Lon, were a vampire, and we were smugglers together before you settled down with your harem. And you, Joshua, saved my life once; and I aided you on your quest. And your best friend was Beauty Centauri' – her face became wistful now – 'the centaur whom I grew to love. I sorely wish he were with you now,

but like I said, some things change with each new cycle.'

'His absence pains you,' Lon said softly.

'The difference between what is and what might be,' she smiled with a great sadness. 'Still, I hope to touch him on the journey ahead – the journey to our pasts. Touch him even briefly, to fill the emptiness he left in me when he died . . . God, I hate him for that . . .'

She remained quiet for a moment, and cried, I think, though no tears came. Then she stopped, and smiled. 'Sixty-seven million years is a long time to have to be strong – I guess I'm just a bit wearied of it. Sorry. You'd think when they figured out how to bioengineer all the weaknesses out of humans to make Neuromans like me, they'd have done something about emotions like regret and longing. Maybe it was just poor quality control in my series,' she laughed. Then she pointed to her dry eyes. 'No tears, though, see? Counterproductive in dry climates – tears waste critical body fluid. So I guess *some* of my circuits are still intact.'

'I think you've got some great-looking circuits,' said Lon.

'You always were the charmer.' She shook her head happily. 'But anyway, that was my time. There were other times before that one, too, and they all coexist – some of them in those tunnels we just left behind us. Accessible through those bridges in the rock. I built those bridges. Never mind how; the technology is unimportant. It relates to microscopic masses dense enough to locally warp space-time. The bridges are actually just nodes of intersection, points where this time crosses the path of a moment in an earlier cycle. I've created about a hundred of these nodal openings.

'And what we have to do is, we have to save the universe.'

'Save the universe,' said Lon. 'Right.'

'What drivel,' Darwina whispered angrily. 'What unmitigated – '

'Let her finish,' insisted Torrie.

'Let her go back to where she came from,' said Dar.

'That's what I'm trying to do,' Jasmine spoke softly, her unrelenting focus defusing our hysteria. 'See,' she instructed, 'the universe is like a spinning top, spinning around the axis of time. The trouble is, the energy of the top is running down, and when it runs low enough, the top will topple – the *universe* will topple – end over end, into a timeless kind of chaos. I'm making this a little simplistic for now: we can go into details later.'

'Timeless chaos is not my idea of simplistic,' I mentioned.

She held up her hand. 'Stay with me. The thing is, the universe of this current time frame is even more likely to topple now, because the *last* go-around witnessed the birth of a strange, nearly omnipotent child who caused a week of cataclysmic events that all but broke time's axis. This child warped space and time, tore it nearly apart before she was through, and the world has been sitting mindlessly on the brink ever since. I can't emphasize this enough: time's axis is indelicately precarious at the moment. Teetering, in fact.'

'Like your mind,' muttered Dar.

'And the only way I could come up with to right the current axis – to speed up the spinning top so it rights itself – is to bring energy into the system. Inject energy into the universe-top so it spins faster, so it comes upright, so it regains its balance, so it doesn't fall.

'But the problem is, you see, we can't create energy *de novo* in our own universe – what we make in one place has to be lost elsewhere at the same time. *At the same*

time – that's the key. The only way to inject new energy into *this* universe is to extract that energy from *another* universe – the universe of a previous time. So there it is.'

'So there what is?' I was getting confused, and I wanted to understand her. I had to understand her. She was telling her *story* to *all* of us, but somehow, I felt, *speaking* to *me*.

'So we've got to go back into the tunnels, go through the time-nodes I've opened, and bring as much energy as possible back with us from previous times into *this* time. And that infusion of energy will make the wheel of this universe spin faster, thereby righting the axis of time.' She looked intense. 'Once more: there are no certain futures yet, but many pasts. In these previous ages there was plenty of energy, and now there isn't, so we've got to bootleg energy from any of your pasts and get it into the present. Before the present universe collapses.'

'You're mad, of course,' said Dar. She was restrained but furious – that anyone would suggest that she, of all people, should go back into those tunnels.

'What do you mean by the "axis of time?"' I said. 'I mean, what are you talking about? What – '

'It's . . . the stuff of time,' she tried to make it comprehensible. 'If it falls, if it breaks, it's not just the end of this present time – time is *always* ending, and beginning again. It's that word "*always*" that would vanish. It would be as if the present time – and all the *past* times – had *never* existed. No memory, no history, no past, no pasts – and with no past or present, then no future.'

'Sounds rather like a bad hangover,' said Lon.

'This all sounds rather like a bad joke,' said Darwina, 'so if you don't mind – '

'Bear with me,' Jasmine stopped her. 'Let me tell you what you'll find when you go through a node.

'You'll find people, usually. They'll be doing all the same things they were doing in that place, during that time – only not quite. Because they aren't actual people, see: that time is over and gone, and those people are long dead. What you'll actually be seeing are *images* of those people – that is, the light waves propagated by those people when they *did* exist, light waves traveling along parallel to us, accessible as perceptions to us now only if we go through the open nodes to see them. It sounds impossible, I know, but it's true. True as I'm here.

'You'll come upon people living in not too dissimilar times and places from your own. Sometimes they'll be nearly transparent, because the light waves will be so diffused and diffracted by now; sometimes they'll be nearly solid, because resonance with your own time will be so strong. Occasionally, you'll be able to sense what many of them are *thinking and saying,* because the electromagnetic waves propagated by their brains during their lives have *also* continued traveling, right along with the light waves.'

I thought of the translucent people in the war room – people almost like me, whom I could almost understand. Like dreams. Jasmine continued.

'So these people will be insubstantial to you, since they no longer exist as actual matter; but they can at least partially perceive *you,* too. They're only light-wave images of people, but they maintain a consciousness sort of like the consciousness they had when they existed as matter, a consciousness related to the electromagnetic waves their brains produced and radiated, when they first existed.

'So! They're semivisible, thinking semithoughts, semi-perceiving you with their semiconsciousnesses. And it's these image-people you've got to get back through the

nodes to this present time, because the energy of the electromagnetic waves that *constitute* them is what will infuse *this* time with *new* energy to speed up the gyroscopic universe of the present, so time's axis will straighten. Get it?'

I looked at her dumbly. 'And if we don't bring these semipeople back through your tunnels, the current universe is going to end, so the future will not exist?'

She looked hard at me. 'The current universe won't end, no. It will *never have been.* Try to imagine it – you will never have existed; nor anyone to remember you; nor flowers, nor song. Nothing that *is* will *be* or *have been.* No time, no past. Can you even stand to *think* of the emptiness of that?'

'There's not a chance in a million that – ' Darwina spat.

Jasmine's eyes flashed. 'If there's a chance in *ten* million that I'm right and in a hundred million that you can help, how dare you mock me, how dare you be so glib.' Her voice was like a whisper from the tomb. She stepped close to Dar. 'Have you never loved anyone, woman, that you can be so off-handed with his memory.'

Darwina just glared. Torrie touched Jasmine's hand. 'You loved him well, this centaur you call Beauty.'

Jasmine smiled. 'Forever.'

'I'd like to meet him,' said Torrie.

'Come with me to that time, and I'll introduce you. Reacquaint you, in any case – you were married to him once. Rose Centauri is what you were called then.'

'Rose Centauri,' she murmured.

'But why is this happening now?' I persisted.

'Because of the Child – she who warped space and time with the power of her mind. A child with power far beyond her understanding or control. She brought us to the edge. It's all described in here.' She handed me the

journal of the Joshua from her time. 'It's funny – he asked me the same thing once, asked me why it was all happening. I told him it was so there could be heroes, and people to remember them.'

'And now you want someone to remember us,' said Lon.

'I want there to be something to remember.'

'And all we need to do is suck a little energy into the world through these holes you've made.'

'Nodes,' she nodded. 'Unfortunately, I don't know exactly how much energy is *needed* by this current time to pull the axis upright, but I suspect it'll require bringing thousands of these ghost-people back with you. Oh, and incidentally, since they do lack substance, by and large, you won't be able to cart them back. You'll have to get them to follow you back somehow.'

'Follow us back,' said Lon.

'Yeah. I mentioned earlier that I was awakened several times over the eons, anticipating your return. Well, each of those times, before returning to my state of suspended animation, I crossed a few nodes and lured as many ghosts back into this time as I could. I got hundreds back, maybe, but as I said, thousands are needed. And, we're at the critical nexus now – it's up to you, "once sea-swallowed, now cast again . . ."'

'"And by that destiny,"' Lon continued the quote, '"to perform an act whereof what's past is prologue, what to come, in yours and my discharge."'

Jasmine smiled at him. 'That was always one of our favorite poems – in the last cycle of time.'

'One of my favorites now,' said Lon. 'I never realized it had been around so long.' He was being sarcastic, but he was both moved and shaken by Jasmine's familiarity with the poetry. She was beginning to grow on him.

She went on talking about the nodes. 'You've got to be very careful crossing over. Those nodes are time-contracted places, from this frame of reference. Time spent on the other side is almost like no-time.'

'What's to become of us?' asked Torrie. 'I mean, you know the fate of our counterparts in the last cycle. Can you predict what our fate will be?' She spoke as if she believed it all.

Jasmine shook her head. 'Too many particulars change from time to time.'

I still didn't get it, though. From life in the university to life in the universe was too great a leap. Or maybe too much order led inevitably to this much chaos. It just seemed so – irregular. 'Why me?' I said.

'It's always been that way,' Jasmine said simply. 'You've always been a perfectly ordinary human, dropped by time's wheel at the center of perfectly extraordinary circumstances. That's your destiny. What you do with that destiny is your choice.'

My choice.

My destiny and my choice.

Her words began exerting a profound effect on me. Terrible promise shaded every inkling. Terrible cost.

I could confront the future. Danger loomed there, and memory. Dire struggle awaited me, strained to haunt me, trembled to stalk me. I could seize these shadows, though. Much might depend on my actions. Jasmine seemed certain of it.

Her charge electrified me. Here was the universe, bobbling in my hands. I quivered lest I drop it. Lives were in the balance – planets, and suns. Time itself. I had to face the choice, that was my destiny; and then, if I dared, I could choose to wrestle the void.

The grave power of this prospect glinted in my vision,

glinted amid the scattering of lights that I suddenly recognized as the herald of a seizure. My hand began to twitch. The perfume . . . and then the visions came: the earth, breaking apart, boiling in liquid fire, melting; shorn, rumbling, sucked into a time-hole, gone as if it had never existed, its living forms vanished without a soul to remember it once had a history, once had a name, once was. Out of this blackness a man reached for his child, but before they touched, both burst into flame.

Worlds raced around suns, reversed direction, became glass, shattered into dust. The universe of stars disappeared, leaving a universe of timeless, unending void. Void without space, tumbling dizzily over and over into the emptiness of its own depth, falling aimlessly, out of control, over, and over, and over, and over, and . . .

I woke up.

Jasmine was holding me on my side; Lon had a towel in my mouth.

'You're okay now,' she said. 'You just had a little seizure.'

Torrie wiped my brow.

'He's fine,' said Lon.

Jasmine looked concerned, though. 'This makes things a little tougher. You take medications for the epilepsy?'

I shook my head.

'It just began happening a few days ago,' said Lon. 'When we got to the city.'

I thought of the compulsion that had dragged me into that strange city, coinciding with the first of my seizures.

Jasmine nodded. 'When he started getting close to the nodes. See, in the last time-cycle your previous incarnation also had seizures – induced by high-frequency radio transmissions. Those same transmissions are reaching you now, and if you go through the node into *that* cycle, the

seizures will get much worse. Of course, your ancestor in that time minimized the problem by wearing a metal helmet to block the radio transmissions.'

'A soldier of time,' said Torrie. She looked like she was feeling a bit seizurish herself. 'We've been chosen for this,' she said almost reverently. 'Great purpose, great design. I can feel it.' Her eyelids fluttered a little.

'I've had epilepsy since childhood,' said Dar, 'and all I've ever needed for it was Dilantin.' She sounded sullen.

'So you shouldn't have any trouble at all,' grinned Lon. Then he turned to Karl. 'Nor you, my old friend. This is beginning to sound like one sortie I'd hate to pass up. To smuggle spirits into our world for a beautiful woman? What do you say?'

Karl smiled his slow smile. 'If I could witness once the fires of the last world, I would give the rest of my toes.'

Darwina's mood looked blacker still. Jasmine sensed the tide turning toward her and resumed. 'Of course, there are lots of other dangers I need to tell you about. First, there's the question of the energy itself – it can be potent. Some of it's ultraviolet, for instance – it can blind you. There will be infrared that can burn you. It can be explosive at times. It may be so dense at times that the people or things it comprises actually seem to have substance.

'And then there's the timesickness, which is like a resonance that develops between you and your earlier incarnations. Makes it hard to know sometimes what your own time is. Sort of a chronogenic loss of identity.'

'Like jet lag,' I rasped. I remembered well, though, my feelings beyond the node, where I'd seen my ancient self in that strange war room: it was frightening, and moving, and electrifying – and I wanted to do it again.

Jasmine seemed to read my thoughts. 'And it can lead,'

she said, 'to the greatest danger – getting lost in time. Never finding your way back to your own time. That would be terrible for the universe – it would be a further loss of energy from this time.'

'Doesn't sound like it would be much fun for the person who was lost either,' said Lon.

'Depends on who you're lost with,' Jasmine replied. I thought of Di, of being lost in a time-warp with one of her incarnations for an eternity. That didn't sound like the worst thing that might ever happen.

'And of course the nodes themselves can be problematical,' she continued. 'You've got to enter at the *edge* of each opening in order to get whipped around the vortex to the other side. And you've got to enter and exit at exactly the *same* edge and the same angle – altering your position of reentry could throw you off years in time.

'But it's not all bad – you won't get hungry, beyond the nodes, or age very much. Time through the nodes is time out of time.' She paused, with a desperate look. 'And if we fail to bring sufficient energy back to this time, we'll know soon enough – if the Magellanic Clouds begin to slow their Doppler effect in the next fifty years, we'll know we're losing. And if they actually cease dopplering, it'll be too late. Beyond our help and beyond hope. The final catastrophe will then be unavoidable.'

'What is this Doppler effect?' Karl asked. He'd made up his mind to see the fiery embryonic world that held the seeds of his beloved jungle, and now he wanted to know everything he might need to know to preserve this ancestor-time from oblivion. For if Jasmine was right, all of these previous cycles would vanish with the collapse of our universe.

'A shifting of the starlight to the red end of its spectrum,' explained Jasmine. 'It's happening all the time; it

means the stars are racing away from us. Getting dimmer. When the Timefall comes, the stars will slow and stop, though. No more red shift. And then the stars will begin plunging back down toward us – they'll glitter brighter than ever before, until the night sky is spinning like a great radiant diamond; and then all the magnificent celestial facets will converge, and the cataclysm will be upon us.'

We were lost in thought and wonderment.

'But the first thing we have to do is get the jewels from the eyes of Goranchacha's idol,' she added as an afterthought. 'Combined with the emerald from the eye of the black skull you found – the skull of your previous incarnation – they form a special three-lens telescope that will locate all the nodes for you – '

'But I have Goranchacha's eyes here,' I said, pulling them from my pack.

She seized them happily, looked through them at the rising of the moon. 'So you do,' she said, handing them back. I peered into the jewels, into the moonlight. Futures danced within. Dark and brilliant possibilities.

'Of course, I know where most of the nodes are,' she went on, 'but then something may happen to me. There has to be a way for you to continue the work, even if I'm gone – '

'You are gone,' said Darwina, pointing a pistol at Jasmine's chest. 'Far gone.'

She'd pulled it from the supply pack in the canoe without being seen. She stood back now, shaking a little. 'I'm leaving. You can stay here in your bloody tunnels until you rot for all I care. I'm going home. Come on, then, everyone into the boat.'

There was a long, tense pause.

'You can put the gun away,' Jasmine said. 'I won't stop you.'

'Nobody's going to stop me. I said get in, everyone.'

Another pause. 'I think I'll stay awhile,' said Lon. This grandest of adventures with this brassy lady was opportunity knocking if ever he had heard it. Jasmine touched his cheek.

'And I,' said Karl. 'And Fernando. Seeking him with the skull of black coal and green eye whose gaze – '

'Fine, then fine. Josh and Torrie and me, then. Come on, then.'

That's when Torrie began having her worst convulsions yet and fell into the canoe. I went to help her, and so did the others, but Dar held them back with her gun and shoved off. With just the three of us in the boat.

Jasmine shouted from the shore. 'I beg you, don't leave with Joshua – he's critical to this expedition.'

'He's critical to *my* expedition,' yelled Darwina.

'Joshua!' Jasmine called. 'Remember your destiny and your choice. Remember what close friends we were once. Remember Di is alive in there. Remember the Timefall. Remember – '

But I saw Dar's hand come down with the butt of the gun on my head, and then everything faded away.

I awoke later that night, floating down the river, full of mixed feelings: anger at Dar; fear for Torrie and my own lost self; separation anxiety from my abandoned comrades; but also some relief, if truth be known, for this temporary lifting of the burden of decisions with which Jasmine had weighted me – decisions about struggle, and cause. The universe could end within my lifetime – or I could die trying to save it. Something else I realized in my half waking from Darwina's blow: I loved this woman

Jasmine. I felt I'd known her across all time, and always would – if time remained.

I tried to sit up but was seized by a monstrous headache and an overwhelming lethargy. I wanted nothing so much as to sleep for the time being. Even so, I did get up, to protest to Dar to go back. But my head began to throb as soon as I moved, and I slumped back down to the hull of the canoe. For the time being, I slept.

The time, being.

And Dar just kept steering the canoe, south and east, toward the red guidestar.

All night she steered, and when the stars disappeared, we rested on the bank. I awoke intermittently. We tended Torrie, argued, dozed, but Dar always kept a hand on her gun; and when night came again, our sorry crew shoved off.

On the second day, after I'd regained my senses, I suppose I could have taken Dar's gun while she slept. But I had little confidence I could find my way back to the caves alone, red star or not. Besides, Torrie was developing bad fevers, and lapses of consciousness – she needed civilized attention, not jungle potions. I think I was a little febrile myself, alternately convulsing, vomiting, and desolately confused.

For six days and nights we proceeded like a boatload of seizures.

On the seventh night we came to a peaceful village, with a church, a road, and a shortwave radio. And so we were saved.

Of the rest of our journey home, I recall little. Dar apologized for her behavior, but she didn't look very sorry to me. In any case, she got us on a plane to Los Angeles and herself on one to London. By this time I was no longer putting up a fight. I was no longer certain what

was real and what was imagined, and needed the recuperative hand of time to give me direction. Torrie was in no state to argue.

Dar, it turned out – since she'd been in the jungle since 1947 – had never seen a jet plane, and was somewhat unnerved by the sight of the SST. She held her own with the present day, though, confronting it one eye at a time. She wired her London bank for money, in fact, and found herself quite well situated – her investments had compounded substantially during the intervening years.

So we parted, all of us too sick and uncertain to hold much of a grudge, promising to write, and Torrie, at least, promising to go back to the jungle.

We checked directly into the UCLA Hospital, just a few months after our expedition had begun, which was early September 1976. So it should have been around December. And December it was.

Except the man at the registration desk told me it was now 1981.

PART TWO
Déjà Vu

CHAPTER 10

The Fourth Man

As I said, the events of the days following our escape remain thoroughly hazy to me. Between the fevers and the recurrent seizures, I could barely function. But the hospital became my home for a time, and it was nice enough under the circumstances. My neurologist, Dr Hoffman, was nice enough, too, I suppose. He kept reassuring me that everything possible was being done for me, which somehow only depressed me further. The fact of my deepening depression in the face of physical improvement (fevers resolved with antibiotics, seizures well controlled) worried the doctor, causing him to call in for consultation his older brother, a psychiatrist also named Dr Hoffman.

The second Dr Hoffman was earnest and seemed to feel my frequent crying jags were appropriate and well founded. I wasn't depressed so much as I was grieving, he put it.

Grieving is right. I was disconsolate. Di was dead. Di was gone. Di no longer existed except in my memory. Even more disturbing, my memory placed her death five years ago – which made sense, since she'd been killed in 1976 and it was now 1981 – but it made no sense, because we'd only left a few months ago. How could I fathom such paradoxes? I couldn't.

There was my own near death to deal with, too. And Torrie's mutilation. And Lon. And Jasmine, that strangest of missing links. I brooded constantly, obsessed with these things. The world seemed a bleak and insufficient place.

Two things turned me around. The first was the cat.

How it ever made its way up or down to my seventh-floor hospital window ledge is beyond me. Cats have ways, I suppose. This one was black, bloodstained, and bedraggled, with that wild look in its eye, like a mad cackle. I opened the window, reached out, pulled the creature in – she clawed my arm up and hid under the bed.

I fed her secretly. From my lunch tray. She was suspicious at first – wouldn't take her cat eyes off my face, though I held a bit of chicken Kiev directly under her nose. She changed her tune after she tasted it – adopted me on the spot.

The only thing about her not black was her eyes: cold, teal, deep as a frozen lake. I named her Ice-eyes.

Kept her up there, under wraps. I knew the hospital would make me get rid of her if they found out, so I became a master of clandestine maneuvers. I insisted my door remain shut at all times and that people knock before entering. Ice-eyes knew what was what, too. At the first sound she'd scamper under the bed or into the closet, to hide.

We ate our meals together, too. Shrimp cocktail was her favorite; she loved to bat the little critters around the floor like hockey pucks before devouring them. After eating she'd curl in my lap and methodically, almost arrogantly, lick her entire body clean. I would stroke her head. She would lick my arm. We attended each other.

She was phenomenally bright, I thought – watched TV with great curiosity or stared at the pages of books I was reading as if she were intently trying to figure them out. Frequently, when I started to turn a page, she'd stick out her paw, hold the paper down a moment, look up at me with tilted head, and then let me proceed.

For a toilet she used the flower box that sat on the

window ledge where I'd found her. The flowers started doing poorly, I'm afraid, though I was good about cleaning up the box. Once – it had started raining, so I'd unthinkingly closed the window – she used the bathroom sink in which to empty her bowels. Before I was aware she'd done so, I was startled by a knock on the door. Ice-eyes hid in the closet, and the nurse came in to put a clean cup in the bathroom.

I heard a little grunt as she entered, then a lot of water-running, toilet-flushing, disinfectant-spraying. I couldn't imagine what she was doing in there. When she left, she gave me the most repulsive look.

I had no idea why until my visit from Dr Hoffman (the psychiatrist) the next day. He was rather perplexed and asked me why I'd done it. Done what? I wondered. Apparently, the nurse had told him I'd been shitting in the sink; she would not tolerate it.

I only smiled, and apologized, and promised it would not happen again. Dr Hoffman was a bit rushed and had to leave, but indicated we would talk about the episode in depth at a later date. I nodded earnestly and opened the window to the flower box.

Ice-eyes and I had somehow entered into a conspiracy – of concealment, of mutual nourishment. I suppose she was just someone who needed me, and that's what I needed. All I know is, her coat, day by day, began acquiring a certain sheen, and as I observed this transformation, I began feeling stronger, as if my skin, too, were taking on a new luster.

I saw, in Ice-eyes, my inner self: secret, curious, uncertain, dark.

Healing slowly now, but healing.

The second thing to help pull me out of my spiraling depression was Torrie.

She *really* went through hell that first week back – surgery to remove the infected jewel from her brain stuff, intravenous antibiotics, anticonvulsants, anthelmintics (it turned out we both had parasitic infestations, in the bargain). She made it hard for me to maintain a good head of self-pity.

I sat with her during her first, mostly unresponsive days. Then when she started being able to walk, I walked with her, up and down the corridor. She had a left-sided weakness now – a limp in that foot, a slight droop to her smile on that cheek – and a strange, sort of fey manner as well.

Not that my own personality hadn't become a bit strange, I know, but hers was something special. Canny, somehow. She said the emerald had imbued her with the notion of its crystalline harmonics. She resonated.

I am – at least, I once was – an intellectual. Yet I harbored an occult fantasy about Torrie. Though I didn't, and don't, believe in souls, let alone in the transmigration of souls, I did believe that in some inexplicable way Di's soul had entered Torrie. I saw Di in Torrie's mannerisms, in her speech, in her moods. It was almost as if Di still lived.

Of course, I knew this wasn't really so: I wasn't yet so mystical in my worldview. It was simply a case of wish fulfillment on my part. I was projecting.

Still, it drew me close to Torrie and eased my pain considerably.

So that by the end of two weeks of in-hospital medications, perambulations with Torrie, and therapeutic cat-purring sessions, both Doctors Hoffman were well pleased with my progress. Hoffman the elder cautiously estimated I wouldn't need to be an inpatient for too many days longer. Hoffman was in agreement.

* * *

Lightless tunnels opened into each other, diverged, intertwined, doubled back, grew lighter, grew vertical – blossomed out. Out of the catacombs onto dry land. Smoky, bright. Explosions everywhere and people screaming. Not people, no. Animals.

A shadow passed low overhead, then swooped up with a rush of wind: it was a man, with huge leathern wings, with long claws, with green eyes.

Hoofbeats approached. From the left, out of the fire. A herd of bulls with human heads bore down on me, bellowing, and then *I* was bellowing, and the sky turned black but for a negative image glowing in it, an image of twisting corridors, fading to total blackness . . .

I woke up.

Torrie sat on the floor beside me, holding me on my side. Gently, she pulled the wadded washcloth from my mouth; it was soaked with saliva, and a little blood. I looked up.

It was Torrie's room in the hospital – I remembered it now. She sponged my head. A long string of spittle leaked from the corner of my mouth and hit the floor. Torrie wiped my mouth. Why was I lying on the floor?

Oh, yeah.

'I just had a seizure, didn't I?' I whispered. My throat was hoarse. I tasted blood where I'd bit my tongue.

'Yeah, but don't . . . let it bother you,' she said with her lopsided smile, 'great men are always . . . ahead of their time.' She had a slight hesitation to her speech now – a 'case of the pauses,' she called it.

I sat up shakily. She wrapped me in a blanket and rubbed my shoulders. 'Want to go for a walk?' she said.

We took a long walk through the hospital. Down stairwells, around lobbies, across conference rooms, into the basement. Past the medical students' lounge, the laundry room, the laboratories. I took her hand. I almost

felt like an innocent, strolling with my girl. *Daisy, Daisy, Give me your answer, do.* We stopped in front of the morgue. 'My doctor tells me I'm leaving tomorrow.' I let go of her hand.

'Oh,' she said softly. 'How . . . wonderful for you.' She noticed the door beside us. 'Want to go in here?' she whispered.

I shook my head.

We started walking again. 'You won't have to stay much longer,' I assured her.

'I don't care, really,' she shrugged. 'I just wish I knew what happened to my mind. I mean . . . I know I lost some of my brain. But why does it feel like I'm . . . just now losing my . . . mind?' The pausing in her speech pattern was getting worse.

I stopped, pulled her to me, hugged her.

'I'll . . . dribble on your neck,' she warned. Suddenly, she pulled away and began walking down one of the cross-corridors. 'Look, here's Physical Therapy!' she called. She opened a side door, and I followed her into the darkened room.

It was a room of shadows, filled with mysterious equipment of all kinds: exercise machines, parallel bars, massage tables, tubs, weights, and pulleys. The only light came from streetlamps shining through the exterior windows. No one else was here.

'This is where they . . . help me work on my limp,' she said.

She went over to the treadmill and took a few steps. I looked out the window at the night sky. Orion winked at me, vigilant, unswerving.

I walked back to Torrie. She was standing beside the whirlpool now, dangling her hand in the water.

'It's still . . . warm,' she said.

My stomach fluttered. I put my hand behind her neck,

pulled her mouth to mine, kissed her. She was passive at first, then tentative. I moved my hands gently over the flannel of her thin housecoat – her back, her chest, her waist. She pulled me closer, then suddenly began crying.

I held her.

'Are you . . . going to . . . make love to me?' she said.

We slid to the floor, still holding each other, both half-shivering, half-impassioned, emotionally rocky physical wrecks. We kissed again. I felt right on the edge. So elated, so depressed. Seducing a woman with a literally battered psyche, less than a month after my own wife's violent death. Or was it five years? I felt guilty, yet so close to Torrie – spiritually, metaphysically. Like a twin almost. Did that make this incest? I didn't know what it made it. All I knew was, it made me crazy.

And she looked as breathless as I felt – all beautiful, moist-eyed, vulnerable, so sensual in spite of her cropped hair, or maybe because of it, and her fingers under my shirt . . .

Half-undressed, there on the rug, we made love among the machines.

Afterward, we cooled out in the still-warm whirlpool bath, floated there like embryonic spirits awaiting birth.

And after that we snuggled in her hard hospital bed, rarely sleeping, conscious of each other's hungry touch all the long night long.

I left the hospital next afternoon, Ice-eyes perched on my shoulder. No one could believe she'd been in my room the whole time, but there she was.

I took a cab to Lon's house. It was all closed up, vacant for years, it looked like. I broke in a back window and set up shop.

The water, electricity, and phone were still on – that kind of stuff was paid automatically by Lon's business manager, Neal. There was food in the fridge, too old to

be rotten, and a rather angry good-bye letter from Melinda dated January 1977.

My own possessions, I'd found out, were being held in storage by the university, my apartment leased to a new junior professor. I felt attached to none of it anymore, though. To nothing, in fact. I felt like a new human being, with no past and an infinite number of futures. Or was it the other way around?

In any case, I wasn't concerned in the least about my immediate needs – I was rich, for one thing. I'd brought back a pocketful of jewels, appraised, while I was in the hospital, at more than I'd ever likely spend. No, money wasn't the problem. The problem was what to do with my life.

I turned to the journal – the journal Jasmine had given me, written by the Joshua she knew, a journal that was, by her account, 67 million years old.

It was the diary of a simple man on an intricate quest. His brother and his wife, Di, had been kidnapped, so Joshua had set out to rescue them in the company of his friends: Beauty, Jasmine, Lon, and a cat named Isis. His journey was personal but touched and intertwined with the vital moments of the epoch. He was not a hero, yet his simple resolve had heroic effect.

I found myself moved by his story. His crises seemed not nearly so far removed as the millenia would indicate.

The book culminated with the calamities of which Jasmine had spoken – the disastrous keeling-over of time caused by a demented, telekinetic child. What Jasmine hadn't prepared me for was the identity of the child: it was the child of Joshua and the queen of the city.

My child.

My child with the queen. I was staggered. Was this prophecy? Destiny? Charade? In a past life, it seemed, I

had made love to a queen and begotten a girl-child with powers.

So had I in *this* life been raped by the queen of that jungle city.

And where would *that* conception lead?

Jasmine said few things were ever exactly the same from cycle to cycle. Maybe there would be no child this time; or maybe the child could use its powers to right time's axis; or maybe there would be a child, but . . .

I read the journal again and again. It was filled with nuance. It felt indescribably familiar, yet opaque through large sections. It imbued me with a profound, if quiet, excitement, and I began to regard it less as a historical document than as an instruction manual.

Three weeks later Torrie, too, was discharged from the hospital and came to live at Lon's with me. We were essentially shacking up together for a protracted convalescence.

Rapidly – obsessively, I think – we'd grown quite dependent on each other. But, then, who else could possibly understand what we'd been through?

We made love constantly, passionately – desperately. It was as if we'd both been raped in the jungle – some deep core violently penetrated – and now we were trying to reassert our capacity for love, for human contact; but we couldn't expose our rawness to anyone else, only to each other. And to each other we pressed our wounds to obliterate the pain, to make the violated boundaries of our selves less severely demarcated. We'd have fallen into each other if we could.

The two of us rattled around that huge, rambling house like ghosts in a Gothic mansion. We rarely left. We had pizzas, Chinese food, and groceries delivered. We had the phone disconnected. Dishes piled up, laundry collected in corners. Our day-night sleeping patterns randomized. The

place took on a dissolute, almost deranged air.

This frayed ambience was decidedly enhanced by Ice-eyes' presence. She became a sort of familiar – skulking about in odd corners, sniffing at the furniture, discovering niches and vantages. She stalked lizards and birds in the backyard, occasionally bringing some prize inside and dropping it smugly at my feet for inspection. She favored each of us periodically – though certainly not regularly – by sleeping on our feet for a few hours during the night. Invariably, she'd rise, though, with just enough commotion to half-wake us; through lidded eyes I'd see her shadow float by, shift to the floor, click away into the darkness – just another ghost.

She still felt most attached to me. She'd sit in my lap for hours sometimes as I stared out the kitchen window, her claws almost imperceptibly extending and retracting with gentle pressure, like a kitten nursing. She had her sullen moods too, though – didn't we all? When that happened, you couldn't put a hand near her to pet her without getting a deep scratch down the back of your wrist for the effort.

My seizures returned – but slightly – so I began juggling my medicines a bit, trifling with my states of mind. Once or twice, the convulsions wouldn't stop, and paramedics had to be called to drag me twitching into some local emergency room. I never stayed long, though. I'd played as much as I wanted to with the seizure; there was no point in wasting the hospital's valuable time beating a dead fit.

Does it sound so crazy? Maybe it was, a little. It's hardly more than a standard deviation, though, isn't it – experimenting with metaphysics, with obsessive love, with alterations of consciousness? Doesn't everyone sometime? It's only that we were playing hardball – seizures and anti-convulsants instead of marijuana, psychodramas

that included friends lost in a jungle tunnel. Lost in time.

Whom the gods destroy they first make mad.

Once we had simultaneous seizures while making love. Can any of you know what we knew?

Enough. So it was madness, perhaps. For a time it made us feel well. There was a measure of peace. We were looking for our peace in that house of echoes.

After a while I did begin to feel less gaunt. I think, finally, we started to mend. I asked for, and received, an extension of my extended leave of absence from the university. They were 'very understanding' about my 'condition,' as the departmental secretary informed me off the record. That was funny; I didn't understand a thing.

So as my strength returned, I became more convinced of the need to rejoin my friends in the jungle – needed it for, if nothing else, a sense of closure. I wanted to see Lon, to touch Jasmine, to see if she was real. To see if I had a child by that wild jaguar queen. To touch my destiny.

Here I'd been, taking all this time off, and what I really wanted, in some deep way, was to take time on. I felt the way some soldiers feel coming home from a war – I missed the vitality of walking death's edge, of conversations with darkness. Such soldiers inevitably reenlist, or become soldiers of fortune. A soldier of time, Torrie had said.

Yet at the same time I was afraid – for Torrie, for myself, for my sanity. How could we possibly hope to embark on a trek like the last one, just the two of us alone, wrung by convulsions?

We discussed these matters one evening on the rug in front of the fireplace, with Dvorak's *New World Symphony* on the stereo.

'All that stuff is important,' she told me, 'but . . . it's

not the main thing. The main thing is . . . the Timefall.'

'I don't half-believe any of that now. That was in the jungle. This is civilization. This is the twentieth century. That was – '

'That was . . . eternity,' she smiled. 'I've seen it again, Josh . . . in my seizures. The different times . . . the universe. The entire universe is in every cell in your body, Joshua . . . if you look, you can see it.'

'What if I don't want to see it?'

'People like you, Joshua . . . you can't help yourself. Like me, too. We're like . . . blind visionaries.'

Blindly, we rolled around the floor half the night. It felt like we were rolling down a steep hill, unable to stop, ready to take off at the slightest bounce.

I woke up next morning in a kind of jangled, spacey clarity. The seizures were behind me – temporarily, at least – I could sense that. What was ahead was less apparent. I needed time and space to think, to consider my life. So I went wandering in the wilderness of LA.

It started out unassumingly enough. I told Torrie and Ice-eyes I was going on a long walk, not to wait up. Then I just strolled out of the Hollywood Hills, down to Sunset, and started heading west.

Once again, I had cause to wonder, as I walked, if it wasn't all epileptic phantasm: reviving a multimillion-year-old woman; a lake that was a slime-mold; seeing a golden statue with my face. Surely, some of these images were flights of altered consciousness; yet surely, some were not. And just as surely, all my friends were gone save Torrie – and Ice-eyes, who couldn't speak.

I walked. For two days I walked. I slept wherever I found myself when sleep came. I didn't eat, drank little. I spanned the concrete basin of the LA River; I slept in Hancock Park, at the edge of the Tar Pits; followed the

tracks downtown, dozed in a barrio alley, cooled my feet in Echo Park Lake, ran from two teenage muggers who caught me and beat me for having no money; I lost my shoes. I meditated on the universe and the Chinatown lights.

I meandered through Griffith Park, feeling like something between a contemporary urban Buddha and a psychotic derelict. The park at night was a wash of sexual trystings, half-seen shadows, insistent noises, lurking shapes. Like a land of dream. It made me feel somehow alive, close to my inner core. A brooding excitement filled me, staying me from sleep now, readying me for – something.

I came to the observatory. The telescope was trained on the Hercules Cluster – an aggregation of thousands of stars, the program guide said, that looked like a single star to the naked eye. But through the twelve-inch telescope's resolutions, they were seen to be a conglomeration of specks. So far away, many of them may have become extinct millions of years ago, but the light they'd given off was only reaching the earth now; so we were just seeing them, as they'd been, those millions of years earlier. We were seeing their past.

The few other tourists on the observation deck kept regarding me with discomfort and soon left. I must have looked like a crazed hobo. When I was alone with the guide, I asked him if it was possible to see the Magellanic Clouds from here. No, he said, you have to go south for that. Colombia? I asked. Yes, that would do.

Sparkling lights flittered across my peripheral visual field. 'Now *there's* a cluster for you,' I said thickly.

'What?' asked the guide. But that was the last I heard before launching into my next convulsion.

* * *

When I came to, I was in some emergency room being taken care of by some doctor named Kahn.

And he was the fourth man.

When Jasmine had taken us through that node to the ancient time in the war room, I'd seen myself walking with Lon, Di, and a fourth person who was unfamiliar to me, a person I'd addressed as my brother.

That fourth man had the face of this Dr Kahn.

I stared at him now from my hospital bed as he shone lights in my eyes and listened to my heart. I, too, listened to my heart: Trust this man, it said; trust him like your brother.

Kahn had to understand. I had to *make* him understand.

I told him about the end of time, and the android creatures called Neuromans, and how one of them still lived. I took some artifacts from my pocket – mementos: a piece of the quill feather I'd used to unlock Di's cage in the castle; a small ruby.

Kahn listened, and I could see he thought I was crazy. 'But you're my *brother,*' I said, 'you've *got* to understand.'

He said gently, 'I'm not your brother, but I'm trying to understand.'

He was a skeptic, but not unkind. He believed in his little universe as I was growing to believe in my larger one. We weren't so different, really – both scientists at heart, our faith resting on what we could observe and deduce. My powers of deduction were no greater than his; I had simply seen more. His life, like most, was sheltered by choice – for who among us can live without shelter?

So I saw in Kahn someone truly like a brother, someone I might have been but for a path not taken, but for the path I *did* take, leading inexorably to the edge of the void.

So for even just a moment, I wanted him to share my lookout.

'It's like the dimmest stars,' I said. 'You know how when you look up at the night sky sometimes you can see a star out of the corner of your eye, but when you try to look right at it, it disappears?'

He didn't know what I was getting at, but he tried to reassure me. 'There's a rational explanation for that. The edge of your retina has more rods in it – rods are the receptors that only see black and white, and they're much more sensitive to light than the color receptors near the center of your eye, so your peripheral vision can pick out dimmer objects than your central vision.'

I smiled; he sounded so like me when I lectured a student. 'Yes, but that's not my point,' I said. 'The point is, when we look directly at the star and it disappears, we assume there's nothing actually there, we assume what we saw from the corner of our eye was a fantasy, a trick of perception: since the star wasn't there when we looked right at it, it simply didn't exist in fact.'

'So?' he said.

'So? You don't find that disturbing?' I demanded. 'You don't find it maladaptive in the extreme – from an evolutionary perspective – for a person to disregard information he derives from his more sensitive peripheral visual receptors, and to rely instead on a contradictory message from his less sensitive, though more commonly used, central vision?! I can assure you, as an evolutionary biologist I find it a counterproductive mode of behavior not only for the individual but for the species. You disagree? People could become extinct acting that way!'

He knitted his brow, nodded contemplatively as he considered my assertion, before he spoke. 'Face it,' he said, 'people are assholes.'

We had a good laugh, sealing our fraternity forever.

'You got *that* right,' I said, wiping my eye. I was feeling considerably better.[1] 'All I'm saying,' I went on, 'is that some truths have to be glimpsed. They're elusive. They dissolve under cold, close examination – but that makes them no less truths.'

He answered almost apologetically. 'My truths are all bright stars.'

'Nothing wrong with that as far as it goes,' I said. 'Only I think you have a more sensitive appartus for picking up some of the more flickering truths – you just discount it because you use it so rarely. I never used mine at all until I learned how on my recent travels.'

'And what do you make of your new flickering truths?' he said.

'Ah, there's the rub,' I said, wilting. 'I don't quite know.'

'Well, then,' he smiled, 'you're not so different from the rest of us.'

A nurse approached and told him the kidney in Bed 4 was acting up, would he please come? He excused himself to me, but I held him back a moment and gave him another token: a seed from one of the red fruits that hung in the grove surrounding the idol of Goranchacha. A proof.

I lay there in the ER for a couple of hours, staring up at the ceiling, listening to the sickness and death all around me scrabble at the door. X rays were taken of my skull, blood tests of my blood, polygraphs of my heart. I heard a man clutching at his chest, a child screaming, a woman crying, a lonely whine. Could I live in this world again?

I heard Kahn call Dr Hoffman about me. I couldn't

[1] So I suppose, therefore, his claim to being a healer was legitimate, though his commentary on my analysis suggested that like most physicians – contrary to his own estimation – he was no scientist.

catch the specifics, but I got the drift. It made me feel extremely third person.

When he returned to my bedside, I sat up, resolute. 'The way I see it,' I said, 'there are really only two possibilities. Either I'm nutty as a *Snickers* bar, or this stuff happened. But I have to believe what I remember; so if I believe it, the question is, what do I do?'

'Why do anything?' suggested Kahn. 'Just accept it and move on to something else. The rest of your life is waiting.'

'That's very therapeutic, I'm sure, but we're speaking of the end of the universe here, potentially. Doesn't that phase you?'

'Frankly, Joshua, I don't see it. I think you had a series of traumatic emotional upsets in the Amazon jungle, and you got a serious knock on your head, and now you have seizures, and a kind of haphazard support system at home, and . . .'

Somehow my case had gotten misrepresented. That being the case, there seemed no point in pressing the matter. So I just left. Sometimes that's the strongest point you have.

I was frustrated by my inability to communicate the nature of time and the universe to Kahn – but maybe it was always in the nature of the fourth man to be my devil's advocate, my flip side. No matter. I knew my spirit now. Kahn would not deter me.

I went straight home from the ER. Torrie and Ice-eyes were really excited to see me. Made me feel like I was where I belonged.

In spite of all my medications, my seizures grew much worse over the next day or so. More and more, too, they were accompanied by the glaring black-and-white images of tunnels writhing before me – flashing mazes, pulling me in. Always the same, too – the same labyrinths, the

same seizures. Much as I wanted to return to the jungle now – to wrestle with my new glimmering truths – I was reluctant to venture too far until these convulsions were at least a bit more stabilized.

And then suddenly they were gone. Just gone. I woke up and I knew it. I brought my hand to my head to scratch it . . . and found I was wearing a thin metal skullcap of some kind. It felt like aluminium or paper-thin tin. When I started to remove it, to see what it was, Torrie stopped me – she was sitting beside me.

'Leave it,' she whispered.

'What is it?'

'A helmet.'

Shakily, I got out of bed, wobbled to the bathroom, and looked in the mirror. It was a child's toy headpiece, something from Flash Gordon, I think; maybe what Ming the Merciless wore. A smooth, form-fitting yellow-red-and-blue-painted aluminum bonnet, coming to a V down the center of my forehead, wrapping around the top and side of my skull, leaving space for the ears, curling up in a blunt Saf-T-Lip (pat. pend.) at the back of my neck. It was covered with bold lightning bolts, sizzling five-pointed stars, broad bands of color, and was tied loosely under my chin with a red plastic strap. I looked quite ridiculous.

I had to laugh. Tears on my cheeks, I stumbled back to Torrie, and we fell into a long embrace, laughing or crying, I don't know which.

I sat down on the bed once more. 'My convulsions have stopped,' I said. My eyes felt wild.

'The helmet blocks the radio transmissions from the last cycle . . . coming through the node . . . the high-frequency ones that cause your seizures. Remember? Jasmine said so.'

I nodded, hardly daring to believe she was right.

'But you know,' she went on with a twinkly smile, 'it doesn't look half-bad on you.'

It was the last obstacle overcome. There was now nothing to prevent me from going.

We spent a couple of weeks getting ready, but there really wasn't all that much to do. I got copies of all my hospital X rays and tests to file away with my last will and testament – for historical purposes. When future generations of children asked their parents, 'What was he like, this man who saved the universe,' their parents could say, 'He was like this: he was lost and his motives were mixed, and his white blood cell count was six-point-two and his potassium was four. That's what he was like.'

I bought a toy kaleidoscope at Woolworth's, pried out the lenses, and replaced them with the two emeralds from Goranchacha's eyes and the one from the eye of the black skull that still sat in the secret room behind Lon's library. When I held the jeweled telescope to my eye now, I saw an intricate weaving of lines, like the veins of a leaf or the cracks in a crystal. Branching lines, like a labyrinth.

It gave me a feeling of déjà vu.

But I knew it wasn't déjà vu. It was the maze from my photseizures; it was the time-tunnels to which Torrie and I were now preparing to return.

Everything seemed to be meshing so neatly, so quickly. Such phenomena Jung would have called synchronicity – meaningful coincidence. But these things were rooted, I felt more and more, in our resonance with our selves from previous times.

I see I'm beginning to sound cultist, but how else to explain the meaningful coincidences on the journey we'd made and the one we were about to make?

Not to mention what happened at the party.

The last day before we were to leave for Rio, Art

Reingold, one of my old colleagues from the university, called. He'd just heard I was in town, got my number, hoped I was doing well, etc., etc. Could I come to a party at his place tonight? Big bash, end of semester, he'd love to see me.

I thought not and begged off. But when I told Torrie, she insisted I call him back to accept. She hadn't been to a party in six or seven years, she might well be spending the rest of her life in the jungle, she wanted one last taste of civilization and its discontents, and besides, she felt like celebrating.

So we went. I wore a cowboy hat to cover my Space Cadet helmet.

It was a huge old house in Brentwood, maybe a hundred people there, mostly academic types, drinking, debating. Torrie went straight to where the music was blaring, to dance with herself, or whoever wanted to join in.

I got a drink and wandered out to the garden. There, sitting alone by the pool, was Kahn, the doctor who'd seen me in the emergency room two days earlier. And he was playing with a toy gyroscope.

Talk about synchronicity.

I'd felt intuitively[2] in touch with him in the ER; but now, crossing his path again in such a different context – while he toyed with a model of Jasmine's universe – it seemed, like all the other miraculous events that had befallen me, both implausible and inevitable.

I walked up to him. 'Hi. Remember me?'

He stared at me quizzically a moment, then broke into a smile. 'You're looking a lot better, cowboy,' he said.

'More vertical, at least. Mind if I join you?'

[2] Intuition, it may be recalled, is a recognition of patterns established during previous cycles of time, and repeated now, with variation.

'No, sit down. You a friend of Gail's?'

'No, Art's. That your gyroscope?'

He shook his head. 'Just found it here. Haven't played with one since I was a kid.' He pulled the string hard, until the wheel was a blur, then set the point of the wheel's cage down on the deck. It hummed, balancing there without moving.

'It's amazing, you doing that,' I said.

'Yeah? Why?'

'Well, it's just that I'm going back to the jungle tomorrow, to help my friends down there, and it all revolves around the universe being like that gyroscope.'

'Oh, yeah?' He seemed pretty interested, if a bit loaded – two empty martinis sat beside him; he nursed a third.

'Yeah. I mean, remember that stuff I was telling you in the ER? About Neuromans, and the castle in the jungle, and the idol of Goranchacha, and the fall of time?'

'Yeah?'

'Well, that wasn't just postseizure babble. That was true.'

A shadow briefly crossed his face. 'Uh-huh,' he said tentatively.

'And you and me,' I continued, 'we knew each other in another life. Or our doubles did. We're two sides of the same coin, though: I'm the romantic and you're the skeptic. Like brothers. We *were* brothers, in fact, at least once before. I saw us, beyond the node. You were the fourth man.'

He looked at me like he didn't know what to say. The gyroscope between us started wobbling ever so slightly, the axis of its spin leaning in small, slow circles around the point at which it touched the ground.

'Tell you what,' I said. 'You interested in cosmology? Philosophies of space-time, the workings of the heavens?'

'Sure,' he smiled noncommittally.

I knew I had him, though. These doctor types all have pretentions to understanding the Way Things Are. Maybe after they get to play God long enough, they feel like they know Him well.

'Okay, let me give you an analogy,' I said. 'This isn't what the universe *is,* but the universe behaves *as if* it were like this. Okay?'

'A model of the universe.'

'Right, a model. Now we're talkin' the same language.' The language of science, trying to approximate time's delicate dance. 'We have terms. The universe can be explained *in terms* of this model.'

'You have a theory,' said Kahn.

'You could think of it that way.' In the religion of science, a theory is like a rosary.

'So what's your theory?'

'It's a concept of time, primarily. It views time as cyclical. For example, picture the universe as a spinning top – or gyroscope.' We looked at the toy on the concrete beside the pool as I talked. 'The total energy content of the universe is a function of the speed of the spinning of the top, and time is the axis around which the top spins. But in addition to spinning, the axis itself circles slowly, around the point where the *tip* of the axis is touching the surface it's on. It's called precession, this rotation of the axis. Well, time's axis has precessions, and every time it makes a complete circle, we're back to the same place in time.'

We both stared at the gyroscope. As its spinning wheel got slower, the arc of the precessions of its axis got bigger – it wobbled in wider and wider circles.

'But as the energy of the system runs down,' I went on, 'the axis of the spin swings wider off the center until the center can no longer hold – and the whole machine tumbles . . .' The gyroscope bobbled too low – its rim hit

the deck, it skittered across the concrete and flopped into the pool, tumbling slowly, end over end, twelve feet through the brightly lit crystal blue water, coming finally to rest on the bottom.

'End of universe,' I said. 'Unless we could put energy into the spinning wheel, make it spin faster, bring the axis more upright, tighter to the center.'

'Smaller precessions,' said Kahn. Humoring me.

'There you go. Trouble is, the only way to do that is to bring in energy from another universe – the universe of the last precession.'

'So that's where you're going.'

'Right, to a previous time, to bring back energy.'

He tried to get into it. 'Well, okay, but if time keeps repeating itself, then there's no free will, everything we do is predestined and endlessly repetitive. So what's he point?'

'Each cycle is a little different, though, and the differences are crucial. For example, during the last cycle the axis was tipped almost to toppling by a telekinetic creature who could warp space and time, so we've got quite a job ahead of us trying to straighten the axis out again during *this* cycle.'

'Can I tell you something, you won't be offended?' he asked. I shrugged. 'You *sound* crazy,' he said, 'but you *look* like you feel very together.'

'You don't believe me.'

'I believe you believe it's true.'

'If it's not true, how come I left in 1976 and came back three months later and it was 1981? I'll tell you – it's because time is locked in those tunnels. It's time out of time. You spend a few days in there, a few *years* have gone by out here.'

We stared at each other – without concession, but not without humor. In fact, a moment later he raised his

glass, smiled, and sang softly. '"The fundamental things apply, as time goes by."'

I started to pick up my own glass but slipped and fell, cutting my hand. The good doctor immediately examined the cut – a lopsided Y-shaped laceration at the ball of my left thumb – and applied pressure with his cocktail napkin.

'Nasty cut,' he said. 'You'd better get down to an ER where someone can sew it up.' His instincts were good. His instincts were to help.

I pressed my hand to his, blood-brother-fashion – it took him by surprise. I'd done the same with Lon – how long ago? – to seal our fate. 'Your laying-on of hands is all the healing I need,' I said.

He smiled at me appreciatively. 'Man, you are far out.'

I smiled back across the gulf that separated us. 'Man, I am farther out than you will ever know.' My hopes for getting him to see the light were by now dimmer than the farthest stars. Still, I gave it one more try. 'I think it was the astronomer Hoyle,' I noted, 'who said "the universe is not only stranger than we imagine, it's stranger than we *can* imagine."'

'Very likely true,' he mused.

Perhaps all wasn't lost. 'So a man of science needn't necessarily lose his sense of wonder.'

'A man of science must necessarily not,' he said, a bit pompously.

'So you say.'

'Look, just because I try to be objective – '

'Ah, but there's no such thing as objectivity.'

'Objectively, the universe exists – and will, I imagine, until it meets its entropic doom in a hundred billion years or so.'

'But what if doom came in just a *hundred* years? And what if someone told you you could prevent it?'

'I gave at the office,' he smirked.

'And what if doom meant nothing would ever exist again – and since that meant time, too, then nothing would ever have existed before either. You, here, now, me, this conversation – it didn't happen: we were just figments of the imagination of a universe that never was.'

For just a moment, I saw an inkling pass over his face – a sense of what had been, or what was to come. It flickered across his cocky brow, this inkling, like the shadow of the fourth man. And then it was gone, and Kahn the rationalist was back in the pilot seat.

But I'd cracked his armor.

'Josh, listen,' he said, a bit patronizing, a bit genuinely trying to touch. 'We're all lost in the world – lost and alone, with no one to take care of us. Everything seems incomprehensible, and we try to make sense of it, but we can't. But you know what? You don't *have* to make sense of it. You just have to keep on until somebody gives you a gold watch, and then you get to sit on the porch until it's over.'

I smiled beneficently. 'You love illusion more than you know,' I said, a bit patronizing, a bit genuinely trying to touch. 'Watch for me in your dreams.'

He looked curious, but before he could reply, Torrie walked up.

'Oh, there you are,' she said. 'I don't feel very partyish . . . after all. And we ought to be going anyway . . . there isn't really all that much time.' She smiled at Kahn. 'Hello.'

'Hello,' he said.

'Good-bye,' she said, and we walked away.

'Get that laceration sutured,' he called to me, concern in his voice.

'Good-bye,' I called back, boldly waving my cut hand. On our way out, I stopped by the phone in the kitchen, found a personalized black phone book beside it, looked

up Kahn's address in it, and copied it down.

Then we left. I never did see Art, or his friend Gail, who'd invited Kahn to the party – they were evidently the instruments of time, facilitators of my rendezvous with Kahn, so their place in the history of the universe is assured – if such a thing as history is to exist, in such a thing as the universe.

The next morning I broke into Kahn's house while he was at work. It was small potatoes after all I'd been through.

I left Ice-eyes there for him. She needed someone to take care of her, and he needed someone to take care of him, lost in the world as he was, so it was right that they should live together. Ice-eyes knew this was her new home right away – she ran all around the house, examining every room for smell and spirit, finally disappearing to someplace I couldn't find her.

I left a little note and two rubies on the kitchen table for Kahn, explaining that Ice-eyes now lived here. He could cash in one of the rubies for her care and feeding and keep the other for himself.

I hoped to see him again someday.

And then we flew to Rio, I wearing a blue wool stocking cap to cover my tinny hood. It set off the metal detectors at the airport, but they only made me take it off for a minute, and then I could wear it again, so everything was okay.

In Rio we hired a professional guide to take us up the Amazon. For two weeks we had surprisingly few adventures, and no seizures. We worked our way back by memory and recontact with the people who'd helped us get *out* when we'd left with Dar, months earlier. Finally we arrived at that tiny Brazilian village with the church and the road and the shortwave radio, the village we'd

come to after six nights on the river, following the red star south and east, with Dar at the helm.

Dar was gone now, of course. We'd tried to reach her in London, to see if she wanted to return with us, traced her from Victoria Hospital to UN Liaison to the anthropology department at the University of London to an apartment at Lynton Mansions to No Forwarding Address. So long, Darwina S. Vine.

We let our guide go, and the bearers with him, though we kept two big motorized rubber rafts with lots of supplies.

And one night we set off, heading north and west upriver, with that same red star planted firmly behind us.

Six nights we traveled on the river; six days we rested on the bank.

We shared a feeling of calm excitement, of homecoming – of great expectations. We spoke little, choosing rather to savor every smell, every sound, to examine these sensations minutely and to hold them as long as they would last, like clinging to a moment of déjà vu before it slipped away or like pressing a flower to keep it forever.

Early on the seventh night we heard the rushing of the falls, and saw them in the moonlight two bends of the river later. The moon was so bright it cast a shimmering, nearly colorless rainbow through the mists.

We grounded the rafts up on shore and stood before the cliffs that bound time. Beneath the waterfall before us, like a dark open mouth, yawned the portal to these other worlds.

The time of biding was past.

We hugged silently, then hopped across the stepping-stones into the roar of the maelstrom.

CHAPTER 11

Timetripping

I entered the cave first. We stood together, letting our eyes get used to the dark, before turning on our flashlights. When we did shine them around, we saw the many exits, each winding into a different tunnel. I took the toy kaleidoscope from my pack and, with intense anticipation, held it up to my eye – a clear, green path emerged, leading directly into the fourth tunnel. I led the way.

The trail was convoluted and lengthy, but not treacherous. The tunnels were narrow or dimensionless or steep or jagged, but the scope always showed me the way. The path sometimes feathered out in several directions, but always one main branch was visible through the tube. We followed this branch until we came at last to a flat dark wall. Dark to my naked eye. Through the kaleidoscope it glowed red, bright with implications.

This was the first node.

I laughed once – a vacant laugh. I felt wired. Ready for everything. Reckless.

'Let's go,' I murmured.

Torrie gave me an intense, lingering kiss. The passion of imminent danger.

We kept our backs flat to the wall, and entered.

I found myself in a stairwell. It was dark except for the bare red light bulb screwed into the ceiling. It looked like the access stairway of a modern office building, actually – concrete-block walls, steel-bannistered steps doubling back and forth, up and down. The door to the landing I occupied – the one I'd just come through – was open,

only blacknes beyond. Suddenly, from out of its void, Torrie emerged.

We looked around. 'Kind of like the last place we went into,' I said.

'The last *time*,' she corrected.

Two flights up we heard a door close. Without a word we took the stairs. On the second landing above us, the door leading out of the stairwell was shut. I opened it, and we exited.

We found ourselves in an enormous lobby of a partially bombed-out building – a hotel or something. Broken furniture was strewn everywhere; a huge chandelier listed, shattered, in the middle of the floor; a ragged hole filled one wall. The giant plate-glass windows that faced the street lay in piles of shards all over the rug. Outside, hysterical people ran in all directions.

We walked to the empty windows and looked out. Fires burned in the distance. Something like an air-raid siren began to wail. The crowds in the street before us were screaming. Rumblings shook the ground. The cornice of a structure across the road broke off and tumbled into the masses. People were crushed. We stared, openmouthed.

A group of refugees staggered into a foyer nearby and huddled there, talking. I looked closely at them. They were short – under five feet – and their torsos seemed disproportionately squat compared to their legs. They wore strange, tubular clothing. Their faces were somehow odd. Their eyes were set too wide. They had no ears. Like the giants we'd seen in the war-room-node so many months ago, these people weren't quite human.

One of them saw us standing off to the side. He screamed – an unearthly scream – and ran away, stumbling, into the melee.

I looked at Torrie with dazed recognition, profound awe. Once again, we were in another time.

* * *

For another minute we just stood there, gawking.

The entire sky suddenly erupted in a silent lavender light. I closed my eyes, held my hand before my face, turned my head. The intensity dimmed after about fifteen seconds. I looked up to see a large mushroom cloud filling the horizon.

Almost instantly, the shock wave hit. The floor buckled; we were thrown to our knees. An impossibly loud roar filled my ears; typhoon winds shipped the room, rolling us across the ground. Angry heat seared our faces and burned the backs of my hands. The curtains burst into flame.

The whole building was shaking. Outside, high-rises collapsed, crushing and burying hundreds of people. The wall behind us began to crack.

That's when I saw them. Jasmine, Lon, Karl, Fernando. Across the street, dodging fires.

'Lonny,' I screamed.

They looked up, saw me, and started running toward us. The bedrock shook violently, though – they kept falling, picking themselves up, lurching forward. When they were ten feet from the front door, a small vehicle came screeching around the corner, headed right for Jasmine. I ran into the street, yanked her out of the way, and we all made it back into the lobby.

'What's going on?' I shouted.

'Not now,' Jasmine yelled. 'Let's get out of here first.'

I couldn't have agreed more.

We dragged ourselves toward the door to the stairwell. The stairwell was filled with smoke. Eyes stinging, we raced back down the two flights of stairs – the stairway itself was now tremoring wildly. Rubble started careening down all around us. The roar buffeted my eardrums. A beam, dangling electrical wiring, hit Karl a glancing blow

to the right shoulder. He screamed amid a shower of sparks and crackling light.

We reached the lower landing as the building crumbled all about us. Tripping, coughing, pushing each other, we plunged through the darkened doorway through which we'd first come.

On the other side it was dark, still, and quiet. We were back in the cave. Dark, dead-end.

Suddenly, the brightness of the wall increased to a burning orange red for several seconds, and then snuffed out completely. The cave was now totally black, totally quiet.

I slumped to the floor. Torrie turned on her flashlight, panned it around. Lon felt all along the wall we'd just come through. It was solid now. Damp, cool stone.

'This node is closed,' whispered Jasmine.

Everyone sat down. I shivered a little. Nobody spoke. We were each of us sorting out this barrage of images, impressions, emotions.

Lon finally looked over at me and grinned. 'So what the hell are you doing wearing that ridiculous hat?'

We hugged like long lost brothers. Soon we were all embracing, kissing, babbling. It was a grand reunion.

'I was afraid we'd never find you,' I said, 'and here you are without hardly looking.'

The reason we'd come upon them so quickly, Jasmine told us, was that this was the closest node to the outer world, and they'd just entered it a minute before Torrie and I did.

'A minute before?' I said. 'But we've been gone months.'

'Months in the outside world,' said Jasmine, 'but much less in these tunnels. From our perspective, you and Torrie and Darwina left down the river just a few hours ago. We slept on the bank overnight, then reentered the

tunnels, went into this first node, and a minute later you showed up. And lucky for me you did – another minute and we'd have been trapped beyond the node for all eternity.'

We looked at the wall again: cold black stone. Completely unyielding. Its other side was now buried in the rubble of that time.

'Very scary,' I whispered.

'By the way,' Jasmine wondered, 'what happened to Darwina?'

'Went to London,' I said. 'Went home. We tried to locate her, but . . .' I shrugged.

Jasmine nodded like she was having a conversation with herself, but said nothing.

Lon examined Karl's injured shoulder. It appeared to be burned – scorched and blistered from the upper chest down to the elbow. Karl sat there impassively as Lon debrided flecks of debris from the wound.

Fernando crouched in a corner by himself. He winked at me once, to reassure me, then looked uncertainly to Karl for a cue. Finally, Karl spoke.

'He with the emerald eyes, who made the jungle green by his gaze, he with the skull of black coal which is all that was left from the fires of the last world – it is with me now that we have just witnessed these fires, which gave birth to my jungle-mother.' He looked as if he'd had a sacred vision.

'That was a nuclear bomb,' said Jasmine. 'We were almost killed – by an atom blast that happened hundreds of millions of years ago – a blast that's still happening, just across the node. But the node is closed now. Buried in the blast.' She patted the solid wall. 'And the blast was obviously strong enough to disrupt the channel I constructed between the two times.'

Had we waited a minute longer in that place, we would

have been closed off from returning to our own time.

I held the telescope up to my eye. Bright, jeweled veins of light twisted up the tunnel, splaying off in ten different directions.

'Well, there's still lots of other nodes,' I suggested meekly. 'Right?'

Lon laughed, half in resignation, half in bravura. 'Well, I'm up for anything,' he announced. He'd gone from hippie to smuggler to adventurer, as the situation demanded and his whim decreed. He was an extraordinary man, and I dearly loved him. Which reminded me – I'd brought him a present. So I reached into my pack, pulled out his favorite satin tuxedo, and presented it to him. And to everyone's great delight, he put it on. 'If you know how to dress,' he smiled, 'you can go anywhere.'

'I have told you my mind,' added Karl. 'To meet he of the black skull, I would go far.'

'Far is where it is,' said Jasmine.

'Not far at all,' said Torrie. 'It's right in here.' She pointed to her heart.

Fernando didn't say anything. He just followed Karl, completely content with his old friend's decision. It was quite clear he was willing to follow Karl to the ends of the earth. It was less clear if he understood that we were going considerably farther than that.

For me it was a watershed moment. Diversely motivated, poorly outfitted, haphazardly prepared, yet somehow together, we were on our way. I had a hundred questions I wanted to ask Jasmine, but there was plenty of time for that later. Time for everything.

We walked back along the tunnels down which we'd come. Using the scope, I guided us to the next node around the bend. We looked at each other, held hands, flattened ourselves against the wall, and sidled across.

To emerge on a lifeless plain. Nothing but grainy black

sand, and what looked like glass where the sand had melted. A high red sun and a thin, cool wind. This, and only this, in every direction.

Behind us was a dune, at the base of which was the dark portal through which we'd come, visible only as a textural difference in the black mound. Had we walked fifty feet, we'd never have found it again.

We stood there ten minutes, though – unmoving, listening, feeling the desolation.

Then without speaking, one by one, we went back. Into the caves.

We sat in the darkness for a minute. Finally, Torrie spoke. 'It should give us hope. Even from that . . . life like ours can flower again.'

We moved, without further discussion, to the next node. It emerged, on the other side, from a deserted shack at the end of a deserted street that ran down the middle of a shanty town. We set off down the street.

Some of the houses looked burned out, some just weathered. It was dusk, but no lights shone from any window.

At the corner we heard voices.

We approached the house from which the voices were emanating and looked in the front window. On the floor of the bare front room, two people sat by a small cookstove. They were foul people – drooling, bickering, tattered, with bleeding sores on their faces and matter oozing from their ears. They were eating the remains of a third person.

I gagged. The sound attracted the attention of the diners: they looked up; they saw us at the window.

One picked up a gun and fired it at us, but we were already running. They gave chase.

We could hear them – feel them – behind us, smacking their lips, crackling obscenely, gaining on us. We raced

into the entry shack and came out in our own caves again. They were right on our heels.

We kept running. With the telescope to my eye, I followed the main floor path, turning through tunnel after tunnel. The territory was so strange and disorienting to our pursuers, we managed to put a little distance between us. In ten minutes we emerged from the catacombs into jungle proper, rushed into a grove of gaint ferns, and crouched there, panting.

Half a minute later the foul ones came out of the same cave, ran five feet into the undergrowth, and stopped. They looked around incredulously, suddenly realizing they had no idea where they were.

Astoundingly, they looked different to me now out here. No less horrible, but significantly less substantive. In fact, they were now nearly transparent. I wondered if we'd looked as ethereal to them, on their side, as they looked to us here on ours.

There was a noise some distance away – an animal thrashing, it sounded like. The ghost-people heard it, too; they tore off into the brush after it – kept going, until we heard them no more.

We sat there, breathing quietly a minute. Then Jasmine began to smile. 'Well, you did it,' she said. 'You brought back new energy from an old precession.'

She was right. I felt like shouting, just from emotional overflow. A moment before, I'd been terrified, running scared from these demented cannibals slavering after me; suddenly, they'd become apparitions, and now they were gone. I felt powerful. I'd just affected my universe. We all had. It was a heady feeling.

Karl scratched his beard. 'I think I see now where the ghosts came from to this part of the jungle.'

Lon stood up, rubbing his hands together. 'Let's go get some more.'

* * *

Through the next node we discovered a peaceful village of wattle and daub homes, cows in the field, music in the saloon. We spied on a few families; they seemed quite homey. Things were even more diaphanous here than they'd been in some of the *previous* previous precessions. I don't think they could see us very well at all.

Night was approaching. We wandered into the village square, where a large bonfire burned. People stood around, warming themselves, talking. We watched from some bushes for a time, then Lon nudged me and said, 'Check this out.'

He trudged into the clearing hands raised over his head, fingers wiggling, moaning 'Oooooohhhhhboogabooga-booga. Ooooooooooooooooooooooooboogaboogabooga . . .'

The people in the square were riveted. Some screamed and ran away. Some waved torches at Lon, trying to force him back. Some held up pendants – stylized tridents worn around their necks – to ward him off. He just kept slowly walking, though. Karl walked behind him, to shield him from danger, like a great, bearded zombie. Bodyguard for a wandering spirit.

'Evil is among us,' someone groaned.

'Summon the vicar!' someone else shouted. 'The dead walk!'

'We need no priest. Come, we are many! Back to Deathland with these demons!'

Lon was hopping up and down now, being as scary as he could – not a great performance, I thought, but then I'm no critic. In any case, things seemed to be getting a little out of hand, so Karl stepped up, grabbed Lon, and started pulling him out of the light. Karl's potent appearance inflamed the situation much more, though – half the crowd screamed, ran, or cringed; the other half swore

oaths, brandished torches and tridents, and began chasing us into the woods.

The woods where the node was.

We brought eleven over with us this time; lost them near the river, at the southern cave exit. But it gave me pause this time.

'These were people,' I said to Jasmine.

'Essentially,' she nodded.

'I mean, they weren't so bad, really – like that first bunch we brought over, I mean, they were a little backward, or superstitious – '

'Primitive,' Jasmine helped.

'Yeah, primitive. But not, like evil. I mean, we've stranded them here now – in our time, hundreds of millions of years away from their lives . . . I mean, it doesn't seem quite fair.'

'No,' she smiled. 'It's not quite fair. These people are sacrificing a great deal for our universe. But believe me – and you'll have to take this on faith for the moment – if they're wise, they can find great solace here. And if they're not, they wouldn't find much even close to home.'

Torrie said, 'I never found much comfort close to home.'

Jasmine said, 'It's really all a question of knowing where your true home is. I think you'll find that, in general, those who followed us back here didn't have all that much back *there* to keep them. These things have a way of settling out.'

The thing that struck me was the ease with which Karl had fallen into his role, as if he knew these people, was a part of them, had always been of them. I mentioned this, too, to Jasmine.

'These are primitive times,' she said. 'Primitive peoples, full of magic and the earth. Karl doesn't have far to go to be one with them.'

'Like I do.'

'You have less far to go than you may think. A time will come when your own primitive self won't be far from your senses – and you'd best be open to it, or it'll snag you and turn you until you *never* find your way home.'

Once we emerged on an upper floor of a huge, darkened mansion. There were so many rooms, and it seemed like such a clear, well-ordered place, we decided to split up and meet back at the node in fifteen minutes.

We each took a different wing. I quickly went through room after room without seeing a soul: libraries, studies, laboratories, storage closets, guest chambers. Finally, I came to a bedroom elegantly appointed – at its far wall, a large four-poster, and in the center of the bed, a sleeping figure.

I approached. As I neared the foot of the bed, I could see it was a young woman under the covers, her hair splayed across the pillow. By the time I reached the bedside, I could see clearly: it was Di.

Almost. Slightly older, not quite solid. She slept fitfully, struggling with her dreams. A tear came to my eye, she was so beautiful, so – haunting. I touched her cheek – soft, like a cloud, almost too soft to hold. How many times had I stroked that cheek, comforted those night terrors? My heart twisted with love, with grief. Gently, I brought my hand down the slope of her neck, cupped the fullness of her breast in my palm, it tingled with a strange energy, an unearthly, impalpable delicacy.

She opened her eyes. Shock filled her face to see me there. She pulled back. Then disbelief, poignant longing. She brought her hand up to caress my cheek, but her hand went through me. Or maybe my face went through her hand. She began to cry.

I backed off.

Lon stood in the doorway. 'Josh, let's go. We can't find anybody to bring back.'

I left her there, sobbing, holding herself.

Once again, we hadn't been able to say good-bye.

I told Jasmine about it. She nodded. 'That's part of what you have to learn, part of finding your primitive self, as I was talking about before. That's the self that knows how to say good-bye.'

'He wasn't around – my self. Only Di's self was in that house.'

'Well, sometimes he's just not there. Keep your eyes open, though – he's a great one for hiding.'

'Maybe, sometime, if you see him but I don't . . .'

She shook her head. 'No good. You've got to see him yourself – that's the only way you can be sure who he is. He might not even look exactly like you, so I'd never know at all – but you can feel it, if you're open to it – you'll know it's him, and then you can learn from him – who he really is, how he feels, how he does all those darkish and magic things you might've forgotten. Like how to touch, or say good-bye, or hear the spinning of the earth.'

'Have you forgotten?'

'No, I never lost my core – kept her with me, even in my gloriously "sophisticated" years.' She smirked sarcastically. Then, more serious: 'That's one of the reasons I want to get back to the last time so badly – so *I* can say good-bye properly. To my dear centaur, Beauty.'

She wandered from me then, lost in her memories. I didn't tell the others of my experience with Di's ghost; but in passing, Torrie had seen me beside the bed and it had given her an idea. On our next foray she posed as a succubus – entered the boudoir of some unsuspecting sleeper, hovered seductively nearby, calling until he awakened, and then she beckoned.

She enticed seven back to our world that night – to the land where *they* were *our* dreams, instead of vice-versa.

Lon, of course, not to be outdone, became incubus to dozens, luring the willowy souls back across time, dangling the promise of astral sex before them, then retreating like a satin-tuxedoed dream-lover to his den.

Poor souls. But they had just as much opportunity to turn their losses to gains as we did, so I gradually stopped worrying about them and left them to whatever opportunities they could create for themselves.

We tried to manipulate each encounter in such a way as to get the 'visionaries' of that time to accompany us back to ours. We did this through intimidation, love, curiosity, supernatural terror, sexual tension. People in some times, it turned out, were more suggestable than others. The inhabitants of these periods were much more willing to believe we were visions of some kind and follow us. It was these times that we concentrated on. Other times were full of skeptics; these we avoided. The results were that hundreds of variously strange, lonely, angry, bitter, scared, or enraptured beings returned with us, only to get disoriented in the tunnels and then lost beyond the caves. These phantoms wandered around our jungle, directionless, haunting anyone they came across, looking for the doorway back to their own time. Some of them undoubtedly strayed out of the jungle completely, wandering over the vastness of our world.

It is these lost image-people, meandering about the planet, who are taken for the ghosts, spirits, devils, gods, visions, visitations, space aliens, and hallucinations of our own time. It is the lost image-people that Jasmine brought back to our time cycle, over the centuries, who have been recorded as the ghosts of our more recent past. And it is these same lost image-people who, becoming disoriented in our jungle tunnels, stumbled into other nodes, to

become lost in other times, where they became *those* times' demons and ghosts.

We'd opened a can of worms, I began to realize. They wriggled, spiraling, into the folds of time's fabric, and nothing would ever again be the same.

I was getting a bit carried away. Or maybe I am in the telling. It was like a big wave, though, or a fast dream. I was never quite sure it *wasn't* a dream. Torrie, too, was beginning to act a bit hypnagogic, going in and out.

'High risk and high stakes,' said Lon. 'It's a smuggler's rush. I haven't felt this alive since the old days when I was carrying my own gems across the borders.'

Strange borders, these.

We came at last to a time that felt immediately different. Special, familiar – alive.

We emerged in a large dark tent.

'This is the last cycle,' said Jasmine. 'The one that ended sixty-seven million years ago.'

'When the dinosaurs died,' I said.

She whispered. 'Have I told you what the dinosaurs of your past really were? They were giant lizards and dragons that the scientists of my age created with genetic engineering. And I'll tell you again why your dinosaurs all died. Because the strange, mutant child with telekinetic powers increased the gravity of the earth, so nothing large could stand or fly; and then she rained meteors down on the planet.' She paused.

'My daughter,' I added.

Jasmine nodded. 'You'll have to deal with that in this time,' she said. 'And the knowledge you gain will inform you.'

'Inform me about what?'

'About how to deal with your daughter in your *own* time.'

'But I don't have – '

'Your daughter with Queen Namsháya Moon-Goddess Jaguar-Woman. The daughter not yet born.'

It had been on my mind, of course, but completely suppressed, or repressed, or denied for some time now: a child would spring from my jungle union with that barbarian queen.

'Hopefully, we can *all* learn from our experiences in here,' Jasmine went on. 'It's a time close to us all. And it's on my mind that this new daughter of yours, Joshua, might someday be enlisted in our service.'

'I've read the journal of my earlier self – the one from here – and he describes the child as just another lost soul, finally. Looking, never finding.'

'That's the great value of retrospect – if we have the sense to use it.'

'What else about this time?' I asked. I was anxious to explore it, to touch it. We all were – Torrie played distractedly with her hair; Lon stared out the flap of the tent we were huddled inside.

'You'll see yourselves here most clearly. It'll be tempting to stay – but remember why we came.'

She ushered us out the doorway.

It looked like a marketplace – a dusty street of tents, vendors, jugglers, fantastic creatures, masked harems, vague translucence, reedy music, and glaring sun.

We immediately set out to pull people back to our time, and it was embarrassingly easy. The market was a natural setup; we simply lured people into the tent to buy our goods, and once in the tent, we led them into the caves. One of us then merely guided them out into the jungle and left them there.

We rotated the job of hawking the wares in front of the

tent. As soon as one of us took a customer back through, another of us stepped up to drum. We advertised whatever came into our minds, or whatever the interested party seemed to want – girls, boys, silver, silk, drugs, clothes, weapons, food. We made it a game to guess what a passing prospect might fancy, and then cater to that whim. If he limped, a medical miracle awaited inside the tent; if she wore jewelry, we had jewlry fine; if they looked weary or dry, we could supply wondrous drink and rest – but a little way inside the tent.

We did this for hours. The supply of buyers seemed unending – a gold mine of energy for our toppling universe. At last, though, the temptation to explore this cycle proved too great to resist, so we decided to make short jaunts while the others kept the energy-transfer operation going. Lon and I made the first foray with Jasmine.

It was quite the exotic place. Merchants sold oils, teas, incense, livestock, statuary, slaves, cloths, spices, gems, grain, blades, toys. Magicians did sleight of hand, beggars tapped their cups, dancers whirled with scarves and snakes, sex was offered casually or furtively. Creatures not human strolled nonchalantly among the crowd: a man sprouting giant leathery bat wings from his back walked two humans on a leash; a woman with six arms caressed a minotaur; a griffin preened.

Lon turned to me and said, 'Well, Toto, I don't think we're in Kansas anymore.'

We came to a larger street, filled to overflowing with hundreds of milling creatures. For the first time it was open enough to admit a wider view of the environs. What I saw, looming perhaps a mile distant, was a castle. We stopped.

Giant, lumbering, stone, it commanded the sky. It was

terribly reminiscent of the castle whose ruins we'd viewed in our own jungle city, and I said so.

'It's the same castle,' said Jasmine. 'It survived the ruin of this time nearly intact and made it all the way to you, to the city in the tunnels.'

It seemed unimaginable, but once again, little was left to the imagination; there was the castle. We walked toward it.

About a hundred yards up the road, we came to a low wall with an open gate. It marked the end of the bazaar. Beyond it, and surrounding the castle proper, was a standard fortress village. Stone or thatched huts, street-lamps, shops, fountains – well, not quite standard. The people all had wings.

Leatherish bat wings, like the few we'd seen in the marketplace. Hundreds of them, talking, walking, a few flying low. We started to walk in, to get a closer look, but a guard stopped us at the gate. He, too, had wings.

'Hold on there,' he said gently but firmly. '*You* know there's no humans allowed in this part of the city.'

'We're just . . . looking for a friend,' volunteered Jasmine.

'Not in here, if he's human. Say, you're a funny-lookin' bunch,' he squinted.

I think it was the intense glare of the sun that saved us. I think it probably made *everything* look a little hazy, a little thin.

He continued speaking, as if in answer to my surmise. 'This weather we're havin', I suppose,' he nodded at the sky. 'It's not natural, I tell you. Too bright one day, too dark the next. Thunder when there's no clouds.' He leaned forward intimately. 'It's that child in the castle, you want my opinion. The new queen. She turnin' things upside down. There's trouble afoot. I tell you, confidentially, there's a lot of us won't be here much longer.

Things don't settle down, we're leavin', make no mistake. So I'll tell you – you want to slide out while there's still time, I've got openings in my harem. You come along with old Zed, and I'll take care of you proper.' He winked.

'Well,' nodded Jasmine, 'we'll certainly keep that in mind.'

Zed shrugged. 'It's hard times, as well you know.' He stretched his wings, then wrapped them around his body. 'There is one place you might be safe if you don't fancy the harem life – a little human camp, just sprang up overnight, about five miles south of here in the old oak grove. Don't know where they came from, or what they're doin' here – but say, you might stay there.'

Jasmine thanked him, and we moved on. 'Why don't we head back?' she said. 'Torrie's probably getting worried.'

'This place is so strange,' I said, 'but . . . compelling.'

'That human camp he was talking about,' she said. 'That's where you lived for a time, Joshua. And I.'

'Me, too?' said Lon.

Jasmine smiled sadly. 'You were dead by this time, I'm afraid. And in any case, you know' – she hesitated – 'you were a vampire.'

'So you've said.'

'Like Zed, the winged man we just spoke to. But don't be so disparaging. Many of them were the aristocrats of my time.'

'And me?' he said. He wanted to be her aristocrat.

She shrugged. We walked back to the marketplace.

The weather was getting a bit odd. Lightning streaked the cloudless sky. You could hardly see it, the sun was so bright, and it made no sound. It seemed to upset the people in the market, though. They began pointing, mumbling, quickening their pace. Vendors closed up

shop, browsers scurried out of sight. In fifteen minutes the crowd palpably diminished. It was a trifle worrisome, although we could now locate our tent without difficulty.

'What's going on here? Why's everybody . . . leaving?' said Torrie.

'I think they're troubled by the weather report.'

We stood, waiting for Karl and Fernando to return from their last sale in the tunnels, as the bazaar continued to thin out around us. By the time they got back, the streets were fairly empty. We decided to go out the southern gate of the city, to check out the encampment Zed had spoken of. It was a road Jasmine seemed well acquainted with.

A rushing river flanked the city's outer wall; we had to cross a drawbridge. Standing outside the city, we could see it was perched on high cliffs overlooking the sea. The river flowed all around the walls of the enclave and tumbled over the cliffs in a roaring spray. With the ocean at our right, we began walking south.

Karl seemed as perky as I'd ever seen him. 'Smell the air here,' he beamed, expanding his chest. 'Is fertile.'

'Smells like ozone to me,' said Lon.

'Your nose has been corroded by too much city,' Karl said gently, if a bit patronizingly.

'Smells like home to me,' said Torrie.

Jasmine walked by my side. 'It's only as I've said,' she smiled. 'Karl feels at ease in the company of *any* of his primitive selves; Torrie feels particularly in touch here, because of the nearness of her closest preincarnation; and Lon feels a little detached here, because *his* shadow-ancestor from this time is dead.'

'And me?'

'I guess we'll find out.'

It took us about an hour to reach the oak grove. The trees were a few acres deep. They blocked out enough of

the sun's blinding radiance that the true translucence of everything became apparent to us now: trees, rabbits, plants – all had a smoky, somehow insubstantial appearance, like old holograms.

We could hear voices laughing and talking, deeper in the forest. Occasionally, when someone strolled nearby, we hid behind trees. Once we came upon a couple lying in a glade, passionately embracing. She was human; he was one of the winged people we'd seen so many of in the city. A vampire. We paused a few moments, we were so taken by the sight. The woman's head was thrown back, her mouth was open, her tongue on her lips; the winged man had his hand between her legs, his teeth in her neck. He was sucking her blood.

We neared a large, sunken clearing filled with people, all dancing, singing, and story telling. We crouched in the bushes near one group of revelers, listening to them swap tales. They spoke of themselves as Scribes, people who worshiped the written word. They spoke of their lives in the caves that apparently laced these cliffs. They told harrowing stories of escapes from vampire harems or from Neuroman experimentation labs. They told of faraway lands where giants lived, where sorcery was commonplace, where writing wasn't illegal, where humans were kings and animals had lost the power of speech.

They were interrupted by a loud voice in the clearing: 'You here today – all of you – you're my family!'

The crowd cheered wildly and repeated the word back to him like a litany: 'Family – family . . .'

We tiptoed to the edge of the open space and looked down. As the crowd chanted, the speaker in the center waved and smiled.

He looked just like me.

Beside him stood a woman who looked very much like

Torrie; and a centaur; and the same Jasmine who stood beside me now. The self-same Jasmine.

The speaker – the Joshua – suddenly turned to the centaur with a queer look in his eyes, muttered something, and began walking north, alone. Toward the castle.

I had to follow – how could I not? He was my ancestor, my precessor. He was me. I had to be with him.

One by one, my comrades joined me.

Jasmine, I think, came along to keep an eye on me – to see how I handled this reckoning with my spectral double. But she had mixed feelings about leaving the grove, and I'd glimpsed the reason: Beauty, her long-lost centaur. Still, she left with me, not yet ready, herself, to say goodbye to the mythic lover.

Torrie, too, was clearly ambivalent about departing from the encampment, for *her* counterpart was *there* and tugged at her with the same impulses I was feeling.

Karl and Fernando seemed content to wander wherever, as if they were at peace with it all. As if something about its ancestralness sustained them. Primitive souls in a primitive universe.

And Lon just loved it all – Jasmine, the adventure, the wildness of it.

Flocks of huge white birds passed overhead, flying low, their thirty-foot wingspans casting chill shadows. Then suddenly – in a moment's time – the sky turned a deep purple black.

As Joshua approached the city, we could see caravans of people making a disorganized exodus north or east. Droves of the winged vampires swooped out the main gates and away, over the sea, screaming in a shrill, high-frequency whine.

Inside the walls the city was in chaos. Large clusters of vampires and other creatures were shouting, running around madly, as if they were ants in a burning box.

Many of the tents in the bazaar were, in fact, burning, as were numerous other structures throughout the city.

Joshua walked through it all calmly, almost like an automaton – inexorably toward the castle from whose turrets black smoke rose. I started to follow him, but Lon held me back.

'Hang on, sport. I'm not much interested in getting trapped here because our node gets buried – and it looks to me like this place is going to blow.' Lon loved the dangerous edge to it all, but totally foolhardy he wasn't; and he always had a keen sense of when to stand, when to run, when to fight, when to hide. And he was saying now it was time to run. Jasmine was looking at the sky, nodding in agreement, and even Karl had his legs set instinctively wider apart, braced for something unexpected. Only Fernando continued to smile, unconcerned, so in tune to the quaking ground he seemed to be dancing with it. It tore me up to admit it, but Lon was right – we had to get back to our time before the portal was sealed off. I wanted badly to stay, though, wanted to follow Joshua, to meet him, to gaze upon him, to somehow lose myself in him. My chest was tight with wanting it. My hands were tremulous.

Torrie felt the same, I could see. She kept straggling, gazing back toward the woods where her own counterpart waited. Lon had to keep pulling her ahead. 'Torrie, come on! We can talk about it on the other side!'

'What other side?' she snapped.

We moved forward through the frenzied streets. People were dashing, wailing, glancing at the sky. Acrid black flakes began to float down like an evil snow. Humans were pulled into empty tents and houses by hysterical packs of vampires. Wild dogs roamed freely, their fangs dripping blood.

We neared our tent. Torrie looked more and more like

a terrorized bird with a broken wing. Her eyes darted back and forth, unable to fathom what was happening. Tents began spontaneously bursting into flame. The ground buckled.

Jasmine and Lon pulled me forcefully to our tent. Explosions erupted all around us; the sky itself seemed to warp.

Out of nowhere a band of vampires descended upon us. Shrieking, hissing, they gnashed at us, swung their razor talons.

The talons hurt. They had energy and impact. My neck flushed with searing pain; I stumbled to the ground.

Black smoke filled the air; there was a beating of great wings, the sparking of grounded electrical discharges. I felt a blow to my head; my helmet went sailing.

Strong hands gripped me by the wrist. I was pulled along the ground. My strength was gone, though, and my will. Into what lair was I being dragged, in what time? To await what torture? So this was the end. My mind swam in dizzying circles.

I went under.

CHAPTER 12

Saying Good-Bye

I awoke back in our own tunnels. It was Karl who'd pulled me through the node while the tent was burning, while the ground was shifting.

I was alive.

We all were – Karl, Fernando, Jasmine, Lon . . .

'Where's Torrie?' I sat up hard.

No one spoke, but the answer was clear. She was still in that time.

I slumped against the wall as Jasmine began treating the burns on my neck. And I thought of Torrie.

Her final regression to that time wasn't really so surprising, just infinitely sad. She'd simply succumbed to the timesickness.

She'd begun to resonate with her earlier incarnations in these ancient times; and the last cycle was the worst. Seeing her analog there in that clearing – feeling her presence, sensing the woman – Torrie had truly begun to lose her sense of self, of her own time, of her place in time. Her identity had started to merge.

I knew, because it was happening to me. I'd been feeling increasingly disoriented for days, but seeing myself in that last precession – my preincarnated self – nearly took my breath away. It gave me a physical tingling to observe him, a combination of horror, exhilaration, deindividuation, diffusion, communion, timelessness – that was it. A feeling of timelessness. How else to say it?

I was timesick.

Numerous after-the-fact rationalizations sprang from this fever, reasons why I needed to be in that other

timezone. Some of them were very potent. It was a way I could see Di again, for example – at least, a previous version of Di. And if I couldn't hold this image-Di, I could look upon her, sense her, experience her, be with her.

And the previous Joshua, my namesake – I could observe him, watch what he did, how he acted. Could I learn from his mistakes? Jasmine seemed to think I *had* to learn from him to make myself whole, the better to do our work.

Our work – that was the critical thing. Jasmine was so certain, so compelling in her fears for our universe; Lon seemed totally in her thrall, Karl set on exploring the roots of his jungle-mother, Fernando his faithful companion. And I? My Di had gone, and now my Torrie.

If Jasmine was right, we were tugging the stars back into place. There was nothing to do *but* go on.

With the helmet gone, my seizures returned. They were worse near certain nodes, presumably because of influences emanating from those times. These nodes we avoided.

The telescope was gone, too – Torrie had been carrying it. But remarkably, during the seizures, the veining time-tunnels were clearly imprinted in negative relief in my mind. It was very like the perception you get when you stare into a bright light and then close your eyes tightly; sometimes you can see the actual veins in the back of your retina, or so it seems. The images would fade slowly as my waking consciousness blearily returned.

I discovered I could follow these patterns, if I hurried, as I regained my footing and awareness; so we followed my seizures from node to node. We became, I may say, rather adept at luring people back, at least when the time was right. Once we piped away an entire village of

children from a rat-infested seaport town. Got the rats, too.

It was hard, sometimes, getting them to follow us precisely, back out the same edge of the node through which we'd come. For ourselves, we always entered a node at its most left-hand aspect – to be consistent – and returned, from the other side, through the right-hand edge; so we reproducibly popped back out in the same place, and time, from which we'd started. Our ghost-followers weren't always so exact, though; sometimes they'd plunge after us through the *center* of the node, or even the opposite edge. When that happened, we lost them into a slightly different time. No time to go back for them, though; we always went on.

Yet successful as we were, my heart was growing wild – for these jaunts took me progressively farther and farther from the precious time I longed to inhabit. The time of my last self.

Penetrating the next node, we emerged in the same tunnel we'd just left on our own side, except it was only half-solid. We walked up two or three familiar turns and back again. No doubt about it; here was a mirror image of our own time, in another, earlier precession of time's axis. It wasn't the very last precession – that's where Torrie was. But it bore a very close resemblance to our own frame of reference.

I half-expected – with both trepidation and wanting – to see our shadow-selves here, lurking about their shadow-tunnels in search of a way out. That's not what we saw, though. What we saw was a dragon.

That is, it was what I imagined dragons would look like, more or less, if they existed, which this creature seemed to do. A small dragon, to be sure – twenty feet long. In fact, it gave the impression of being stunted, or

maybe just adolescent. Scaly, pudgy, bare nubbins of wings sprouting from its back, it lumbered toward us on four stumpy, clawed feet, nearly filling the tunnel.

We were taken off guard, and for some long moments just stood there. The thing got closer.

'Is that . . . a dragon?' Lon asked.

The thing opened its sauroid jaw, gnashed its teeth. Sparks flew from the jagged cutting edges. It repeated the action; this time one of the sparks ignited a spume of gaseous vapor the beast was exhaling, and a rush of translucent flame blew out of its mouth and down the tunnel at us.

We ran away. Ran in the opposite direction, as the violet flame-radiation scorched our backsides. We passed through three corridors quickly, then stopped.

'Dragon is what it is,' said Jasmine. 'We had similar beasts in my time – stupid, but dangerous. They can fly because they're filled with methane from bacterial decompositions in their intestines; they can expel it and ignite it, too, and those flames are pretty intense even across *this* time-frame. So I'd say we'd best avoid this critter until it blunders elsewhere.'

We heard it roar again.

I got up to run deeper into the caves, but Jasmine held me in check. 'Wait, we can't go too far, or we'll never find our way back,' she cautioned.

'We must remember every turn,' Karl agreed somberly.

'Left, left, right.' Lon nodded.

We heard the dragon scraping its massive body nearer. We took the next left and trotted down a long tunnel which opened into a large cave.

Boulders and pieces of broken stones were scattered everywhere. What looked like a rockslide was piled up along one wall; beside it a great pit sloped down into darkness. Out of the pit crawled an adult dragon.

Easily four times as big as the pup that was following us, this old mother looked completely unamused. We couldn't go back – the juvenile was blocking our exit – so we ran right past the pit, into the next cavern. Unfortunately, there was a shelf and a ten-foot drop into the next cavern. We dropped.

No one was seriously hurt, though it was a jolt. We flashed our lights around: the cavern was endlessly big, its extent immeasurable. Studding the floor at irregular intervals was a field of pointy stalagmites; and interspersed among these stone spikes were holes in the ground, vertical shafts maybe four feet in diameter, of unknown depth.

The mother dragon waddled to the edge of the cavern and looked down. We dispersed behind six stalagmites, just in time: flames shot past us, red and blue. We cowered behind the stone.

With a great wind, the beast took to the air. It soared above us, rose, banked and began to turn, to make a pass at us from behind. We followed it with our lights.

As it completed its banking maneuver, its wingtip scraped the sidewall of the cave. Astonishingly, it spun out of control and came crashing to the floor fifty feet away, impaling itself on the spearlike formations.

We all walked toward the body of the dragon, gingerly picking our way around loose debris and precipitous openings. When we reached the thing, it was still alive – barely. Torn, battered, held fast to the ground by the stony spikes, its massive chest rose and fell in labored respirations. One eye was still open.

I approached its recumbent head, big as a refrigerator. The open eye tracked me, watched me, fixed on me – liquid, sad, wondering. Then it turned glassy, and the beast was still.

'No wonder they're extinct,' said Lon. 'That was the worst flight I've ever seen.'

I didn't want to hear jokes, so I started walking back. When I was halfway to the first cave, the child-dragon appeared on the ledge. It shrieked once and leapt toward me.

I froze. It opened its mouth. When it was hardly ten feet away, Fernando came charging up behind me throwing me to the side, tumbling in the opposite direction himself. The smaller dragon thrashed right between us, scraping along the ground directly toward the dead behemoth that was its mother.

I saw Karl running to where Fernando had fallen: the brave Indian was tipping over the edge into one of the shafts. I raced, stumbling, to him – but was too late. Both of us reached the chasm just as Fernando fell in. Jasmine and Lon were there a second later.

We shone our lights into the abyss: down, down, he fell, straight down without stopping, never hitting bottom. He called out as he was falling – a long, loud, single word: 'Cosiyaaaaaaaan . . .' The shout got softer and softer, his body got smaller and dimmer as he receded into the endless hole. Then he was gone altogether, and all was silent.

'What . . . what did he say?' I whispered.

'It was his name,' said Karl. 'His true name.'

We walked in silence to the ten-foot shelf that rose to the first cave and scrabbled up the footholds to the higher level. For several minutes, we sat there. Looking back, I could see the shimmering image of the whimpering baby dragon, nuzzling its dead mother.

We got back to the node without mishap – right, left, right, right. On the other side – on *our* side – we took the same path to the caves we'd just vacated in that nether time. Left, left, right, left, down the long tunnel to the

first cave, across the cave to the drop-off into the huge cavern. And there it was.

The same cavern, the same stalgmites, the same bottomless pits. And there, twenty-five yards in, a pile of bones.

We slid down the short cliff and retraced our steps across the craggy surface. Two enormous, fossilized skeletons lay before us. One was much bigger, sprawling back among dozens of stalagmites. The smaller one's skull, upturned, nestled under the chin of the larger.

'Dinosaurs, I would have said.' I picked up one of the cervical vertebrae. 'Allosaurus, I'd have sworn. I'd have written a paper proving it, with lots of footnotes.' I carefully replaced the neck bone. Over near the jaw, a loose tooth lay on the floor. I picked it up.

Two inches long, triangular, flinty. I struck it on the ground. Sparks flew. 'In case we run out of matches,' I said, and put it in my pocket.

We walked to the hole that Fernando – Cosiyan – had fallen into. We looked down.

It was still black as time.

And now we were four.

Karl had a hollow look. Just going through the motions. Life without Fernando – Cosiyan – would be a bleak exercise for him.

Lon seemed confused. It had all been like a lark before this, his most challenging smuggling operation ever – sneaking contraband image-beings across the border of time. And Jasmine was his tutor. But things were going sour now. Di dead; Torrie, Fernando, lost in foreign prisons. The accumulated weight of these losses was beginning to tell on him. Who would fall next?

And it didn't seem like we'd pirated nearly enough energy back yet to make those losses worth the price.

Didn't seem like it to me, *or* to Lon, I think. Which meant, maybe – horribly – that it was all for nothing, that their sacrifices had been in vain, that they were trapped for eternity in those timeless, nightmare worlds.

It was a grim thought. It led nowhere but to fatigue of spirit, or further sacrifice.

'This is hard,' I whispered to myself.

Jasmine overheard me. 'But we will win,' she asserted.

'What makes you so sure?'

'Because so much is at stake. Because we'll just do whatever needs to be done.'

'What if it's beyond us?'

'In a finite universe, nothing is beyond rescue. And no one beyond heroics. At some level we all intuit that we're part of the universe, a tiny swirl in the pattern – and if the whole weave can be undone by the unraveling of one loose thread, it can just as surely be tightly knit again by twining the same stray ends.'

'What if I can't find my thread?'

'We each of us know what needs to be done and what we need to do,' she reassured me. 'We know because we're part of it. So just do what seems right – and most likely, it will be. That doesn't mean it's not dangerous, but it *does* mean your actions can affect the outcome of things. All of ours can. Fernando's sacrifice may have *enormous* consequences we can't predict.'

'That sounds altogether too religious for me.'

'Mystiscientism. All the rage in the times before the Cataclysm.'

'What happened, exactly – in your time?'

'Well, the sky cracked open. The earth altered its rotation. There were floods, and fires, and quakes and destruction on an inconceivable scale. Most everyone died. And no one was left to remember except me.'

'That's a powerful burden of memories on one person.'

'You can't know what it means for me to share some of it after all these centuries.'

'Some memories can kill you,' I said tightly.

'If you let them,' she agreed. 'You've got to make a truce with your memories, though, Joshua – otherwise you'll walk through life looking over your shoulder, afraid they're going to stab you in the back.'

I smiled wanly. 'The one that weighs on me is already buried to the hilt between my shoulder blades. My wife . . .'

'Your wife, my centaur, Karl's friend – everyone is haunted by someone, Joshua. At some point you just have to make a truce.'

I noticed that Lon was walking directly behind us, listening. Listening hard, was my sense. I never knew what ghosts he carried with him.

Anyhow, that's the only way I can explain what happened next.

We came to a node that was flaring, flickering bright orange.

'Must be a lot of energy coming through here from *that* side,' Lon commented. But no sooner had he spoken than the light snuffed out.

'Explosion, probably,' Jasmine suggested. 'Node probably just got buried under the rubble in there.'

Lon got a funny look in his eye. 'Could be,' he nodded. 'Like the one where Torrie got lost.' He walked up to it.

'What are you doing,' I said.

'Going in. Wait for me.'

'Don't . . .'

'I'll just be gone ten seconds,' he promised. 'Just see what's going on.'

'That'll be ten *minutes* out here,' I reminded him.

'Okay, ten minutes, then. I've got a feeling about it.'

Without waiting for a reply, he went through. The rest of us sat there, brooding, musing, resting.

Five minutes later the bright orange glow returned briefly at the node, then went out again. Shortly after that, Lon returned. His hands were badly reddened, and half his face.

'Firestorm,' he choked. 'Just this side of the timecrossing, some kind of fire door has fallen in place, though. I moved it for a second, to look. It was a furnace out there. Like the inside of a star or something.'

He was pretty hyped up. It must have been overwhelming.

'I'm going back,' he said.

'What are you talking about?'

'If I can keep that door open, all the energy out there will pour in here. It'll be worth hundreds of mystics following us back one by one, looking for nirvana.'

'You can't keep that door open. You'll be fried in thirty minutes.'

'I have a plan.'

I'd heard that before. He ran up and down the tunnel collecting the largest rocks he could find – at least basketball-sized – and rolling or lugging them back in front of the node. 'Come on, give me a hand,' he grumbled. We all pitched in.

When we had about twenty of them – enough to make a small wall – he began rolling them into the node, where they disappeared.

'What the hell are you doing?'

'Making a wall. In the node. At least, when I get in there, I'll pile all the rocks up into a wall to hide behind. Then I'll prop the door open while I sort of lay low behind the rocks.'

'And what do you plan to prop it open with? This is

your dumbest idea yet.' I was more than annoyed; I was scared. I didn't want to lose Lon, too.

He smiled a gloating smile. 'Wait right here.'

He walked down the corridor, cold sweat soaking his shirt. At the corner, where we'd all leaned our packs, he stopped, pulled out Karl's four-foot blowgun, and brought it back. Straight, hard-fired stonewood. 'Voilà,' he said to me. And to Karl, 'May I?'

Karl shrugged. Lon looked at me, softened and hugged me a long minute. 'Man, I'm about to score the biggest lid of energy this old universe has ever seen.'

Karl scratched his beard. 'I think is maybe a job for two.'

'Forget it,' said Lon, 'this is – '

'Is *my* blowgun,' smiled Karl.

'Property is theft, you always said.'

'*Sí*, but not community property. I think, if we go in there together and share this tool, then you can hold the door open sometimes, and when you get tired, I will hold open the door, so the light will always come through. This is more better, I think. Also, it happens much that you need my help, so I think better for you now if I am around. Also, it is on my mind that these may be the fires of the last world, from whose ashes rose he of the charred skull, whose gaze made green my jungle-mother. Also, now that mi Fernando falls ever in darkness, I would lessen his shivering by bathing in this bright heat – for still we are together in some ways, and that which warms me greatly will warm him at least a little. For do I not even now feel his chill? Also, thou government spy, I am an anarchist, and I will go where I will go.' He brought himself up to his full height, which was considerable, waiting for an argument. But it didn't come.

Lon bowed low. His satin tuxedo was torn and smudged. Time-worn. 'Age before beauty,' he said. Then

he laughed and laughed, like the last of the pirate-kings. It was a roar of equal parts stormy bravado, dark glee, jolly self-ridicule, and sheer delight at life's insanity. He laughed in the face of his fate and his free will, laughed to be so outrageous, laughed as a posture, laughed that he was alive.

I had to smile. Here he was about to do something real scary, laughing because he was scared. It made me feel kind of proud of my own fears, like they were what made me human. It was a source of great joy to have fears and to act in spite of them.

To me Lon said simply 'Good-bye,' and took the blow-gun, with Karl, into the node.

The aged rock remained dark to us for nearly fifteen minutes. We sat quietly on the stone floor, wishing and wondering.

And then it lit up. A horizontal band of orange at first, widening slowly to a blazing window, the light pouring through to us in a flaming ichor from the time-slowed space of the node.

And crouched down in the glare of the firestorm, just two shapes at the base of the flames – human, fetal shapes – Karl and Lon huddled, heads tucked into their chests, behind the shielding stones of the precarious wall: from our perspective, frozen in time.

I had not thought those two would succumb to time's din. I'd thought, of us all, Karl knew his center, Lon his comforts. I'd thought they would walk me through these terrible times, and when I finally fell, they would carry on. I'd thought – but what does it matter what I'd thought?

Suddenly, now, I had this terrible, empty foreboding that they were gone forever.

Thus does time reduce us all to memories.

* * *

And then there were two.

Jasmine and I roamed from precession to precession, raiding time's labyrinths, bull-dancing the ghosts. Without the scope we relied primarily on her memory and my seizures to guide us; in some way these tunnels had become a place completely of our minds, which we followed, inexactly, twisting around from time to time.

It was exciting, actually, exposing myself almost carelessly to danger in a way I'd never done before. These places and times were so surreal, though, and so intricately bound to my seizures, that I brought a sort of dream-bravery with me to the encounters we had there.

I charged through flame and laser-blast with bravado; taunted explosions which, even time-diffused, had force enough to kill. Yet I survived.

With time, my exhilaration intensified; with time, I sailed.

Yet I was aware now of a deep and abiding emptiness within that no amount of adventure or plunder could fill. Abstractly, I felt I was doing something noble; but it seemed a hollow exercise.

I began to change.

I accompanied Jasmine, but I no longer concerned myself with hijacking the pellucid characters who peopled each precession; I only looked in, to see if this was a time I wanted, a time of my choosing, and then stepped out again when it was not.

So I weaved, dreamily, through these many worlds. How long, I've no idea. Always, in my mind, a single type of image held, though: reunion with Torrie, reunion with Di, reunion with my self. Seducing energy-forms remained a goal, but this notion came and went on the winds of time.

It was during this period that I began keeping my own journal in earnest. An accounting of all that had befallen

me, it was an anchor of sorts, something to focus on. I modeled it along the lines of the journal kept by my Joshua-precessor, the diary Jasmine had given me – for, in fact, he was becoming some kind of model for me.

Though I'd never spoken to him – barely *seen* him, really – just that brief glimpse of him, to know that he existed, had moved me in ways I couldn't explain. Like a peek at a whole new universe – *inside* me. And then it was snatched away.

I had to see more.

'You're moping,' said Jasmine.

'I'm not moping.'

'You're timesick,' she nodded.

'I'm just tired.'

'Joshua, like I said – you have to make a truce with these memories. Otherwise you'll reverberate among all your pasts like a dozen ghosts on a TV screen: you won't be able to see the real image for the shadows.'

'Maybe I need a new set.'

'What you need is to confront the noisiest ghost-image and make peace with it.'

She took me to a familiar node. It had a look about it, like a recurring dream.

'This is where we left Torrie, isn't it?' I whispered.

'Not exactly,' said Jasmine. 'We went through this node at its left edge. But the doorway spans a number of years: the *right* edge enters the same cycle, but maybe thirty years earlier than the left edge. So to find the people I want you to meet, I'm going to have to map the node. You wait here – this may take a few hours.'

She entered near the left side, disappearing into the rock. I sat down and tried to rest. Fifteen minutes later she backed out of the rock, drawing a chalk line down the floor behind her. 'The node where we left Torrie isn't

completely buried,' she muttered. Then she reentered at the right side, and again came out drawing the chalk line.

Next she drew an arc connecting the two lines, bisected it, and delved into the third quadrant of the node, pushing the chalk before her.

This went on for two hours, in and out, line after line drawn along the floor, some diagonal, some curved, until at last she emerged smiling and said, 'Well, I found it.'

'Found what?'

'The time I wanted. It's about five years before where we crossed over with Torrie. It's right at the end of this mark . . .' She drew an X at the tail of one of the lines. 'Let's go. And don't stray off the mark, or you'll get lost God-knows-when.'

She pranced unerringly along the spoke she'd laid down. Into the stone, I followed.

We came out in a stormy night on a dark street. Lightning flashed deep inside the great purple clouds; a cold wind blew at our faces. Occasional specks of rain nipped my cheeks.

Lightning splashed again, illuminating, in silhouette, half a mile up the road, the castle.

'Follow me,' she whispered.

She took me through winding streets, from corner to recess. Lights glowed from the windows of some of the houses; there was laughter within, or muffled voices. A few times we hid from passing strangers; all were tall, wrapped in giant wings, like strange larvae, or cloaked demons.

Once someone saw us, and we ran. Jasmine led me up an alley to a shaft which connected, a hundred feet down, with a series of underground tunnels that laced the cliffs beneath the city, then took me up a similar shaft that emerged out an open-mouthed cannister on another darkened street corner.

Again, we crept up shadow streets, sidled along walls, crouched in alleys. Finally, Jasmine pulled me down beside a partly open iron back door. 'This is it,' she whispered. 'Bal's house – Eighteen Street of Wings.'

'What is it?'

'The peace table,' she smiled. 'Go in. Be cautious; be open; be clear. Make the best peace you can.'

'Aren't you coming in?' my voice rose.

She shook her head. 'It's for you. I'll be waiting right here. Take your time, but don't take all night.' She smiled reassuringly and backed into a shadow.

I pushed open the door; it felt like a spider web. I entered the house.

There was a dim corridor, perforated at intervals by entryways. No one home. I tiptoed along the paneled wall, stopped, and peered into the first room off the hall. It was a large kitchen lit by flickering electric bulbs. An older man stood at the sink washing dishes. I left him undisturbed and proceeded silently to the next door.

Here was a great dining hall: a long wooden table surrounded by thirty chairs, and windows floor to ceiling, overlooking the night. At one end of the table three people sat playing cards – two young women and a young man – chattering gaily. I left them to their game and continued my cat walk down the corridor.

I didn't know what I was looking for, but it wasn't in there. I felt flushed with expectancy, though – a sort of fear, longing, and magnctic charge that made every step I took seem meaningful.

I paused a moment before peeking into the next room. Many voices inside, rising and falling. Taut, subtle, I gazed around the lintel into the murmuring chamber. There, in candlelight, lounged twenty people: men, women, boys, girls; jeweled, perfumed, naked, veiled, sitting, reclining, smoking, laughing, teasing, dancing,

sleeping, weeping, pale, thin, and generally purplish about the neck. I knew at once this was a vampire harem.

My hair stood on end; I held my breath. Carefully I studied every face. None were familiar. None sensed my presence. My chest constricted with anticipation. Tremulously, I moved on.

I made to inspect the next room down the line when something caught my ear: at the end of the hall, a room, and somewhere inside, a delicate, crystal voice, singing.

I walked up to the door and looked in. It was a bedroom, lit by candles and orange lanterns. Mirrors lined one wall; a large downy bed filled another. Standing before one of the mirrors was a girl.

Lithe, pretty, she danced with herself, humming a wandering tune. She appeared unclothed at first, until I realized hundreds of long, fine threads hung loosely from her neck to the floor, swaying vaporously as she moved. Her back was to me, but I could see her face in the mirror. It was Di.

I stepped into the room and stood there watching her. A young Di, almost adolescent; her pallor was pronounced. She danced in place, her feet barely moving. Slowly, she turned, hugging herself. When she was facing me, our eyes met; she gasped and halted, her eyes wide.

I shivered. 'Don't be frightened,' I said.

She took a step back but was stopped by the wall of mirror. 'You're Joshua's ghost,' her voice cracked. 'Oh, God, you've come to haunt me . . .' She looked left and right for escape.

'No, no, I'm not dead,' I assured her. 'I mean he's not dead, I mean . . . I won't hurt you, please don't run.'

She remained standing where she was, pupils still dilated with uncertainty. 'Who are you, then?' she challenged.

Salt stung my eyes. 'I'm . . . I . . . just came to say

good-bye.' I didn't know I was going to say that; it made my legs wobble.

Her posture softened. 'But you've only just come,' she said. 'That makes no sense. And if you're not Joshua's phantom, why do you look like that?'

I took a few steps forward. 'I . . . come from another time,' I explained haltingly. 'In my time . . . I knew you.'

'I think I'm imagining you,' she pouted. 'I think you'd better go.'

'Do you . . . want to come with me?' I asked. I wasn't sure what that would mean.

She looked slightly uncomfortable, then sad, then haughty. 'I'm quite happy here, really.'

I walked directly in front of her; her backside was pressing the glass. She was so lovely. Up close, I could see that the thousand long, dangling silk threads were actually sewn into her skin around the circumference of her neck. Her neck was a blur of yellow-to-purple bruises up and down the line of both jugulars. We were of a height; her eyes stared curiously into mine.

'Well,' I whispered. 'I'll be leaving, then.'

She gazed deeply into me, searching, remembering. My heart filled to bursting. She raised her arms, right one to the side, left one forward. I took her right hand in my left, encircled her waist with my right arm, and we danced.

Slow, stately, passionate; I could scarcely feel her at all. Full of grace we turned, specters of each other's lost love, touching in the most delicate of embraces.

'We'll be, again,' I whispered.

'When?' she said.

'In time. Watch for me. I'll see you . . . when the stars return to this night. Until then, this is an ending.'

Our lips came together, touched. A current electrified me from the point of contact to my depths. Her lips were

the softest of lips, almost the memory of lips.

And so we kissed. I stood back when we parted; she gripped the mirrors for support.

'Good-bye,' I murmured.

'Good-bye,' she called. She trembled against her reflection: image and image, fading in candle glow. 'Fare you well,' she echoed, as I backed into the hall.

Free. I felt thunderingly sad; but free. And a thousand pounds lighter.

I looked down the corridor – still empty. Stirrings continued to emanate from other rooms. I ran down the hallway, slipped out the back door.

'Jasmine,' I uttered into the shadows.

Something moved, over near a doorway. I stopped. Before I could even raise my arms, it lunged out at me – big, dark, strong, it was on me, its hands were on my mouth . . .

'Sshhh,' it said.

It was Jasmine.

'Hunters on my trail,' she barely phonated. 'I decoyed them from you, but I think they followed me back.'

We stayed low, moved across an alley. The moon broke from behind a cloud, revealing a cluster of figures in silhouette thirty yards away: wings, hooves, hands, horns, beaks, tails, talons.

They saw us.

With a shriek they descended.

'Come on, then,' snapped Jasmine, and ran for the end of the block. I needed no further encouragement.

It took us a minute of sprinting back streets to reach the node. The hunters were only fifteen yards away now; I could hear their breath hissing. Jasmine paused to locate her exit marking. One of our pursuers shot a weapon; its beam of light hit me in the hip, and I fell. Jasmine picked me up, found her line, and walked across the node.

In a moment we were back in our own time. And a moment later all those stalking horrors were rushing in after us: vampires, griffins, harpies, minotaurs, manticores. Jasmine put me down, and we ran.

They gave chase. They were only ghosts, but they were scary. Flapping, bellowing, scrawking, they'd have devoured us if they could.

We led them through tunnel after tunnel, finally coming to the jungle beyond the cliffs. There we hid in a camouflaged niche we knew as the hunters ran by in confusion on their way to eternal wandering. Their evanescent shapes receded into the dense undergrowth, and they were gone.

'Good-bye,' whispered Jasmine.

I looked out into the jungle a long time; time-warped by the nodes at its core, the Amazon had aged much more slowly than the rest of the planet. Its ancient plants felt suddenly like home to me now.

I looked at Jasmine a little sadly, a little anxiously. 'I have to go back,' I said. 'Back to where Torrie is.'

Jasmine just nodded.

I was afraid to say it, but I did. 'I have to be with my other self.'

CHAPTER 13

Doubles

Thirty minutes later we were standing before the node we'd just escaped, with Jasmine's chalk marks still scribbled all over the ground. And a moment after that we were pushing through the left side of the portal, squeezing past debris that had fallen over the other side. A big rock at last gave way and we were in.

To that place again, to that time. There were no more tents; many of the stone houses were crumbling or half-burned; the bazaar was a shambles. I wouldn't have recognized it but for the hat. For by some fluke or hazard, there in the ash and rubble lay my Flash Gordon helmet, its paint blistered away, its plastic strap melted.

I picked it up, dusted it off, put it on. It seemed a great good omen. Behind us the lightless node was half-buried under loose timber and chunks of earth. We began walking south toward the oak grove.

'It's dangerous for you here, you know,' she said.

'I have to see him. Torrie, too.'

'If you can learn from him, fine. If it's just to wallow in the timesickness, though, I'll have to leave you.'

In the outer city it looked like early morning on another planet. Purple rock formations grew in gravity-defying patterns; liquid fires trickled down the streets, emitting a vile smoke. Meteor showers screamed out of the sky. The castle, a thousand yards to the north, smoked and rumbled above the deserted city. The sun was just breaking over the water to the west.

I reached the small woods in thirty minutes. The plains were covered with shimmering orange pools, phosphores-

cent ice designs, braying beasts. The woods were as I remembered. But in the clearing, the people, clustered around small unwarming bonfires, seemed deeply melancholy.

I hung back, keeping to the shadows, looking in.

It wasn't hard to find Torrie.

To my eye she was the only unequivocally solid being. Truly – in this land of specters, her form fairly demanded to be touched.

I touched her.

She turned, startled, and then, seeing it was me, fell into my arms with a little cry. We embraced, there in the morning mists and the vapors of that time. Jasmine hung back.

'Joshua . . . Joshua . . .' Torrie wept.

'Are you okay?'

'I have . . . so much to tell you . . .'

'And you – what about you?' I insisted.

'This place . . . fills me.' She looked at me longingly.

She and Jasmine greeted cordially. Then the three of us walked a short distance into the undergrowth and sat down.

'What's it all about here?' I asked.

As we lay down in the tall grass, Torrie told me the story. It was a story I already knew well from Joshua's journal, but I listened to Torrie tell it. 'These are Scribes here. They worship the written word. It's a . . . religion, Scribery. The quill is their totem, and there aren't many humans left. And one of them is named Rose.' She paused to organize her thoughts, to let me order mine.

'Rose,' I repeated. 'She's . . . you, here.'

Torrie nodded. 'She's lost, too. But I'm . . . helping her now. We're helping each other.'

'How do you mean?' I asked. But I think I sort of knew.

'I've become . . . her other. Her muse. I follow in her shadows . . . I whisper things to her. It scared me at first. But she listens now . . . I inspire her. We *con*spire. I come to her in dreams.' She flushed with dark delight. 'I whisper as she sleeps. She wakes up sometimes . . . and we talk. We ask each other questions. We give each other solace. We've become . . . secret visitors. Secret sharers.'

She looked down.

'You're a phantom here,' I whispered. I was speaking to myself, too.

'I'm Rose's other. I'm her . . . spirit now. And she's mine. My muse. We bemuse each other.' She touched my hand, took my eyes in hers. 'Stay with us here. I need *you*, too.'

Jasmine spoke for the first time. 'What about the Timefall?'

Torrie knotted her expression. 'We could send people back from here. We could get them to the node and walk them through . . . and then . . . just come back here. We could be guiding spirits . . .'

Lost in time. Was that so bad? It sounded like an attractive proposition at the moment. But somehow improper. I should have been in my own time, facing my own time's problems.

Right?

I couldn't decide what was right; I couldn't figure out what to do, or what to think, or who I was, or who I should be, or why it seemed like such a problem at all.

I only knew that something had ended for me back on twentieth-century earth, something that had been rekindled here and now in this nether time.

'Stay the night with me . . . at least,' said Torrie.

Just the night. It seemed a small thing. 'Sure,' I replied. It would be like a sleep-over at a friend's house – we'd tell ghost stories and giggle until we fell asleep, and then

run through dreamland side by side until it was time to go back to school the next morning. 'But just tonight,' I warned.

Torrie smiled.

Jasmine didn't.

We spent the rest of the daytime hours exploring the place.

Lacing the cliffs below the encampment was the same series of tunnels and caves with which I'd by now become so familiar. Here it was the warrens of this people known as Scribes. We went down there.

Many of the caverns were magnificent rooms, some of them cathedrals to the written word: libraries of handwritten books, reading rooms, paper mills, ink factories, binderies, studies, index rooms, reference chambers, quill refineries, illustration facilities, optometry offices, letter presses, etching stones, lead molds, glass grinders, sewing rooms, tanneries, tooling shops, bookshelves upon bookshelves.

It was a pretty overwhelming display to an old academic like me.

Some of the caves were bedrooms, some were kitchens, some game rooms, some dining halls. There were subterranean lakes, and falls, and engine rooms and laboratories and theaters and dens and rivers and tunnels and museums and conservatories and nurseries and churches and galleries and docks and map rooms and gymnasiums and schoolrooms and baths.

An intricate civilization existed here, rich in nuance, just below the surface. A labyrinthine interior, unsuspected and profound.

We went up again to the cliff tops. Full night had come.

Jasmine headed north – to remember the castle's truths

and lies, she said. Maybe seduce a few vampires out to 1982. Torrie and I went back to the camp.

People were bedded down now; fires were sparking. The air was pensive; conversations were whispered. Torrie led me to a maze of secluded bushes and put her head on my shoulder.

'Well?' she said.

'Pretty odd place.'

'You don't feel . . . your heart here?'

'I don't know what I feel.' I felt lost and found.

'Do you feel this?' She kissed me.

I felt it; I responded. We lay down in the leaves.

'See there,' she whispered. She pointed through the semisolid foliage to a semisolid figure stretched out a few feet away: Shadow-Rose, sleeping.

I gasped. She looked so much like Torrie.

Torrie smiled. 'She likes me to be near . . . while she sleeps. Especially when . . . her Joshua's away.'

It gave me a funny feeling to hear my ether-other referred to, by name, in the third person. 'Where is he now?' I asked. Like I was asking about myself. Like I was schizophrenic.

'In the castle.' She put her hand on my chest. 'For tonight . . . let's think only of each other, though.' And to Rose, she whispered: 'Rest easy. We're not alone.'

Rose seemed to settle into a quieter repose.

Torrie and I made love.

Rose, covered with a fine flush, moaned in her sleep.

It was a strange, dislocated ménage à trois: Rose in our shadow, we in her dream.

When Torrie and I got up in the morning, Rose was already gone. We walked to the edge of the clearing. Voices were being raised – tense, excited, jubilant.

People were arming themselves with knives, swords,

and torches. A large vampire was speaking of battle plans; men were shouting at him.

'What's happening?' I asked Torrie.

'They're getting ready to attack the castle,' she said. 'The final battle for human survival . . . in this time.'

'And you?'

'I'm going to go with Rose. I'm her . . . guardian angel.' She walked a few yards away to where her pack was stowed, pulled out the emerald telescope, and gave it to me. 'If all doesn't go well . . . you'll want this. To be on your way again.'

Fires billowed against the dull sky; distant explosions shook the stone. Torrie and I walked behind the small army like a spectral rear guard. Once through the outer gates, we entered a tunnel and began making our way through the catacombs beneath the city.

That's when the flood came.

A surge of translucent water, roaring through the tunnels, knocking dozens of people into dozens of corridors. Separating me from the rest. It took me forever to get my footing again, and when I did, I was alone. With no idea where I was.

I walked around for ten minutes without success. At last I came to a vertical shaft that I assumed led up to the city, so I climbed the rungs that ran up its side – climbed a hundred yards, I think – and emerged through a hole in the floor of what looked like the dining hall of the castle.

A long serving bench occupied the center of the floor; statuary lined the walls. It looked familiar; but where had I seen it before? When? I'd been part of so many times now.

There were a dozen exits in the chamber. I took one that led to a somewhat smaller room strewn with furniture. So familiar. Drums were beating somewhere out-

side, rising and falling in the distance. A pungent, ancient odor filled the room – distinct but unnameable. Old oil lamps were spaced along massive wood tables, illuminating everything. The chairs around the tables were carved teak, dark with oil and years. The floor was ornately designed ceramic tile – cracked, chipped, still beautiful. Art and artifacts decorated one wall: woven feather tapestries, animal masks, stone bas relief, clay vases.

The building suddenly shook with the rumble of an explosion. Some of the vases toppled and shattered. The image jolted me: broken vases along this wall. Standing on this floor. Where had I seen it before?

One wall contained a large, open, exterior window. The ceaseless drumming wafted in on the night air from the village below. I walked over to the window.

Five stories directly beneath me was a courtyard. Hand-to-hand combat raged there, or rather, hand-to-claw: it was humans versus creatures, and the humans didn't seem to be doing too well. Torches were alight everywhere, dancing about the clearing like elven spirits, like fireflies. The image haunted me in the way dreams or precognitive visions are haunting: evocative, intimating, echoing. I squeezed my eyes tightly shut, but nothing came. I walked around the room.

A large, open-topped, cylindrical receptacle stood in one corner, identical to the shaft I'd just come up in the last room. I looked down; it plunged darkly into the tunnels beneath the castle.

The table was filled with arcane apparatus of unknown purpose. It looked alchemical. Glass beakers, shiny coils, strange books covered with complicated symbols and cryptic writing. Potent secrets.

Sounds of fighting came nearer: clashing steel, screams and footsteps.

I walked over to the other door, in the far wall. It was

open. I crossed into the next chamber, which was lit by a single, guttering torch.

One entire wall was covered with a mural: orbs and bizarre constellations swept over the curved ceiling; there were arcs, lines, geometric shapes, arrows, numbers, figures . . .

It suddenly hit me. I ran to the far wall, deep in shadow; it was floor-to-ceiling cells, like animal cages.

This was where Di had been locked when I discovered her in the jungle city.

These were the same rooms, the same castle – 67 million years before Di had been locked up here. Before the trek that had first led me into the jungle. Before I'd stumbled, convulsing, into the core of this city.

I stumbled backward, raced out of the room – I had to get away from this place, it was literally the stuff of dreams, and it made me feel as if I were falling into myself, endlessly. I had to get out of myself.

There were voices at the end of the hall, shouts and cries that sounded, to me, like my lifelines. I ran toward the cacophony and entered the room.

A great battle was in progress; blood oiled the floor. A small army of humans hacked away at a vicious array of griffins, vampires, manticores, and carnivores. Stabbings, beheadings, and dismemberings punctuated the wails of engagement. The sight of it nauseated me – all this hopeless carnage – but my gaze was riveted. I stumbled among the combatants like a wraith, like an automaton, searching for reason.

It was quite clearly a throne room. The massive stone chair at the center of the fighting was encrusted with jewels, elevated on a dais, surrounded by long ebony tables. I stood behind the throne, shaking.

Somebody screamed above the chaos: 'He is dead! He

is dead! The human they call Joshua has fallen! Long live the queen!'

It was taken up as a battle cry by the mythical beasts; they surged forward mightily, all but overpowering the shrinking human forces. I seemed to be witnessing the extinction of the human race by an onslaught of its own nightmare creatures. Weakly, I stood upon the dais.

'No,' I whispered, 'I am not dead.'

A mortally wounded man on the floor by my feet looked up when he heard me. Light filled his eyes, and he pointed in my direction. 'He lives!' the man rasped, and then louder: 'Joshua lives!'

A few people nearby looked over and took up the shout. For a long moment there was a palpable lull in the battle as heads turned to view me, and then the fighting resumed, twice as ferociously. Only now the humans began to rally.

A cohort of the viler creatures lumbered toward me, blood on their fangs and murder in their eyes. Some were stopped by an inspired human guard that formed around me, but some at last broke through, crazed with hatred.

My back was to the wall, but I remembered this wall: it contained the secret stone panel through which the Watcher had taken me, up to the tower. I pushed up on two irregular bricks, and the door-sized section opened. I stepped through, closing it only moments before the minotaur broke his horn on the wall trying to gore me.

The same circular stairway took me up to the flat, open tower that overlooked the entire city. Purple black clouds filled the sky, creased by lightning, billowed by thunder. A violent, ozone wind tugged me to the low stone wall at the very lip of the fortress.

I peered over the edge of the tower at the city below. The torches had multiplied a hundredfold; the drumming of explosions swelled out of the darkness. It thrilled me:

the lights, the pulsing rumble, the musky air, my connection to it all, my potency within it.

I stood. The wind caught my hair, splayed it like fire. I felt – immortal. I felt the crowd below sense my presence, touch my spirit.

Lightning struck the turret above me, wreathing the entire structure in the green phosphorescent glow of Saint Elmo's fire. And this glow, shining from behind, radiated through and illuminated me. Like a vision. A spirit resurrected.

Far below, somebody saw it. 'He lives!' I heard the cry.

'He rises!' shouted another.

And then, as in the throne room, hundreds took up the chant: 'Joshua – Joshua – Joshua . . .'

And once again, the tide of battle began to turn in favor of the human rebels.

Their spark would not die this day.

I looked over the ruins of the castle, filled now with struggle and hope. My vision extended beyond the city, beyond the occult jungle, beyond the spinning stars. Struggle, hope. I held – I was – this moment.

I closed my eyes, savored it, breathed it into my lungs.

For just that instant, the universe was within me.

I exhaled. The earth came rushing back to my feet. I wobbled, but maintained. Solid ground, once again, though I felt like I'd been through my own mortal struggle.

Still on the tower, still alone; what next?

I checked around the corner, found a vertical shaft, and climbed down its iron rungs to the catacombs far below. Rushing water splashed near my feet – a shallow, underground river ran through the tunnels here. Decaying matter floated down the main tunnel – the sewage of the apocalypse: rotting torsos, grimacing heads bobbing darkly, like half-remembered fragments of another life.

I walked to the next cross-tunnel. A body slumped there, partly in the water, partly out.

It was Joshua – my own preincarnation.

He looked like he'd been thrown out death's back door. Filth clung to him, matted his hair, stuck to his torn skin and shredded clothes. But he breathed.

He looked like I felt. How can I describe it? I was *one* with this thin soul before me. I trembled at his nakedness. He trembled in his sleep.

'What's happening to me?' I thought.

'You've come from the astral plane,' he answered in my mind. 'You've come to haunt me.'

I felt waves between us, soundless but resonant. I thought to him, '*You* are the ghost; not I.'

'I am who I am,' he projected. 'You're only my echo.'

'I am who *I* am,' I echoed.

'Then what's the matter?' he said.

'There is no matter,' I said. 'There's only space, and the energy that flows through it, and time, which is the consciousness of space.' Suddenly, I knew that – more certainly than I'd ever known anything.

'Why did you come here?' he said.

'To see *you*. To *know* you.'

'You know me.'

'Who are you, then?'

'I'm the knowledge of your self.'

I looked at him lying there: an ordinary man. Beaten down, but not beaten. Torn by struggle and hope. Hurting, taking stock. 'What will you do?' I said.

'Rest awhile. Talk to you, it would seem.'

'Why talk to me?'

'Because *you* are the knowledge of *my* self,' he smiled.

I tried a new tack. 'And what have you learned from this knowledge?'

'How to listen to my spirit. How to speak to my spirit.'

'So you know to speak. What do you say?'

'Only that you infuse me. You are my future. Be near, or far – but do not leave me.'

'But . . . what if I *must* leave you?'

'Then you will wander blind, and so will I, as unknowing as a universe without time. And your spirit will die.'

His words made me shiver, and I backed away into the darkness. To desert him, he seemed to be saying, would mean my own *personal* timefall. A life uninformed by selfconsciousness, history, inner spirit. If I was his future, he was certainly my core. Now that I knew him, he was *part* of me. I could no more abandon him than tear out my heart.

Reemerging in the outer city, I wandered for some time. The climate underwent frequent, and radical, changes. Blinding sunlight to blinding darkness. Boneshivering cold, equatorial heat. Earthquakes, ocean fires, viscous rain.

At some moments the sky seemed to rip, letting the void's black fluid spill out. The earth itself began spinning faster, so nights and days lasted only a few hours, and time seemed to rush around like a broken-winged bat, too quick to follow, all aflutter.

I trickled toward the camp to the south. The humans there huddled, awaiting news of the war.

I walked around for hours without a clear idea of what to do, though I felt profoundly and intuitively clearer about who I was.

I staggered through the rubble of the city. Creatures were still fleeing. I climbed over a low mound of stone; I could tell by its relation to the castle that it wasn't far from the node, though by now most other landmarks had been wiped away. On the other side of the wall a figure crouched – fierce, ready to attack. I wasn't even up to

flight, though. Weakly, I said, 'Hello,' and spread my arms open to what the universe held in store for me: let come what may.

'Joshua!' cried a voice.

I squinted into focus.

It was Jasmine.

We hugged. 'I think I have to stay here,' I said. 'My past is here, and somehow I think my future.'

'And now two more old friends,' she smiled sadly, and led me over behind a pile of rocks. There, in the debris, lay Lon and Karl, badly burned, barely moving.

'What happened?' I whispered. They looked to be in such pain, tears blurred my vision.

Jasmine knelt down with me, beside Lon. He lay there on his side, sweating, tremulous. His eyes were glazed, his skin deep red; the skin on his back looked practically charred in places, and blistered. His teeth were chattering, but he smiled as he held my hand.

'Radiation burns,' Jasmine said softly. 'The skin will heal in time – but the damage inside is grave.'

'Lon.' I whispered.

'"Bitter knowledge we gain by traveling," as Baudelaire used to say.' Barely able to talk, he was still cavalier enough to quote verse.

'They were propping up the door at the node where we left them,' Jasmine explained. 'Lon looked in from time to time – it seems there were people in there, just barely visible through the firestorm. And then the flames started diminishing, and it was actually starting to cool down – and I guess that's when Karl thought he saw someone. Someone he wanted to see closer. So he jumped up and ran in.'

'Through the node?' I demanded. 'Into the fire?'

'I tried to stop him.' Lon picked up the story. His eyes were closed now; he seemed completely spent. But rather

would he die than miss a chance to tell a good story. 'Tried to stop him, but he was too strong and too fast. Probably chewing those coca leaves again. So I had to run in after him. It was cooler than it had been, but still way too bright to see much – I kept shielding my eyes, sort of crab-walking backward, tripping over every damn thing around. Last thing I tripped over was Karl.' He paused – whether for effect, or to gather his strength, I don't know – coughed once, and continued.

'And old Karl was kneeling down, just staring straight into the burning center of this whole holy hell, leaning over the body of this huge bearish man, crying "It is he! It is he!" Well, I didn't get a good look at the body, but from what I saw, the fellow was nearly burned to a crisp – I mean he had to be dead, but his arms were still moving, like they were reaching out, almost – must have been the heat of the fire, just shortening the tendons at the back of his elbows, so the arms kept extending. That's probably why his fists opened at the end, when the arms were all the way out – the flames, pulling those hand tendons back to snapping before they burned through completely – that's probably what it was, but I'm damned if it didn't look like he was reaching up to give something to Karl. And I'm damned if Karl didn't take it!' He opened his eyes wide, incredulous at his own story. The effort was too much for him, though, and he soon settled back to talking less forcefully.

'I couldn't breathe for the heat,' he rasped, 'so I rapped Karl a good one on the back of the head and began dragging him out of there. But as I left, I glanced at the dead man's face. And I'm double-damned if it wasn't Karl.'

'No, was not Karl,' came a third voice beyond.

It was Karl speaking. I looked up and took closer notice of him for the first time. He was propped against a rise.

His skin was a crusted dark brown; his eyes, which were staring blankly ahead into space, had changed their pigmentation – altered, or burned away by the radiation, I assume – so that now they were a clear, crystal green. I passed my hand before his face; there wasn't even a flicker of movement: he was totally blind.

His voice was hoarse. 'No, was not Karl,' he repeated. 'It was he with the emerald eyes, who made the jungle green by his gaze; he with the skull of black coal which is all that was left from the fires of the last world. The one true ancestor.'

Jasmine gave him water. 'Rest, sir,' she told the old guide.

Karl drank, and smiled. 'I sought much the true seeds of the mother-forest – and he gave them to me. He kept the last seeds of his burning world hidden from the fires, hidden tight in his fist – and when he saw me, he opened his hand and gave me the seeds to sow again when the flames had died. To carry on for him.' He sank back exhausted.

'That's when I found them,' came in Jasmine. 'Lon was struggling at the node, trying to drag Karl back across. I jumped in and pulled them through. The burns' – she shook her head – 'are pretty serious, I think.'

'But as you see,' Karl grinned harshly through his pain, 'I have the seeds.'

Deliberately, he opened his fist against the charred flesh. There, in his shocking palm, lay the seeds: oval, shimmering, ephemeral. Deliberately, he closed his hand around them once more.

I looked again at Lon, only half-blind, only half-dead. 'Will they live?' I asked Jasmine.

'"Doctor, doctor, will I die? Yes, my child, and so will I,"' she answered quietly. 'Yes, they'll live for a while. I can't say how long. Longer, if they stay in here, I think –

I told you, time in here isn't like time out there . . .'

'How is it you were there to help them?' I asked her.

'I stopped there specifically – on the way back from the jungle city – to see how they were doing. I saw – just in time, it would seem.'

'The city?' I asked, but before I could pursue my question, Karl stood, by what could only have been a massive exercise of will. Slowly, he cast his blind, emerald gaze in all directions. 'There is a desert, not far?' he said. 'I can feel it.'

Jasmine held his arms, turned him, pointed him toward the Ansa Blanca to the southeast. 'There,' she said quietly.

'I would go there,' he rasped, 'before my strength altogether leaves me. I would plant these seeds.'

'But it's a desert,' I protested.

'It is unspoiled,' he agreed. 'Also, I have here a bit of soil from my own jungle, to nourish the seedlings' – he reached into his pocket and came out with a handful of dirt – 'and I will bring some water. Also, there is much energy in this desert. Perhaps my seeds will grow into a new jungle some day.' He smiled at a space between us.

Lon stood, and the two old friends embraced for a long time. In a thick voice Lon said, 'I'm not made of your stuff, *amigo*; but I'll walk with you a way, until I have to rest – fool like you, *someone's* got to set you straight.' Then he looked at Jasmine and winked. 'I'll be back for you, though, lover – I didn't come all this way just to walk out on you.'

And off they paced, Karl and Lon, toward the crucible.

Leaving me alone with Jasmine.

'And you?' I asked.

'I'll nurse Lon back to health here for a short while,' she mused. 'And before I leave, I'll see Beauty, the creature of *my* inspiration all these millennia.' She paused

a moment, and I could see she was visualizing this centaur she'd once loved. Then her face turned somber. She stood straight, spoke slowly. 'I've been back, I told you, to the city in the jungle, where they're still waiting for Goranchacha's return. At night I snuck into the Watcher's Tower – she has a telescope there, you know.'

'Yes, I know. I used it. So what?' Something was coming, here. I felt a premonitory chill – and of course I knew, by now, that premonitions were really nothing more than memories.

She looked strained. 'Actually, I *left* the telescope there, in *my* time, in this castle, in that tower' – we looked at the fortress, rumbling in the distance – 'left it there hoping it would still be there in sixty-seven million years when I woke up, so I could use it then, to see.'

'Okay, so what did you see? The dreamstar? The bloodstar?'

'My eye, you know, is far more sensitive than the human eye – I can register the light of a single photon; and I can discern broader spectrums as well – ultraviolet and infrared included. Anyway, the point is, I was checking the red shift – the Doppler effect on the Magellanic formation – because I knew what it used to be, and what it should have been; and now I saw what it was. And Joshua, there was no doubt about it: The Timefall is coming.'

I looked hard at her – she wasn't joking, she wasn't theorizing. She was reporting, and she was scared.

'It's not quite imminent,' she went on, 'and it may still be reversible. But it's accelerating, and much sooner than I'd expected. So we haven't much time.' She paused to let her words sink in.

'How much time?' I asked.

'A matter of some years, maybe. No more. We're losing time every moment, though. Losing time forever.'

I'd never thought of Jasmine as being scared of anything – intrepid, android, full of life's glee, she was the manipulator of time, not its servant. She broke time like a wild stallion.

But she was shaking.

She steadied herself. 'So I'm going back. To some of the high-yield nodes – get as much energy into your time as I can. I've been a little lax, I'm afraid.' She smiled at me, blamelessly.

The impact of her statement rattled me. This was it. The end was near.

'Well, good-bye for now,' she said. 'And good luck to us all.' Whereupon she kissed me and ran off to help Lon and Karl get comfortable. In a few hours she'd be gone, to her mission.

Leaving me alone. I walked back to the southern encampment – ambivalent, confused. There, in a dim corner of a dim cave, I found Torrie. Rose and my spirit-Joshua stood against the far wall.

We embraced as they embraced.

'I don't know what to feel anymore,' I said.

'You can't feel clearly,' she smiled, 'because you try to think too much.'

'I try not to think at all,' said a voice. It was Joshua, my doppelgänger, at the other end of the cave.

'Will you stay?' Rose asked Joshua.

'I don't know,' I replied to Torrie. She stroked my head; I lay down beside her. 'I should leave tomorrow,' I said. 'So much is at stake. The future is at stake.'

'There is no future. No past. Only now,' said Torrie. 'But you can only know that here.'

Rose closed her eyes, sighing. 'I've missed you,' she whispered to Joshua.

'I've missed you,' Torrie said to me. 'We could be happy here. We could pass an eternity here.'

'Nothing is eternal,' said Josh. He drew Rose close.
'This is eternal,' she whispered. They kissed.
'But not if time falls,' I whispered.

I awoke in Torrie's arms; Joshua and Rose were gone.

I got up without waking her, got up clinging to an audacious idea.

I could invent my own life.

Invent it here, if I chose.

Torrie was here; here to stay, it seemed. I felt needful of her in her absence, and solace in her company. With her I was not so alone.

Yet in my own time the universe was tilted on the edge of chaos. Was it not? I could save it, perhaps. And if not, must I not at least try? My good friends had died trying, or been wounded in the extreme. Di, without ever knowing why. Lon, without thought for himself, using himself as a conduit . . .

A conduit. The glimmer of an idea came to me. A hope, no more.

I got up to leave.

Torrie half-roused herself, looked at me blearily.

I kissed her. 'I'll be back soon.'

'I'll be here.' She smiled her fey, lopsided smile and returned to dreaming of our ancestral lovers.

I ran back to the node.

Rubble almost totally occluded the opening, but I managed to slip through. Once in my own tunnels, with the telescope Torrie had returned to me, I quickly made it out to the jungle. Night was here.

I needed to get back to LA, to see if my plan could be implemented. Map in hand, I started walking toward where we'd hidden the raft.

The cool night air revived me, invigorated my spirit. It

was good to be in my own world again. Unexpectedly, I began to cry. The release was welcome.

The raft was gone. Or had I just misremembered where we'd put it?

I walked for perhaps an hour. It came to me, at some point, just how exhausted I was. When had I last slept? My legs were leaden. I found a flat shelf of rock near the river, curled under it, and instantly fell asleep.

I awoke much refreshed, though it was still night. For another hour I trekked downriver, until, to my relief and astonishment, I saw bonfires up in the forest. Cautiously, I approached them. Soon I began to hear voices; and even more amazing: they were speaking English! 'What is it?' someone said. 'What's happening?'

I rushed into the clearing to greet them. Just within the flicker of their torchlight I stopped and slowly straightened.

To my dense, cold horror, I realized they were ghostly specters. They were, moreover, *my own original expeditionary party,* crouching in the jungle for the first time – over six years in the past. Lon, Karl, Fernando, Di – and me.

'Oh, God, no,' I moaned.

'What *is* that?' hissed Di.

'Jungle steam,' murmured Lon. 'No more. Josh's reflection. It's a trick of the moonlight.'

'Quiet,' Joshua said, 'quiet. He's trying to say something.'

I *was* trying to say something to these creatures of my memory. They were all ghosts to me now, and I to them, no doubt, from the way they stared at me in terror. 'No . . .' was all I could say. 'How can this be? What are you doing here? Go away, I beg you . . .'

With a sudden doubling-over of comprehension, I realized I'd witnessed this same scene six years before from

the perspective of the horrified man who crouched beside the fire – only now I was witnessing it from the point of view of the 'ghost' who'd entered our camp back then. One of the 'spirits of the dead.'

With a shudder I realized I'd become my own spirit: I was haunting myself.

I burst into sobs and ran off into the night.

What had gone wrong? What had I done? Had I finally become totally and forever lost in time?

I knew. In a flash I knew: I'd reentered this time at the wrong edge of the node, the opposite edge from where I'd entered the cycle where Torrie now waited. Jasmine had warned us of this – we had to enter and leave at the same point or risk getting deposited in a slightly different moment from the one we wanted. The moment I'd just entered was simply six years earlier than my own real time.

I wended my way back through the tunnels to the node where Torrie now lived. I passed through the node, the same place I'd just emerged a few hours earlier. Once again, I found myself in the last precession.

The problem was all the debris covering the node on Torrie's side. It had merely obscured the correct point of my entry and exit. I hardly paused. I slid under the piled boards and stones, back to the farthest edge of the node, the edge which I'd first entered.

At last, I slipped back into my own time.

Really my own time; I could feel it – smell it, hear it, touch it. I picked up a rock – a solid rock – and heaved it against the wall. It splintered with a satisfying thunk.

I trotted through the caves one last time – getting to know my way around them with facility by now – and exited into the jungle near the spot where I'd stowed the raft. No sooner had I set foot out of the caves, though, than I was thrown against the rock face, with a knife point

denting my throat. The wind was knocked out of me. I stood motionless, eyes closed, waiting for the blade with a mixture of relief and regret – but the blade withdrew. Instead came a chuckle. I opened my eyes. There stood Darwina S. Vine, arms akimbo.

'Bloody lucky you are,' she smiled, 'I've still got my reflexes. Thought you were one of the abos on my trail.'

I just stared at her, and a wild sight she was: a shotgun was slung across her back, with double belts of shells crossing her chest; camouflage paint streaked her face, and grenades hung at her belt. Her head was wrapped in a black bandanna.

'Dar?' I finally got out.

'Right you are,' she squinted. 'Funny meeting you down here again. Maybe not so funny. Life is odd, and that's a fact.'

'What *are* you doing down here?' I asked.

An anger filled her eyes. 'First of all, my family's all gone – died years ago, it seems. I haven't been home since 'forty-seven, remember. And I've grown rich since then – all my bank accounts just kept compounding over the years – but the world's grown poor. Spiritually poor, that is – nuclear war, televisions replacing books, all that air pollution, and water pollution, and food pollution – who needs it? What? Not I. A foul way to live, altogether too busy. Too anxious.'

I just nodded. It seemed a strange commentary from the commando standing before me. She continued.

'Then, too, there was the little matter of retribution, wasn't there?' She began to pace. 'I had a score to settle with this bloody tribe – stealing thirty years from me, never seeing my family again . . .' A tear came to her eye, but she batted it away and went on in an urgent whisper. 'So I put an advert in one of those soldier-of-fortune magazines and rounded up a few good boys, and

we came back here – and by God they won't forget us in that bloody city again.'

'What did you . . .'

'Killed the *Brujo* and his guard. Killed the good Queen Namsháya Moon-Goddess Jaguar-Woman. Freed all the prisoners and shot up the castle. Took 'em by storm and took 'em good. The prisoners ran in every direction. My boys loaded up with jewels from the Sacred Grove, and went their own way home. Wanted me to come with them – "Granny," they call me – but I'm staying.'

'Staying here? In the jungle?'

She smiled with an air almost of apology. 'In the city under the river. Beside that slime-mold lake – '

'With the people of the lake!' I exclaimed. 'But you – '

'I know, I know, I thought they were all touched and I couldn't wait to get out of there. Well, I see things different now. They had a nice, slow pace down there. And everyone treated everyone else like family . . .' She hesitated now, regarding me suspiciously, uncertain if she should say more, then continued in a more guarded tone. 'And there's the baby now.'

'What baby?' I said, though I instantly had an inkling.

'The queen's baby – I took it from her when she died, it looked so small and needful . . .' She paused again. 'Your baby, Joshua.'

She took me around to an overhang in the cliff wall, sheltered from the sun by a plantano grove. There, on a rubber tarp, lay the infant – frail, quiet, with sunken cheeks, dark blue eyes: my eyes.

I crouched down and touched her cheek. It was hot, and dry. 'She's sick,' I said. My heart constricted for her, she looked so vulnerable.

'Dehydrated,' Dar nodded. 'She's got dysentery. Needs a lot of sterile salt water more than anything, but I haven't even got a match to set it to boil, so I was all set to take

her down with me to the lake beneath the river. They have fires, and screal potions, and they're a caring people . . .'

I stared at the child with a feeling I'd never known – a tugging at my soul, a sense of connection.

'I'll take her with me,' I said. 'I'm going back to LA.'

Dar stiffened. 'She'd never make the trip. And besides, I'll take good care of her. And she'll take good care of me. She's all I've got now, really . . .' She waited for my reaction. This child was mine. 'Of course, you're free to visit us down there whenever you want.'

I stared at the baby. She stared directly back at me; she seemed sentient, somehow, full of a deep understanding far beyond my own. She stared back at me and eased my fears.

'All right,' I said. 'I *will* come see you. When I get back.'

Darwina relaxed. '*That's* the ticket.'

'She needs water now, though,' I said, standing. I knew this as if she'd told me. 'Sterile water.' I walked toward the river.

Dar followed me. 'I've already looked around here. This lot's pretty stagnant.'

I stooped by the shore and gathered some dry bush and sticks into a pile. Then I took a long piece of swamp grass, tied a loop into the end of it, and dipped it in the water. When I pulled it back, a small drop of water balanced in the loop, quivering in the sunlight, like a tiny lens. I steaded my arm against my knee, holding this lens above the ground, its focal point buried somewhere in the dry brush pile. And the sun poured through the water drop, and in a minute the grass was smoking; and then it was afire.

'I'll be damned,' said Dar, and ran to get more wood and a tin cup to fill with water.

How did I know this trick? It just surfaced from deep within me, somehow part of that ancient, primitive Joshua who was now part of me, as if I were in touch now with my own magic, the fire of my shadow-self.

We boiled the water, soaked Darwina's scarf in it, and let the baby suck on the scarf. She watched me as she drank, and I thought: Here is your immortality. Here is why time must not fall.

She drank a lot, seemed stronger, and went to sleep.

'Well, I'm off, then,' said Dar. 'See you when you come back – say, what *are* you doing down here?'

I smiled. I didn't know what to say, and she didn't really care, finally. She gathered up her gear, put the child in a makeshift papoose on her back, and set off into the caves.

'Wait!' I called, 'What's the baby's name?'

But she was gone.

I sighed, pulled myself together, and tracked over to where I'd hidden my raft. It was nighttime by now.

I followed the red star along the same trail of rivers that Torrie and I had taken down here. It was slowgoing, all alone, night after night. But I viewed time on a different scale now. A scale that weighed spirits in the balance.

Suffice to say, I made it eventually downriver to Epechuro, and from there to Rio, and from there I caught a plane to Los Angeles.

I arrived home the next day, where it turned out three more years had passed. I'd returned to the jungle in 1982; it was now 1985.

It took me about two weeks to put things in order.

CHAPTER 14

Epilogue: The Last Campaign

The last thing I did before returning to the jungle was to stop in the ER where I'd met Dr Kahn.

He was just going off duty. I asked him if I could buy him a drink. He hesitated at first – it seemed to make him a little uncomfortable – but finally he agreed.

I had to tell him. Tell him everything. He was my reality check, in a way: if I could just recount to him what had happened, what would yet happen, that somehow made it real. For a document to exist, it needs a reader. Kahn was my reader. And, of course, I felt kindred to him, as I've said, and I wanted to share these things: he was, as he'd always been, my brother.

'Your cat is pretty strange,' he said when we'd sat down in the bar, 'but doing well. She still lives in my house, but somehow in a different universe. You know what I mean?'

I nodded and ordered us drinks.

'Anyway,' he continued, 'we get along quite well.' He paused; then: 'I'm glad you made it back in one piece,' he said. 'I didn't exactly expect to see you again.'

'Well, not exactly one piece,' I smiled.

I reminded him of the specifics of the first expedition: the finding of the skull, the emerald-encased maps; the adventures in the Amazon: the jaunt through the tree-tops; the 'spirits of the dead'; the city in the valley of caves, where Goranchacha's idol had kept watch for untold ages; our escape, with Goranchacha's eyes, back to LA.

That's when I'd first met Kahn, I reminded him. Three years ago. In the emergency room, having the convulsions

that had saved my life in the jungle city. Then I'd seen him again at the party and told him all about the nature of time.

Now I told him all about the second expedition: journeying through the time-tunnels to lure phantoms into our universe – lure them by means of seduction, intimidation, curiosity, enlightenment, temptation, anger, or remorse. I told him about precessions full of light, darkness, typhoon, void; times of faith, times of abandon; worlds of dragons, and bottomless pits. I told him about seeing Di again and how it was possible to make peace with your memories, even your most grievous ones, if you chose the right time.

I told him all about the last precession: the castle, so like the castle ruins in the Colombian jungle; the vampire-people, so like and yet unlike the bloodthirsty tribe we'd met in the Amazon. I told him how it was the land of our others, our spirit-doubles, our alter-selves. I told him of the rushing Timefall, and my friends who still waited in the shadowland.

I told him I was going back.

Three years had gone by here since I'd seen Kahn last, yet in *my* travels hardly a week had passed; and I don't think I'd aged a few days.

'Sounds like a dream,' he suggested.

'More like a nightmare.' We were humoring each other.

'And that friend of yours I met – Torrie – she decided to stay, huh?'

'Bad case of the timesickness,' I nodded. 'I'll succumb, too, of course. Eventually. But there's all that energy to drag across first – to keep the universe afloat.'

'Of course. The universe of your self.'

'Oh, the universe of my self,' I smiled. 'You still think this is all my internal reality.'

'Well,' he circled, 'there *are* some physicists who

believe the nature of the universe is reflected – is *contained* – in every cell of the body, like a holograph – all the information of the whole, contained in every part, in every atom, even. So it's possible, in that context, I suppose, that the human brain *can* know the cosmos, that the universe is *not* stranger than we can imagine. So maybe in that sense your internal perceptions are reflecting some kind of external reality.'

'Reality is all a function of time,' I explained. 'Look at the Amazon Jungle. Its reality is determined by how slowly time swirls there.'

He just nodded and ordered another round. 'I wish you well,' he toasted.

'Leaving it up to me, eh?' I needled him.

'It's hardly my field of expertise.'

'Or your responsibility?'

'I view *people* as my responsibility. Not causes.'

'I never thought of this as a cause, exactly,' I said.

'An effect, then?'

'A special effect,' I drank. 'Like my new baby daughter – a very special effect.'

'To your daughter,' he toasted. 'She still in the jungle, too?'

'Yes – with Dar, in the city beside the slime-mold lake. But now that I've finished preparations for my final campaign in these time-wars, I'll be leaving in the morning. So I'll be seeing her soon. But the great thing is, I think I may have licked this energy problem – at least in theory.' I just hoped it worked in practice.

What had struck me was the way Lon had let energy just pour into our time by keeping that node open as a conduit. Of course, there was an energy gradient in that particular case – light from that precession had flown downhill, so to speak, into the darkness of our caves. Wasn't there a way, I wondered, to capture *any* light

waves on one side of a node and transport their energy to the other side?

Of course there was. Photovoltaics.

So I'd called my friend David Turner, an electrical engineer. What I wanted, I told him, was something like a collection of solar cells connected to a simple cable (a long cable, to be sure; how long *was* it across a node?), connected in turn to a socket that could accommodate a very large light bulb. No problem, David told me; can do.

He worked on it with Mark Ratkovic, another friend, who'd done time at the Department of Water and Power. They came up with a solar collector panel, available commercially, which they hooked up to a three-hundred-watt bulb via fifty feet of insulated wire. Worked perfectly: when the sun was shining brightly, the light bulb would flicker on. (Mark said: 'Seems like it would be easier to just open the window shade.')

I ordered a hundred.

The idea was pretty simple, really: collect light-energy in one of the earlier cycles, string the cable across the node, and light up our own tunnels. Maybe save our universe.

I asked Kahn what he thought. He agreed it sounded pretty simple. He ordered another round and asked me what would happen if the cables didn't stretch far enough. It was a reasonable question. I admitted if that was the case, I'd just have to fall back on the traditional method of seeking and luring souls back from the earlier time-frames.

'Doesn't sound to me like the fiber optics are a solution, then,' said Kahn. 'Technology has never been a good substitute for soul-searching.'

I caught the smile in his eye. 'What, then?' I asked.

He shrugged. 'You said the people rallied around you in that last battle, when you appeared after they thought

Joshua the Earlier had died. Why not just wait until he really does die, and then you can *re*appear to them – reanimated, reborn. Hell, you could probably get *thousands* of believers to follow you back here.' He winked.

I knew he was putting me on. But I think he'd stumbled onto the answer.

That's how I was going to save the universe.

I winked back. 'You're not afraid it might give me a messiah complex?'

'I'm sure you can handle it,' he smiled.

'I believe I can,' I beamed. 'I think you've shown me my place in the overall scheme of things.'

'Think you can prevent the Timefall, then?'

'I think we've got a good chance now. With a little messianic movement. And a little help from my friends. Things could be better, God knows. But things could be worse.'

I went on to tell him I was also anxious to spend time with my child. In the last cycle, I knew from Joshua's journal, this child had great powers. Maybe she had powers again. Certainly, I *felt* a great power within her. But then parents always have a tendency to see deep rivers in their children.

And Dar, of course, lunatic Dar. Now *there* was a madwoman. Yet she knew what she wanted and how to get it, and I found a sweetness to her madness that made it hard to begrudge her wanting to live out her years in a colony of gentlefolk beside a strange lake. And her years would be considerable, time being what it was down there. A gentle way too, I thought, for my child to grow.

I intended, finally, to spend a good deal of time with Torrie in the last precession. I loved her dearly, and we had much to learn and share with our precestral ghosts. Of course, I fully expected to have periods away, when I'd go back and forth again, to press on with the original

work, to appear as a resurrected vision to my followers, to lead them to this time, where they would live eternally as spirits – our world their heaven. So much depended on it.

So that was my story. Kahn's eyes were half-lidded by now, but I still detected a hint of skepticism lurking there. This was unacceptable. He required more hard evidence.

I gave it to him.

'Here's the journal of the previous Joshua,' I said, taking it from my coat. 'It tells his story, in his own words. I mean, I couldn't invent something like this.'

'No, no, please . . .' He tried to refuse me, but I pressed on.

'The signs are all there. Call the Griffith Observatory – ask for the number on the last measurements of Doppler effects in the Magellanic quadrant of the sky. And ask again next year, and see if the numbers aren't smaller than predicted – because the galaxies aren't racing away from us so fast anymore, because they'll soon be tumbling *into* us.

'But don't wait long,' I admonished. 'Don't wait another year, and another. Quick, run to your telescope, man – look to the stars. For as the stars go, so goes time. And when the signal is clear, hesitate if you will; but then go. Help me. It can be won.' I clenched my teeth; I wanted him to hear. I tried to make him understand with the force of my wanting it.

I don't think he heard, though. I think deafness was his tragic flaw. Or maybe he'd just had his memory blotted out in another time, and amnesia was his downfall.

I smiled a polite sort of encouragement. He drained his glass. I told him I intended to give his address to one of the spirits I lured into this cycle of time. Perhaps to a Di from an ancient precession.

I told him not to feel guilty if he didn't help – I was

confident that fulfilling my destiny as messiah of a previous time would brace our own universe.

I bought him one last drink, and we toasted.

'To old times,' he said, 'and new. *Bon voyage!*'

His cheeks were flushed with cheer now; I could see he meant it.

I raised my glass. '"*Hypocrite lecteur – mon semblable – mon frère!. . .*"'

I drank.

I threw my glass to the floor, and the bartender kicked us out.

I said good-bye.

In the morning I left.

In the end, I suppose, I'm my own last footnote. Good-bye.

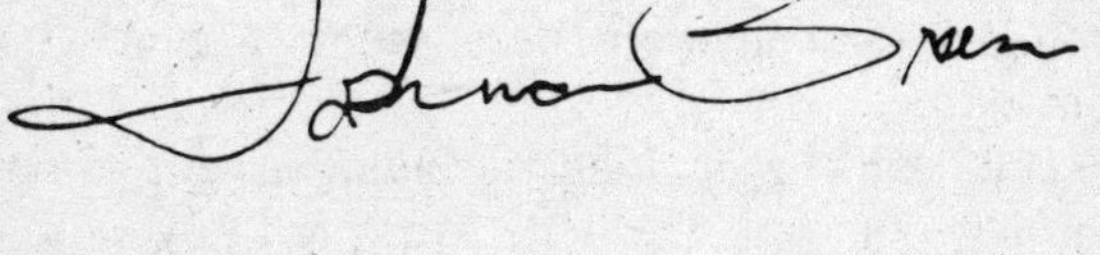

Postscript

Do you remember that huge court, the god's domain,
those bitter lemons where the marks your teeth made show,
the cave whose rash indwellers found death long ago
where sleeps the seed primeval of the dragon slain?
They will come back, those gods whom you forever mourn,
for time shall see the order of old days reborn.
The earth has shuddered to a breath of prophecy.

– Gérard De Nerval, *Delphica* (1850)

– J. G.

Afterword

I hadn't thought about Joshua Green in over three years the night he showed up in my ER toward the middle of 1985. Even so, the moment he walked in I knew exactly who he was. He was the most unforgettable derelict I'd ever met.

He'd made a significant impression on me back in 1982, with his seizures, and his history, and his philosophizing about time at that Brentwood party. I remembered feeling a tremendous empathy for him. 'There but for fortune,' I remembered thinking.

In May 1985 he wasn't having convulsions, though. He just walked in as I was leaving. He looked like a real Space Cadet.

I mean a real one. He wore some kind of Buck Rogers device on his head. He has some kind of plastic pirate spyglass slung over his shoulder. He looked like he'd run out of Thorazine.

He greeted me warmly, asked to speak with me. I told him I was leaving. He asked me out for a drink. I declined. Socializing with patients is a bad habit to cultivate even if they're *not* crazy.

He looked so comical, though, and so lost at the same time – he just plain made me laugh. And he laughed back. 'Come on,' he said.

And of course there were the items he'd pressed on me those three years before: the jewels, the cat who'd now become a great pal. 'I have your things,' I said. He said, 'I have to talk to you about that.' I tried to gauge his eyes. I didn't think he was violent – there was too much humor

in his demeanor; there was an ease about him.

In any case, I was at least curious about the rubies he'd left with me. And I did have a couple of hours to kill before a dinner date, so I relented.

We went to a small pub up the street and took a booth. He bought me a martini and began his story, a condensed version of the manuscript you've just read. He told me of Torrie's timesickness, Karl's and Lon's sacrifices, Fernando's eternal fall, Di's death, his child's birth.

I nodded without commenting. He lost himself in reverie for a moment, then went on with his narrative.

He told me he'd brought scores of image-beings back into our 'precession' – to increase the energy of our 'space-time.' He told me that hundreds of other image-people had become disoriented in the tunnels and had gotten lost in other nodes, where they'd become the 'ghosts' of other times.

He became philosophical. Maybe we're all just ghosts of other times, he said, and we have substance only to ourselves and others of our own precession. If I see a ghost, or have a vision, or run from a dream-character who pursues me for several seconds into waking, am I seeing image-beings from another time? Or am *I* the ghost, lost in someone else's precession. Or is our entire *world* one of these cycling ghost-worlds?

When he'd seen his own ghost on his first jungle trip . . . who was 'real,' and who was the ghost? Or was this visitation not a ghost at all, but merely a precognitive vision of an event that *had* happened in a previous precession and would happen again?

'Past, present, future – they all begin to merge,' he said seriously. 'That's why the *now* is so important. Everything is now. I mean I suppose in some sense everything we perceive is in the past, since it takes light time to travel, so we don't find out about it until after it's happened, and

by that time something else is happening. So nothing really *is* as you perceive it; it only *was*.' He raised his eyebrows at me.

These were not rhetorical questions for Joshua. He wanted answers. What did I think?

I thought I could probably follow him more closely with another martini.

'I know you think I'm not playing with a full deck,' he smiled, 'talking about seeing spirit-images, and other times and whatever. But hey, listen. What about bees? They can see in the ultraviolet spectrum; so what looks like just a white daisy to us is multicolored and complexly patterned to them. They can see all *kinds* of things we can't see at all, things that are colored ultraviolet.'

'People aren't bees,' I noted astutely.

'You learned that in med school, didn't you?' he said deadpan.

'Actually, I was absent that day, but I borrowed the notes from my roommate.'

'Well, I had to take evolutionary biology in grad school, and one of the things we learned was that variations *within* species are frequently greater than variations *across* species. You know what I'm saying? I mean, it's not even out of the ordinary, even in *your* relatively narrow view of the universe, to believe that some humans can see things other humans can't. I mean, why do you think some people have special rapport with animals? Some people are just gifted – or cursed – with extra senses. Maybe *you're* not – but the things I've seen were clear as day to me. Maybe I'm just more than two standard deviations away from the norm.' He winked.

'Well, that's what a bell-shaped curve is for. It's a dirty job living down at the lip, I imagine, but someone's got to do it.' I toasted him.

He didn't mind being teased, though. Maybe that's why

I liked him. He raisd his glass back at me. 'Well, anyway, I'm leaving in the morning.'

'Going back?'

He nodded. He intended to spend time with Lon, Jasmine, Torrie, Karl – share the sunsets of another age with them.

I said that sounded pretty nice. I thought to myself he wasn't really totally off the wall, just basically a sweet guy with a vivid imagination who bounced an occasional reality check.

He smiled like he'd heard what I was thinking. 'You don't believe me,' he sighed.

I shrugged. 'It's your *ghosts* that I have a little more trouble believing in.'

'Quite rightly,' he smiled. 'Believe only in your own ghosts.'

I smiled, drained my glass.

He said he'd send me his *own* journal of these events at a later date. He'd send me his jeweled telescope, too – he hoped, after he was gone, someone else would carry on the tunnel work. He hoped I was that man.

He would work, he expected, until the timesickness overcame him. He had great hopes of bringing thousands of ghosts back here by impersonating himself, in visionary form, and then he planned to retire with Torrie, his dear love, in 'the elder times.' Perhaps with his child.

I drank to his hopes. He offered me a last toast; he smashed his glass against the wall. The barman, whom I knew slightly, was not pleased. He added the glass and a clean-up bill to the tab and ordered us out. I apologized, a little sheepishly. Joshua paid in cash. That's when I noticed the cut on his hand.

A lopsided Y-shaped cut on the ball of his left thumb. Not yet healed.

We sauntered out to the front sidewalk. It had begun

to rain. He pulled his coat collar up. I thanked him for the story and the presents. We shook hands. I wished him well.

We stared into each other's faces for many seconds. Who was he? Who was I? I felt his heart reaching out to touch me. I pulled away a fraction, then held fast; I was touched.

He turned and ambled down the sidewalk. Shimmering reflections of neon streetlights danced in the puddles around his feet, tinting him red and blue. The rain came down harder. I saw him run across the street, against the light, quickly receding into the shadows and colors on the other side. I stepped under an awning to get in out of the rain.

When I looked again, he was gone.

I thought of him frequently over the next several days. One of the sad, wonderful characters of the earth. The events in his life that had led to his current state of affairs, I could only guess. But it was all the more poignant to me that he'd started out, like myself, as an academic.

I read the book he gave me – the 'old' Joshua's journal. It was obviously the product of the psychotic delusions of a crumbling personality structure – all about this fantasy world of mythological creatures, epic quests, and so on. Marginally interesting, I suppose, if that kind of thing interests you. It occurred to me that maybe if he got himself a publisher, he wouldn't need a psychiatrist.

Still, something nagged at me, and it was this: the cut on his hand.

It was the same laceration I'd seen him sustain at that party three years earlier, yet it was barely a week old.

Understand – I'm an emergency-room physician. A connoisseur of lacerations. I can clearly and visually remember every interesting cut I've sewn up in the last

ten years, and I tell you categorically: this was an interesting cut. Complexly Y-shaped ('stellate,' in medical jargon), deep, oddly positioned – it was a laceration I could not have forgotten and which could not have been duplicated.

It was the same cut.

And it was new. Dark blood still crusted one flap; granulation tissue barely covered the avulsed radial end. He hadn't gotten it sutured, as I'd advised him, so it was gaping slightly, and minimally infected.

Barely a week old, in my professional opinion.

And with my own eyes, I'd witnessed the skin tearing, over three years before.

And if it *was* a hoax (which seemed inconceivable on technical grounds), why hadn't he drawn my attention to it?

It was a paradox I couldn't resolve.

Five weeks later I received his package in the mail. Postmarked Bogotá, it contained the handwritten journal of his odyssey, the text of this book, which I've subsequently edited. Also in the package was the small telescope, containing three emerald lenses; a flint Indian arrowhead, labeled DRAGON'S TOOTH; a hand-drawn map of an area south of the Caquetá; a copy of his skull X rays – the ones I'd had taken when he was my ER patient – with a note attached, saying, 'So you won't forget who I was'; and a box full of diamonds, rubies, and emeralds.

I was staggered, to say the least. I read the manuscript, the one you've just read. I held the telescope up to the light: a complicated pattern of leafy veinings glittered across my eye.

The next day I had the jewels appraised. They were worth millions. Somewhat stunned, I opened a safe-deposit box. I would hold them until his return.

I didn't want to hold them forever, though. Furthermore, I wanted to look at his cut hand more closely, and returning these jewels seemed like a good excuse. So in a state of agitated curiosity, I decided to track him down.

I called the paleontology departmental office at the university. A Paula Bookman answered the phone. I said we were trying to locate Josh for medical reasons. She said it was such a shame, such a bright young man, etc., etc. No, she had no idea where he was now.

I called the Doctors Hoffman, but they could shed no light. Neither had seen him in over three years. In fact, the patient had broken two appointments with the psychiatrist Hoffman, so the latter had given strict instructions to his answering service that he no longer *wanted* to see this patient.

I felt stumped.

I talked with Jill Littlewood, a close personal friend of mine with a more intuitive nature than my own. Told her the whole story, described my unease at being the keeper of so much wealth, the guardian of Joshua Green's fragmented estate and mind. Jill said something rather startling. She suggested the story was true.

She said it was just like me to *assume* it was false – because it didn't happen to fit into my own narrow paradigm of the universe; it involved a soupçon of right-brain thinking (which I lacked); it was pseudoscience; it was a subjective experience; it wasn't independently verifiable; and most odious to my sensibilities, it had been asserted by a Known Patient. Therefore, I could not accept it as true. How like me, how so like me.

Did *she* think it was true? I asked.

She answered affirmatively – I think just to be perverse. The point is, she added, it *might* be true, so where was the profit in disbelieving it out of hand?

Besides, Western thinking had largely discarded the

sense of the miraculous in the universe – we had no equivalent of yogis walking on coals. Now here was a scientific theory with miraculous implications; she thought I should be trying to find ways to prove it *was* true and not the opposite.

Fine, I thought – this whole thing had gotten under my skin anyway; I might as well just scratch.

So I reread his manuscript with an eye toward looking for data I could substantiate or corroborate.

The first references that seemed potentially verifiable from the environs of my armchair were the astronomical allusions. I called up Griffith Observatory.

'I'd like to speak to an astronomer, please.'

After a few holds and transfers, I got put through.

'Yes, well, I'm interested in anything you could tell me about specific phenomena that would have been visible from the southern hemisphere during the latter parts of 1976.'

'Mm, not much I can tell you, really, not about celestial phenomena. You mean like meteor showers, comets, exploding novas, that sort of thing?'

'Well, anything. I don't know.'

'I could give you a little planetary info, that's all, you know, appearances and disappearances along the ecliptic, occultations, which zodiac signs Jupiter is in, that sort of thing.'

'Well, sure, tell me whatever . . .'

'Okay, let me just get the ephemeris, here.'

'What's that?'

'*The American Ephemeris and Nautical Almanac* – tells you all that information. Here we go, 1976, let's see, November eighth, there was an occultation of Jupiter that was visible – '

'What's an occultation?'

'When something is occulted by something else, it's

hidden – like when one planet goes behind another one so you can't see it for a while, that's an occultation.'

'Name some others,' I prompted.

'Well, they're not terrifically common, you know, couple of times a year, that sort of thing. Only other one I see here, visible in the southern skies, is September twenty-fifth, the occultation of Venus by the Moon.'

'Ahh, that would be the night Queen Namsháya Moon-Goddess Jaguar-Woman ate the birthstar,' I said.

'Excuse me?'

'Anything else you can tell me?'

There wasn't really. No line on what the bloodstar and the dreamstar were doing around then. No news on the Doppler effect, or changes in the blue-to-red spectrum of outrushing galaxies. I thanked him and hung up.

I now had a single piece of evidence, supporting Joshua's outlandish assertions – confirmation of a celestial event he'd described as having taken place while he was in the jungle city. A piece of evidence that suggested – to me, in any case – that his statements could have been true and accurate in describing the circumstances of his first expedition.

But what about the second expedition? Far more fantastic, it lent itself much less easily to testing hypotheses. Furthermore, it had come after a severe blow to the head, the onset of a seizure disorder, and major emotional trauma related to the death of his wife – all good reasons to make his recounting of subsequent events suspect, or at least open to more liberal interpretation.

But what of the cut on his hand?

Certainly, my researches had not *contradicted* his story. My researches. Research is the way his story had started – Joshua's researches on the black fossilized skull that Lon had had shipped up from Colombia. The skull Jasmine

had said came from the Joshua she'd known in the last precession.

Which reminded me of skull X rays. I looked again at the X ray Josh had sent me in the mail, with its note attached: 'So you won't forget who I was.' Not 'who I am,' but 'who I *was*.' Did he mean this as a clue, a pointer? In conjunction with the researches he'd done on the old fossil skull, it made me wonder.

I called Paula Bookman, the departmental secretary, in the morning. I asked if I could see her; she told me to drop by. When I got to her office, I told her it was of the utmost importance that I be allowed to look around Joshua's office, to get a possible clue as to where he might have gone. I intimated there were medical questions involved.

She took me to a storage closet and unlocked it. Joshua's office had been given to someone else in the intervening years, but all his materials and books were being stored here for when he returned. I thanked her and she left.

The room was a tiny junk heap, piled high, without method. Papers, monographs, memos, books, calipers, glasses, a few numbered bones. I located the fossil spore catalog, with a marker in it on a page showing a *Dryopteris* specimen, and an inset of the Caquetá River. Behind the book pile was a crumpled McDonald's bag; an inscribed pen; a 1976 calendar with meetings scribbled in; a desk photo of his wife Di; the pink latex endocast taken from the skull Lon had given him – the skull, if he was to be believed, of his own incarnation from an earlier time.

They were like fossil remains, these things. The bones of his life. He lived; here was the proof.

I lifted the book off the pile to study it more closely. There, beneath it, I saw what I really wanted. What I'd come for. The X rays.

I picked one up, held it to the light. This was it: the radiogram Josh had taken of the enameled, fossilized skull when he was examining it for Lon. There were three X rays, actually, eight by ten inches each: anterior, lateral, and oblique.

I pulled a manila folder out of my coat. Inside the envelope were Joshua's own skull X rays, the copies he'd sent me of the X rays I'd taken of him in the ER three years before.

I removed Josh's skull films from the hospital folder, held them up to the light, and compared them side by side with the X rays of the ceramic fossil skull.

Perfect match.

Suture for suture, bone for bone, arch for arch. The two sets of X rays were identical in every way – except one indicated bone-density, and the other showed stone-density: one was a living skull, one a fossil.

So what am I to think? Here's a man I've met three times, a charming fellow, really, if a bit odd. He has a seizure disorder; when he cuts himself, he heals poorly; he has a skull X ray that's radiographically identical to the X ray of a purportedly 67-million-year-old fossil.

So what are we to think?

I reviewed Torrie Rosen's medical chart from her stay at UCLA to see if it contributed anything to this story. Nothing in her history or physical examination either confirmed or denied what I'd learned so far, but I was struck by the name on the chart. Last name first, it read: ROSEN, TORRIE. I said it over in my mind, and then out loud a couple of times: 'Rosen Torrie, Rosen Torrie . . .'

It sounded rather strikingly like Rose Centauri.

Rose Centauri, her supposed double in the postulated last cycle of time.

* * *

Most likely it's all a hoax; or else just a madman's rambling tale.

Most likely so.

Or it was as he said when he first stood at the cave entrance to the jungle city: he *was* 'the potent wizard of a magical kingdom.'

And there *is* an entire necklace of pasts draping our universe.

Joshua Green's view of time explains, with complete internal consistency, a number of diverse and often-speculated-upon phenomena: reincarnation, precognition, déjà vu, intuition, second-guessing, second sight, hunches, instantaneous rapport, ghosts, visions, visitations, spirits, UFOs, alien landings, and the impressions we get that time is sometimes fast, sometimes slow, sometimes predictable, sometimes not, sometimes repetitive, sometimes new.

It seems a parsimonious theory, at any rate – much is explained, with little assumed.

I began to wonder about various historical events that had always mystified me, events that bore similarities to this story and were also explained by it.

For example, Cortés' arrival in huge wooden ships on the Aztec beaches – he was taken for the god Quetzlcoatl, who by prophecy was light-skinned and bearded and expected from the east in a floating house.

Or Captain James Cook's discovery of Hawaii. On the day of that island's annual celebration predicting the wondrous, gift-laden return of their lost god Lono – a celebration in which the populace marched clockwise around the island carrying sacred staffs with crosspieces that dangled banners – Cook arrived, sailing clockwise around the island in never before seen ships whose masts

and sails looked identical to the sacred staffs and banners, and bearing wondrous strange gifts.

How could Cortés, or Cook, have been anticipated with such clarity?

Such unbelievably acute prophecies – like the return of Goranchacha to the jungle city – were no mere coincidence, if Joshua's analysis is correct. Instead, all these striking reincarnative promises were fulfilled, just as Jasmine described, when time's wheel crossed itself, precession touching precession.

Cook *had* been to Hawaii before – you can see it, just beyond that node over there.

I had a professor once in medical school who believed dreams were mutations of thought in exactly the same way there were mutations of genes on a cellular level. Dreams, as such, were random recombinations of images, molded by environmental, social, chemical, or psychic pressures; they were nonsense at times, at times detrimental to the well-being of the organism. And sometimes they had adaptive value.

If a mutation of thought resulted in a dream that the species as a whole found useful, that dream inevitably became incorporated into the social fabric, into the being of the race – realized as a work of art, a scientific insight, a philosophical turning, a religious movement. Some dreams were evolutionary breakthroughs.

So even if Joshua's story was a dream, just a dream, what about our fate was he witnessing? What of the human destiny was he in fact evolving in his dreamwork? That's what my professor would have wanted to know.

These are, of course, vacant musings. I've been focused too long on the concerns of this one lost soul.

Like as not, he wrote the entire journal as a metaphor

for the necessity of letting our own spirits inform our daily lives.

Like as not, he was mad.

In any case, I'd reached my limit. What else was I to do?

And so the matter rested.

Until about two months ago.

I was at a party in Pasadena, over at Jerry McGann's. Primarily Cal Tech people – mostly English department types, some visiting scholars, a couple of computer freaks. In the garden, under an unusually clear Los Angeles night sky, nursing a cheap California white wine, I met a youngish astrophysicist named Nelda Lockwood.

She was watching the stars.

'Beautiful, isn't it?' I noted.

'Rare to see it so brilliant.'

We both watched for a time; from deep out of the cosmos's absolute blackness, these tiny motes of white fire, gemlike, elemental, flashing constantly brighter and dimmer, rhythmically almost, like a pulse or respiration.

'They look so still, and they're speeding away from us so fast,' I said softly. It was like being in a temple here; it made me want to whisper.

'Maybe not so fast for long,' she said, shrugging off our mantle of stars, coming back down to earth.

'What?' I said. 'Everyone knows the galaxies are all rushing away from us. The Big Bang, right?'

'Well, maybe so. We've been getting some new data lately, though. There's a fine dust cloud throughout the universe – maybe particulate matter from the Big Bang – but it looks like it constitutes enough total mass to be exerting a significant gravitational effect on all those rushing stars. Enough to slow them down, and stop them eventually – and then start pulling them all back in – back

to the beginning, in the end. The Big Suck.' Innuendo tilted her smile.

'Wait a minute. What are you saying? The galaxies are slowing down now?' I pressed.

'Well, they're just not racing away quite as fast as we thought they'd be, probably because of these newly characterized gravitational effects. So the red shift – the Doppler effect, you know, it measures the rate at which the galaxies are receding – well, it's just a tad slower on our last measurements.'

'Slower,' I echoed.

'Well, I mean don't let it throw you, cutie. At this rate, no one's got to run for cover for another few billion years.'

'"At this rate"?' I gazed into the void. 'And what if the rate changes?'

'Then it'll happen a little sooner. Relax, though – it's not going to happen tonight.' She clinked her glass to mine.

The stars seemed to wink a little brighter.

It's been on my mind since that night. I read the manuscript again.

And again.

People told me I was looked tired. And then one night, the air conditioner broke, with all the bedroom windows open, waiting for the vaguest hint of a breeze to cut the suffocating, unseasonable heat, sweating on the bare bed, turning every few minutes to look for a cooler spot – turning, dozing, waking – I think I saw a ghost. Or maybe I dreamed I saw her – saw her standing in the shadow of the doorway – darkly pretty, dress torn, young, slight of build, insubstantial, haunting: it was Di.

I sat up with a start. She disappeared. I jumped out of

bed, ran down the hall, down the stairs. But she was gone.

Of course, I'd seen her picture in Joshua's storage closet; I'd been overworking, getting entirely too obsessed with this whole affair; moreover, I'd had too much wine with dinner that night. It was merely an unsettling dream, of course.

I took a couple of weeks off work.

'*Hypocrite lecteur – mon semblable – mon frère!*' Josh had toasted me in the bar. Hypocrite reader – my double – my brother!

Hypocrite, I suppose, because I viewed with such distance, such hubris, such smug self-importance, that pitiful dreamer who sat before me.

My double, my brother, I suppose, because we were both academics, intellectuals who prided ourselves on the gathering of data, the interpretation of data.

Mon semblable – mon frère . . .

Was I these things?

Of the cave city he'd discovered in the last precession, where Torrie supposedly now resided, Joshua had written: 'An intricate civilization existed here, rich in nuance, just below the surface. A labyrinthine interior, unsuspected and profound.'

Were we these things?

In medicine we treat the patient with the obscure disease as if it were curable. He is weak with pneumonia. Viral or bacterial? We don't know. If bacterial, antibiotics may save him; if viral, nothing will help. So we give antibiotics. We assume he has a disease for which we have a potential cure and proceed accordingly. If we were right, the patient may live; if we were wrong, the patient would have died anyway.

By such logic I should run to the jungle this very moment – to pull the swooning, sickly universe from the brink of the abyss with the energy transfer which may be the only cure for the tumbling illness that even now tugs at our stars. By such logic I should run.

But I don't.

Why run?

For a psychotic with an unhealing lacerated hand who speaks between convulsions of jungle tribes and long-predicted occultations of neighboring planets?

For two skull X rays that match?

For dreaming of a beautiful spirit-girl on a hot summer night?

For cocktail party chatter about recent attenuations of the Doppler effect?

No, I don't run.

I have a life here. A medical practice, a home, a cat.

I don't run.

But I do watch. In fact, whenever I watch the black and starry sky now, I find myself concentrating on some particularly crystal point of light, trying to sense it, and wondering: is it getting brighter? There – when I looked away a moment and then looked back: didn't it get a fraction brighter?

In fact, I'll be watching the Magellanic Clouds with some interest. Academic interest, of course. But if there happens to be an unexplained slowing of its red shift, who's to say I shouldn't take these maps and scopes on a little vacation into the rain forest. Just a little fishing expedition near a crossing of three jungle rivers . . .

Soul-searching.

Casting for ghosts.

– J.K.
Los Angeles, January 1986

Fantasy authors in paperback from Grafton Books

Raymond E Feist		
Magician	£3.50	☐
Silverthorn	£2.95	☐
Richard Ford		
Quest for the Faradawn	£2.50	☐
Melvaig's Vision	£2.50	☐
Robert Holdstock		
Mythago Wood	£2.50	☐
Michael Shea		
Nifft the Lean	£2.50	☐
A Quest for Simbilis	£1.95	☐
Tim Powers		
The Anubis Gates	£2.95	☐
Patricia Kennealy		
The Copper Crown	£2.95	☐
Fritz Leiber		
'Swords' Series		
Swords and Deviltry	£2.50	☐
Swords against Death	£2.50	☐
Swords in the Mist	£2.50	☐
Swords against Wizardry	£2.50	☐
The Swords of Lankhmar	£2.50	☐
Swords and Ice Magic	£2.50	☐

To order direct from the publisher just tick the titles you want and fill in the order form.

SF1482

All these books are available at your local bookshop or newsagent, or can be ordered direct from the publisher.

To order direct from the publishers just tick the titles you want and fill in the form below.

Name ______________________________

Address ______________________________

Send to:
Grafton Cash Sales
PO Box 11, Falmouth, Cornwall TR10 9EN.

Please enclose remittance to the value of the cover price plus:

UK 60p for the first book, 25p for the second book plus 15p per copy for each additional book ordered to a maximum charge of £1.90.

BFPO 60p for the first book, 25p for the second book plus 15p per copy for the next 7 books, thereafter 9p per book.

Overseas including Eire £1.25 for the first book, 75p for second book and 28p for each additional book.

Grafton Books reserve the right to show new retail prices on covers, which may differ from those previously advertised in the text or elsewhere.